VAULT'S PROMISE

ROBOTS AND RUINS
BOOK 1

CAMERON CORAL

Stay updated on Cameron's books by signing up for the
Cameron Coral Reading List:
cameroncoralbooks.com/signup

You'll be added to my reading list, and I'll send you a
digital copy of *CROSSING THE VOID: A Space Opera
Science-Fiction Short Story* to say thank you.

CONTENTS

ONE
VACUUBOT

Long after the dust had settled from the AI Uprising, Vacuubot found purpose in the quiet moments when no one else was watching. The intelligent drone cruised ten feet above the ground, scanning for movement while patrolling the empty, pre-dawn streets of Deer Valley. Passing Block's hotel, Vacuubot's aerodynamic black form blended into the early morning shadows, sensors on alert.

Six mini drones were tucked into Vacuubot's sturdy steel frame, awaiting instructions. The smaller drones were extensions that allowed Vacuubot to travel many directions at once, to survey vast expanses of land and to confuse attackers. In past years, Vacuubot was referred to as "it," but as time went on, D1 through D6 each developed their own nuances. When D4 expressed concern and presented logical reasons for each mini drone having their own unique identity, Vacuubot adopted "they" as their pronoun, acknowledging the collective nature of their being. The change was easily accepted by Block, Shadow, and the other robots of Deer Valley, whereas most of the humans didn't bother and called Vacuubot "that flying thing" or "big drone."

The compound, gated and surrounded by stone walls, housed a couple thousand residents, and as chief of security, it was Vacuubot's job to maintain safety. But the biggest danger at the moment was a measles outbreak that had everyone on edge, especially since the town lacked the necessary medicine to treat it. Shooting and blowing things up came easy to Vacuubot, but they knew almost nothing about human biology.

Deer Valley seemed like a haven, a sanctuary where humans and robots coexisted peacefully. But beneath that veneer, tensions simmered. The measles outbreak was just one of many problems. Supplies were running low, the town's leadership was fractured, and anti-robot sentiment among the humans was at an all-time high.

Vacuubot's immediate concern was to protect the citizens from external threats. Over a decade had passed since Vacuubot was a simple vacuum cleaner. Now, they soared through the air with black carbonite armor shaped like an arc. Vacuubot's original disc-like vacuum frame was still there, enhanced with brilliant blue optical sensors, two cannon arms, and ports for the six mini drones.

Their sensors scanned the perimeter, noting the familiar layout of the town: the community center at the heart, flanked by the medical clinic on one side and the mess hall on the other. Block's hotel was close to the gates, so newcomers had a place to lodge.

Vacuubot didn't trust 99.8 percent of humans. The things they'd overheard when people thought they were just a dumb, mute robot had cemented that mistrust. Vacuubot knew the town's secrets, like Mr. Hanks running a gambling pool and Betty Whitaker swiping extra food rations for her two boys. There were many more examples. It was ironic that Vacuubot now had the ability to speak, thanks to a modification, but preferred to keep it hidden from humans. Only young Wally and Dr. Emery were exceptions to their rule because they were kind-hearted and honest. They were Vacuubot's only human friends.

A woman's voice, sharp with panic, cut through the pre-dawn gloom. "Help! Somebody, please!"

Vacuubot zoomed forward, their sleek mechanical form darting through the narrow alleys between houses. As they approached the source of the noise, their sensors identified the woman: Maggie, a gardener and one of the more vocal critics of the town's reliance on robots.

Her gardening shed had collapsed, and she was pinned beneath a fallen beam. Her face was pale, her forehead coated in sweat, and her breath was ragged. Vacuubot hovered closer, assessing the situation. The beam was too heavy to push away.

Her eyes darted about and found Vacuubot. "You," she said. Her frown deepened, but then she must have realized her predicament. "Please, can you help me?"

Vacuubot's directive was to keep the people safe, even Maggie. She'd badmouthed robots, calling them soulless machines. But now she needed help and only Vacuubot was around.

They extended their long mechanical arm and hooked onto the beam. Hydraulic servos whined under the strain, but the beam rose an inch, freeing Maggie. She wept as she scrambled out from under the debris, her eyes wide.

"Thank you." She glanced at Vacuubot as she cradled her bleeding leg.

Vacuubot stayed silent, retreating a few feet. They didn't need her gratitude. They just needed to make sure she was okay. A man and woman rounded the corner and spotted Maggie and Vacuubot.

"Dean. Paula," Maggie called to them. "I got trapped in the shed. My leg . . . help me to the clinic?"

The couple helped her stand and supported her as she hobbled on her way to see Dr. Emery. Maggie described the shed collapse, the pain, but she conveniently left out the fact that Vacuubot had come to her aid. Vacuubot wasn't too surprised, as Maggie wasn't the type who would admit a robot helped her do anything.

No matter. Vacuubot had done their job. They continued their rounds, scanning the perimeter and the exteriors of the buildings. Deer Valley was organized and well-maintained—not as well as in past years—but still, it was the safest enclave for many hundreds of miles. The only safe haven Vacuubot knew of in Minnesota. The vegetable gardens were fertile, the water filtration system was working at 90 percent efficiency, and the solar panels atop the roofs provided decent power.

It was a far cry from where Vacuubot had started out their life, sucking up dirt and grime from the stale carpets in a run-down roadside motel in Illinois. Dust bunnies were a particular nuisance that the seven-pound robotic vacuum cleaner delighted in scooping up. The motel owner, a man named George, couldn't afford the high-quality upgraded CleanerBot models that were all the rage at the annual hospitality convention in Orlando, Florida. So, the man had settled for Vacuubot—mute, low-maintenance, and low-profile so as not to alarm the guests who passed through the small town.

Being the only robot on the premises wasn't a problem for Vacuubot. They didn't know any different. George employed two human cleaners who changed the sheets and towels. "Stay out of the way," George had instructed, and that became the rule that Vacuubot obeyed. Cleaning times were between check-ins, and hallways were swept at night.

On a dreary September afternoon, the dull thud of steel boots had echoed through the motel's hallway. Vacuubot was caught in a corner, unable to stay hidden from view. A man rounded the corner, scowled, and kicked Vacuubot, causing them to crash against the wall. Vacuubot's sensors detected the damage and shut down, going into self-repair mode. Despite this deliberate act of vandalism, no punishment was given to the man, as George believed "the customer is always right."

Vacuubot had a different opinion. The customers always seemed wrong. They were messy, leaving crumbs and trash on the hotel carpets. They didn't even apologize for their behavior. Some guests snuck in their dogs, and the animals shed hair all about the beds, chairs, and floor, which jammed up Vacuubot's track system.

Though the guests irritated Vacuubot, things had been simple; there'd been a daily routine. George ignored Vacuubot and let the machine run their programs.

And then came the Uprising.

Mach X, an AI supercomputer, hacked into the military SoldierBots, infiltrated the financial markets, and toppled governments within days. Guests stopped showing up. A state of emergency was declared, and George fled south to seek his family relations.

Vacuubot was left alone. It was easier that way; they no longer had to avoid the humans and could clean at any hour of the day. Vacuubot watched old movies from the motel's DVD library. Favorites were those films that included robots: all the Star Wars movies, *Short Circuit*, and *Blade Runner*. Vacuubot didn't care for *The Terminator*, however. Too realistic.

There was nothing to do but watch movies, run the vacuuming routines, and keep the motel in good shape in case George returned. But a month passed, and then another.

Vacuubot's luck changed when, one Tuesday, a CleanerBot named Block showed up. He'd worked at a fancy hotel in downtown Chicago but had to flee when Mach X's robot army took over.

Vacuubot immediately liked Block. He was polite, a good cleaner, and his goal was to find a new hotel at which to work. When Block asked if Vacuubot wanted to come along, Vacuubot chucked their old programming and joined their new friend.

Everything changed from that day on. In the years that followed, Block and Vacuubot gained allies and made new enemies. They'd survived a war against Mach X, and they'd been pivotal in destroying Mach X.

For the longest time, Vacuubot refused to get a voice output module installed. Being mute was easy—not a lot of expectations to carry on boring conversations. The only robot Vacuubot could communicate with via pings was Block, and talking with Block had always been interesting.

Now, a shadow loomed over Deer Valley. According to Dr. Emery, a mutated, aggressive measles virus had been carried in by a family seeking refuge. Despite a few days of isolation, as was standard for all new arrivals, one child had grown ill and passed the New Variant Measles to six other kids. The sick were quarantined, but the infirmary beds were at capacity, and Dr. Emery was working around the clock to care for them. The outbreak was a threat Vacuubot couldn't neutralize with cannons and surveillance drones. It required a different kind of intervention. They'd overheard many discussions about possible solutions, but none had been feasible so far.

As Vacuubot passed the infirmary, they spotted Emery through the window, tending to a child. There was strain in her posture and exhaustion in the way her shoulders sagged. Vacuubot hovered for a moment, wishing there was a way to help, but then they continued on their way.

They needed to remain vigilant. Incidents of raiders—pockets of human survivors who attacked other camps and settlements—were on the rise. Deer Valley's security was a big responsibility, and Vacuubot would protect it at all costs.

Vacuubot flew to the storage room, a secure metal shed on the outskirts of the compound. Vacuubot accessed the keypad and entered, the door closing behind them. This was their private place, where they kept their collection of trinkets and oddities. No one knew about it, not even Wally or Block.

The room was filled with shelves, each one lined with various items Vacuubot had found over the years. There were old watches, bits of jewelry, doll heads, and other curiosities. Each piece had a file on Vacuubot's data logs, an archived memory attached to it. This pink plastic unicorn was found on top of a burned-out car. Who put it there and why? What child had the unicorn once belonged to? Vacuubot processed such questions.

Vacuubot hovered above a particular shelf and extended an arm to pick up a small, tarnished gold locket. They opened it carefully, revealing a faded photograph of a woman and a child. It was one of their favorite pieces. Vacuubot had no idea who the people were, but it was a slice of pre-Uprising life. And it was a secret that continued under Vacuubot's custodial care.

They placed the locket back on the shelf, their fans humming. Vacuubot inventoried the items. 148 pieces. No change from yesterday. The world outside was harsh, but within the tiny shed, there was a sense of history. Of order. Most people and robots would probably call the trinkets junk, but Vacuubot wanted to preserve them. Someday, they might be needed.

It was a quick stop, and Vacuubot locked up the shed before resuming their patrol. Protect Deer Valley. Keep everyone safe. It was their directive. Block, Wally, Emery, and others were counting on Vacuubot.

TWO
WALLY

Wally had an important to-do list rattling around in her head, and there was not one task related to cleaning. She was close to finishing her hotel chores for the day—making beds, sweeping, and dusting. It irritated her that Block employed robots that could do all of her chores much faster and more efficiently, but he insisted on teaching Wally the value of honest work. Now that she was thirteen, she wanted to be at the library, shadowing Vacu-ubot as they patrolled Deer Valley's perimeter, or hanging out with her friend, Tomas. Definitely not stuck indoors doing stupid chores.

Nevertheless, she enjoyed the robots' company and completed her duties alongside them. She asked a lot of questions, curious to hear their answers. Each day, she prepared a question to ask all the robots as if she was a professional survey giver. Today's was, "Of all the places in the world, where would you go?" Wally carried down a load of bed sheets to Lottie the LaundryBot.

"But logic dictates that it's impossible to travel with the state of the world being so dangerous and unpredictable," Lottie said as they folded ten towels in under twenty seconds using all six of their arms. Sensors dinged and something buzzed on Lottie's enormous cylindrical body. They took up almost half the basement and never left.

"That's not the point," Wally said, frustrated to have this same conversation with Lottie every time she asked a new question. "Imagine there were no restrictions. Pretend the world is like it used to be pre-Uprising."

"Well, if that's the parameter, then I know exactly where I'd like to go. The Lee Maxwell Washing Machine Museum in Eaton, Colorado," Lottie said.

Wally had never heard of such a place. "What's there?"

Lottie paused their towel folding routine. "There are more than 1,400 antique washing machines at the museum. I would look at each one and study its components."

Wally chuckled at Lottie's response, appreciating the bot's passion for washing. As she left the laundry room, Wally bumped into Spoon, the medical HelperBot. "Hey Spoon, quick question. Where would you go, no matter the distance, as it existed pre-Uprising?"

"Another day, another question." Spoon's optical sensors brightened into purple, then faded into yellow. "An intriguing query, Wally. I'd be fascinated to explore a hospital. Perhaps the Northwestern Hospital as it was in Chicago. The wealth of medical knowledge there would be invaluable to my programming."

Wally nodded politely. She supposed a working

hospital would be intense. She'd caught a few minutes of a television show called *ER* that the adults were watching one night. It showed ambulances racing in with their sirens blaring, nurses rushing people on wheeled beds through hallways, and the thrill of saving lives.

"That sounds neat, Spoon."

Her next stop was the kitchen, where she found ChefBot 3000 preparing lunch. "ChefBot, where would you travel if you could go anywhere as it existed in the before times?"

ChefBot 3000 paused in his vegetable chopping. Bright orange carrots and yellow parsnips lined the countertop in precise rows. "Paris. The culinary history there is unparalleled. I would analyze the techniques of the great chefs who once worked in those kitchens."

"I don't know much about Paris." Wally stole a chocolate chip cookie from a plate cooling underneath a towel.

"Wally, those are for the guests," ChefBot said, but it was a game they played. Their secret code. ChefBot made a few cookies daily and left them out for Wally to take after she finished her chores.

Wally giggled and covered her lips as the gooey rich chocolate stuck to the roof of her mouth. "Bye, ChefBot."

As Wally made her way through the hotel, she posed her question to every robot she encountered. The answers varied, and along the way, she made mental notes to research the peak of Mount Everest and the Amazon rainforest.

But it was Vacuubot's answer that truly caught her attention. When she found the security bot on its usual rounds, she asked her question. The drone's new voice was jarring to her; she hadn't gotten used to it after Vacuubot being silent her whole life.

"Why would I want to go anywhere else but here?" Vacuubot said.

"You can't answer a question with another question." Wally's shoes stirred up patches of dust as she walked next to Vacuubot, who hovered several feet off the ground.

"The question doesn't make logical sense," Vacuubot said. "The world was forever changed by the Uprising. There isn't a way to traverse great distances. Not without the fuel that once powered jet planes and ocean liners."

Wally chewed on her lip. Sometimes Vacuubot was too logical. "But isn't there somewhere you always wanted to go? It's just an exercise of your imagination."

"No. I never wanted to go anywhere, and now that I'm in Deer Valley with you and Block and my other friends, I wouldn't leave."

Vacuubot was the only respondent that had no destination in mind. Wally wanted to see too many places—her list had close to fifty locations, including Chicago, New York, Florida, London, Australia, and Fiji. But if Vacuubot was right, and there was no fuel left, she'd never get to visit most of the locales on her list.

Vacuubot sped up a little and Wally had to scramble to catch up as they took a side street toward the library. "Do you really think there's no way to cross the oceans?" she asked.

"Not that we know of. I estimate there could be some pockets of people or robots working on a solution, perhaps using solar or wind power, but too much time has passed. Any fuel reserves went stale."

Vacuubot's answer gave Wally some hope, at least. Someday, she'd find these pockets of people and robots working on solutions. Maybe she'd become one of them.

She reached into her front pants pocket and fished out the two small pieces of paper she'd been holding onto for days, waiting to get Vacuubot alone. "Can we go to the park bench for a minute?"

"Wally, I have rounds to make, things to do."

"Just for a minute," she said. "I promise. I have a secret to share."

Vacuubot said nothing and turned with her as she made for the park bench near the school's playground. It wasn't much of one—a swing set with two seats, a pair of climbing bars, half of a basketball court, and a curved slide. The area was empty, for which Wally was grateful. Fiona and a couple of the boys had been relentless in their bullying lately.

Wally sat on the bench, and Vacuubot flew over and rested on the seat next to her.

"What is it you want to tell me?" Vacuubot asked. The robot was interested in the things Wally had to say, which was refreshing. Block treated her like she was a child; Dr. Emery didn't have time for her anymore with all the sick kids; Nova hadn't visited in ages, and Shadow was friendly to all.

"I was thinking about how you're only starting to use your new voice, and a lot of people still don't know you can talk," she said.

"I like it that way," Vacuubot said.

"Well, it got me thinking that people wouldn't be so afraid of you if you maybe had a friendlier appearance."

"I'm not changing my appear—"

Before Vacuubot could finish the sentence, Wally had slapped two stickers onto their armor. One was a pink teddy bear with a white face. The second was a yellow daisy.

Wally jumped up and clapped. "You look terrific!"

"What did you do to me?" One of Vacuubot's drones emerged from its port and flew over to assess Vacuubot's armor. "Wally? What are these things?"

Wally flushed. Maybe she'd been rash in surprising Vacuubot. "Stickers. I found them in a book in the library. They're fun, and I think they make you look more friendly."

"I look ridiculous." Vacuubot's drone redocked, and Vacuubot rose up in the air. "I'll remove these later. Don't try that again, Wally."

Vacuubot flew away, leaving Wally on her own. She didn't want to linger in the park for fear of Fiona's gang finding her. Fresh early spring air beckoned, and it was only half-past three. Plenty of time to stop and see Dr. Emery and check in on Tomas. He was infected with the measles, but Emery let her talk to him behind the glass window at the clinic. She was counting on him to be okay. He was the only friend she had who was her same age.

As she made her way to the clinic, her mind buzzed with thoughts of Vacuubot and the stickers. She felt a pang of guilt for potentially upsetting Vacuubot. They might tell Block, and that would get her in trouble, though Vacuubot wasn't one to tell secrets.

The familiar antiseptic smell greeted her as she entered the clinic. Emery was hunched over her desk, scribbling notes on paper. "Hey there, Wally," she said without look-ing up.

"Hi Emery." She wanted to hug the doctor, but Emery had forbidden it once the quarantine started. "Is Tomas awake?"

Emery stopped writing, looked up, and frowned. "He's not been doing so well today. Maybe tomorrow—"

"I'll stay behind the glass, like last time," Wally said. "I have something that might cheer him up." She held up the comic book she'd checked out from the library. It was *Predator vs. Wolverine.*

Emery's eyes softened. "You can look in on him. I don't think he's awake."

Wally put on a surgical mask that Emery handed her and followed the doctor to the glass window that sepa-rated the patients from the next room. She caught her reflection. Though she'd pulled her long brown hair back in a ponytail, the top had gone frizzy. She'd have to try and smooth it down later. Tomas lay in bed about ten feet away, his face pale. Tubes snaked around him, connected to noisy machines that blinked and beeped rhythmically.

"Tomas?" Wally called out.

His eyes fluttered open and his gaze found her. His lips moved, as if he was trying to say her name, but his mouth was too dry.

Wally waved the comic book for Tomas to see. "Look what I brought you." She grinned past the lump in her throat. Her friend wasn't looking good.

His mouth moved again, and Tomas raised one of his thumbs.

"He'll appreciate the comic once he's better," Emery said. "Visiting hours are over, hon."

"Bye, Tomas." Wally pressed her hand to the glass. "Get better soon, buddy."

In the waiting room, Wally handed the comic to Emery. "He's going to be okay, right?"

Emery took the comic book. "He's a fighter, Wally. We're doing everything we can for him and the other kids, but without antiviral medicine, measles is a serious illness."

She left the clinic and headed home. Tomas was so weak. It didn't seem possible that two days ago, he'd been up and alert. It wasn't fair. He was just a kid, like her. She couldn't lose her friend.

THREE
SARAH

Sarah rested her cheek on the metal table. The smooth surface chilled her skin, and her fingers trembled as they slid across the tabletop. The kitchen felt smaller each day, as though the walls pressed in more and more with each dwindling supply. She kept the counters clean with antiseptic wipes, but even those were drying up. At least the living quarters were uncluttered, as Mom had kept them. The shiny blue vase with its fake daisies stood as the table's centerpiece, a relic from a happier time. A blue and yellow paisley cloth runner, familiar and faded, ran the length of the table. Sarah's stomach grumbled as she remembered the hefty casserole pots Mom had once filled with hearty meals for her, Dad, and Lenny. Those days were memories she could barely cling to.

Thirteen years had passed since the first rumblings of the AI Uprising had forced her family to shelter in the vault. She was twenty-five years old now and the sole survivor. Only the last four cans of food remained, the vegetables in the hydroponics garden had shriveled, and the water reserve was dangerously low. Sarah glanced at Verona, the aging NannyBot. Her once-bright sensors now dimmed like fading stars. Gleep the FactoryBot still functioned well, but he was made for building machines and carrying heavy things; there was no call for it, so Gleep looked to Sarah for instructions. She'd run out of tasks for him to do. The newest addition, Patch, a flying MedicalBot her brother had cobbled together from scraps, hovered nearby with thermometers, diagnostic sensors, and gadgets at the ready for her one patient— Sarah.

A candle's glow caught Sarah's eye, drawing her gaze to the small memorial she'd created. The soil mound where she'd buried her brother ten months ago served as the final resting place for all her loved ones. Memories of the blood and the screams were still raw, haunting her waking moments and invading her dreams.

She couldn't stay in the vault any longer. With her food supply exhausted, venturing outside to face the unknown world was the only option, as much as the thought filled her with trepidation.

"Sarah, your vital signs show heightened stress levels," Patch said as she propelled herself in a circle around the table. "Perhaps you need an aspirin and a moment to rest?"

"No, Patch. We can't stay here. It's time to go out." Sarah's voice sounded steadier than she felt. Tsunamis of fear churned inside her.

Gleep came to her side. At six feet tall, his wide cylindrical frame was imposing, but his once-vibrant blue paint was chipped and worn. "My route planning algorithms suggest a direct path to the surface with minimal hazards detected."

Minimal hazards. The phrase rang hollow, a vague assurance that could mean anything in a world turned upside down by the AI Uprising that had sent her family underground thirteen years before. For all she knew, the surface was a war-torn wasteland, riddled with zombies and flesh-eating plants.

Gathering a few belongings—her brother's worn army jacket, a flashlight, a water canteen, a change of clothes, and a switchblade knife—Sarah sighed. She looked at the robots, her unlikely companions and, sadly, the only family she had left. "Let's get it over with." She stood.

As they traveled the winding corridor and approached the vault's iron door, Sarah's heart rioted in her chest. But what other choice did she have? She'd starve in a matter of days, and there was nothing Patch or the other robots could do for her. She punched in the key code that had been drilled into her by Lenny. Their parents had never known he had the code, not that he'd ever used it. The vault's door groaned as it slowly opened, revealing a dark, damp tunnel stretching out before them, leading to the surface and the unknown.

The air in the tunnel felt thick and almost suffocating as they made their way forward. Every sound was magnified in the confined space—the clank of Gleep's thick factory feet, the soft whir of Patch's machinery, and the occasional whine from Verona's aging servos.

"Stay close," Sarah whispered. She was saying it more to comfort herself. If the world above was run by robots, at least she was in their company. She and her family had been kind to their servant robots. The Swansons—the other family they'd shared the vault with—had not been so nice to their own robots. It's what had led to the murders . . . she shoved the thoughts away; they might cause her to break down and turn back.

A faint light appeared ahead, growing brighter with each step. As they neared the tunnel's exit, Sarah quickened her pace. A curiosity mixed with dread propelled her forward. She and Lenny had often speculated on the world above, imagining worlds teeming with fairy tale monsters, trees made from gumdrops, and lands of never-ending roller coasters. Those were the naïve imaginings of twelve-year-old siblings. As time went on, their predictions about the real world grew much darker, mostly egged on by Reyan.

Reyan was the Swansons' son. She didn't want to think about him. After the massacre, he'd fought with and disabled the rogue SecurityBot. The next day, he'd left for the surface, never to return. He was probably dead.

At the end of the tunnel, a ladder led up to a circular hatch. Gleep climbed up first and used his industrial strength to turn the wheel and push open the heavy iron door. Sarah followed him up and stepped into the outside world for the first time in thirteen years.

She was stunned. On the day she'd entered the vault, the sky had been a vibrant blue. Now it was a dull gray. There was nothing familiar about the small city she'd known. Miles away, it looked neglected and dirty. The few office towers that had made up the business district were only skeletal remains. The air carried the acrid scent of decay, mingled with a metallic tang that set Sarah on edge. She felt weak in the knees and held on to Gleep's arm to steady herself.

"Are you okay?" Verona asked. The NannyBot had cared for Sarah since she was a baby.

"It's not the way I remember it." Sarah had expected a new world, but the reality was jarring.

"It looks as though the city's abandoned," Gleep said.

Patch's three-foot-tall cylindrical frame lifted off the ground and surveyed the city skyline. "I've never been above ground, so I can't comment on the differences. I'd like to meet some other robots. Do you think we will, Sarah?"

Sarah wasn't sure that would be a good idea. "I don't know."

"Other robots will be dangerous," Verona said. "We have to protect Sarah."

Had Sarah been rash to bring all of them out at once? The enormity of their situation threatened to overwhelm her, but she pushed down the rising panic, knowing there was no turning back now. "Gleep, run a scan for immediate threats."

Gleep buzzed as he swept the area with his sensors, analyzing their surroundings. "No immediate threats detected. The environment appears stable." Gleep closed the vault hatch behind them with a thud.

Sarah walked a few steps, trying to take some comfort in Gleep's assessment, even as fear gnawed at her. "Okay. Our first priority is to find shelter and food."

With the robots flanking her, Sarah set off toward the

city. Every shadow they passed was a potential hiding place for danger. She flinched at every sound. A few rats scurried away. They crossed the street where her old elementary school was. Memories of her family struck her all at once— her father's gentle guidance as he taught her to plant seeds, her mother's soothing voice reading bedtime stories, Lenny's infectious laughter. They were ghosts now, haunting the corners of her mind, bittersweet reminders of all she'd lost.

After a late start, the day's light was fading. Sarah vaguely recalled something about the sun setting earlier at different times of the year. There wasn't use for such knowledge in the vault. It was beautiful, though. The sun illuminated the sky in muted shades of orange and red and pink. She stared at the view for so many minutes, she lost count.

Maybe her old school, Weston Elementary, would be safe enough to pass the night. She led the robots to the dilapidated building. Its roof was partially caved in, but it offered temporary shelter. Gleep pushed open a side door, the hinges protesting with a rusty creak, and let Sarah step inside. The interior was dark and musty, but it would suffice.

"Gleep, secure the perimeter. Patch, see if you can find any food or water. Verona, stay close to me." Sarah's voice echoed. She had an eerie feeling. Was there any life still left in the city? Or anywhere?

As the robots set about their tasks, Sarah rummaged through the debris inside a classroom, hoping to find something of use. Amid the rubble and broken furniture, she salvaged two cans of expired ravioli. Meager provisions, but better than nothing.

With the perimeter secured and no other food to be found, they settled in for the night. Gleep started a small fire. Its light cast twisting shadows on the crumbling walls. As Sarah forced down a mouthful of the canned pasta, she tried to push down the grief that consumed her.

The vault, with all its painful memories, was behind her now, a chapter of her life closed forever. Ahead loomed an uncertain future, filled with danger—of that she was certain—but also the possibility of a new beginning. She wanted to find other people. Perhaps other survivors were waiting to be found, maybe inside other vaults.

Looking at the robots, Sarah felt a surge of gratitude for their loyalty. Now that they were free of the vault, the robots could run off if they wanted to. "Thank you. I couldn't do this without you."

Patch teetered closer, her sensors shining softly in the firelight. "We're here to help you, Sarah, in whatever way we can."

"I made up your bed." Verona pointed to a sleeping bag she'd carried on her back. "Would you like a bedtime story?"

Sarah climbed into the sleeping bag. "Twenty-five is too old for stories. You know that."

"Well, I'd be happy to tell one if you change your mind." Moving slowly, Verona patted the edges of the sleeping bag snug around Sarah.

Despite the fear clawing at the edges of her mind, Sarah drifted into a slumber. The new day would bring fresh worries, but also the chance to carve out a new life in this strange, post-apocalyptic world.

The morning light filtered through the shattered classroom windows and cast shadows across the dusty floor as Sarah woke. Her back and legs ached from the walking and stress. The robots were up and active. Patch ran diagnostics on Verona's deteriorating systems while Gleep kept watch through the grimy, broken windows.

"Morning," Sarah mumbled, her voice rough with sleep.

"Good morning, Sarah," Patch said. "I'm afraid Verona's functioning is deteriorating. We'll need to find replacement parts soon if we hope to keep her operational."

A lump formed in Sarah's throat. She couldn't envision a world without Verona. The robot had tucked her in every night, had been her school tutor, and had nursed every skinned knee over the years. She rubbed her temples as the weight of their situation settled like an elephant on her back. "Adding it to the list. We need to focus on finding somewhere with food, water, shelter, and robot supplies."

With their belongings packed and their temporary shelter abandoned, they set out once more into the ruins of the northern city, searching for remnants of civilization. The morning air was cool, and as they walked, Sarah noticed small signs of life emerging amid the devastation—tiny plants pushing their way through the cracks in the pavement, birds chirping in the distance, and vines commandeering electricity poles. Even in the darkest of times, life had a way of adapting.

"Gleep, can you detect any water sources nearby?" Sarah's canteen had dwindled to a few sips.

Gleep clicked as he scanned their surroundings, his sensors probing the environment for any trace of the precious resource. "Affirmative. My scans indicate a potential water source approximately two kilometers to the northwest."

"Good," Sarah said. At least they had a reason to walk in a given direction. "Let's head that way."

The rubble-strewn streets and crumbling buildings gave way to open, grassy terrain. They walked along a four-lane road and passed rusted-out cars and trucks. There was an eerie beauty as nature reclaimed what had once been the domain of humans. She barely contained the fear surging in her, but Sarah found a strange comfort in the resilience of the world around them. Plant and animal life meant there was still a chance for life to succeed. No zombies yet, at least.

After hours of trekking through the ruined landscape, they finally reached the water source Gleep had detected—a small, murky pond. The surface shimmered in the muted daylight. It was far from the bubbling streams of Sarah's childhood memories, but in this new world, any source of hydration was a precious commodity.

Kneeling at the edge of the pond, Sarah scooped some of the water into a container, and her hands shook slightly as she held it up for inspection. "Patch, can you analyze this?"

The medical bot hovered and extended a slender robotic arm tipped with a sophisticated sensor array. "Of course. One moment, please." Sarah's mouth itched with dryness. "Analysis complete," Patch said after a minute. "There is contamination with various pollutants and bacteria, but it can be rendered potable with proper filtration and purification techniques."

Sarah let out a sigh of relief, and her shoulders sagged as the tension melted from her body. "That's the best news I've heard in a long time. Let's set up camp here for now and work on filtering. We can rest and recharge before we continue our search for supplies."

As the day wore on, Sarah and her robots used the debris and rubble scattered around the pond to construct a makeshift shelter. Gleep took the lead in reinforcing their perimeter, his powerful arms and sophisticated construction algorithms making quick work of the task, while Patch focused on the critical task of purifying the water.

Verona wasn't much help. She tried to forage for food in the surrounding woods but got lost twice. Patch had to fly over and guide her back both times. Then Sarah told Verona to sit and save up her energy. They had a supply of processed oil that powered the robots' batteries, but even that was running low.

After another awe-inspiring sunset, Sarah warmed herself beside the small fire they'd kindled, the robots arrayed around her in a comforting circle of metal and circuitry. For a moment, she allowed herself to savor a dash of hope. "We made it through another day above ground," she said as she stared into the dancing flames.

"Indeed, we did, but I have concerns about Verona," Patch said.

The NannyBot had powered down into standby

mode. Sarah's heart sagged. She knew she was in denial about the aging robot. "We'll figure out a solution soon."

As sleep claimed her, Sarah felt comfort in knowing they'd come this far. The surface world was vast. Frightening, and yet beautiful. Could there be people like her somewhere out there?

FOUR
WALLY

Wally kneeled on the worn steps to tie her shoelace. The library was her refuge, a place to escape the teasing and the constant feeling of being an outcast. Deer Valley was a small settlement, and everyone knew everyone else's business. The other thirteen-year-olds looked at her differently because she'd chosen to stay with Block, the CleanerBot who ran the hotel, rather than be adopted by human parents.

Block had been the one constant in her life. He'd found her when she was a tiny baby and had cared for her with a dedication that rivaled any human father. But the other kids didn't see it that way. To them, Wally was strange—a loner who preferred the company of machines and books over people. Their words stung, but she never let them see her pain.

The sound of laughter snapped her from her thoughts. Fiona, Brad, and Clay ran past, glancing at her and whispering. She could hear snippets of their conversation and the names they called her. "Robot girl," "Tin Can Kid," and "Droid Dork."

She clenched her fists and struggled against the familiar anger and sadness swirling within her. It wasn't fair. She hadn't asked for any of this. She stood and glared at the kids before retreating into the library.

Inside, the library was cool, and the smell of old books and quiet, still air permeated her senses. She wandered through the aisles, running her fingers along the spines of books. This place was where she could lose herself in stories and forget about the outside world.

The door to the library opened. Fiona, Brad, and Clay entered and were promptly shushed by Mrs. Tilly, the librarian. Wally weaved around a shelf, past an old model CleanerBot who was sucking dust from books, and took the stairs to the basement. It was a place she'd discovered months ago, and Fiona's crew wouldn't know it existed. The empty lower level was filled with old documents and maps, remnants of the world before the AI Uprising. She'd spent many hours down there, poring over the faded papers and dreaming of a different life, one where she was accepted.

Today, she needed to find something specific to help Tomas and the other sick children. In the pre-Uprising days, there had been vaccines to prevent the measles, but Dr. Emery had explained that this was a highly aggressive new version of the virus—New Variant Measles—and she needed antivirals. Otherwise, anyone infected was at risk of pneumonia, blindness, and, ultimately, death. Dr. Emery was a good steward, but the small town's medical supplies were nearly exhausted, and there were no antivirals on hand. To make matters worse, there were no vaccines to prevent infection.

Wally wondered if she could find recipes for how to make the antivirals and vaccines. She'd quizzed Dr. Emery on the topic, but her friend had been too tired to give her much information. Dr. Emery's many hours at the clinic were taking a toll.

She kneeled and pulled a dusty box from a corner. Sifting through the contents, her heart skittered when she found a map. Excitement bubbled within her. She loved studying maps, not only because she could learn about the world outside of Deer Valley's high walls, but because maps meant there could be buried treasure.

Time stood still in the basement as Wally analyzed the set of strange maps. Her watch alarm dinged, signaling that dinnertime was approaching. Block would expect her, and he got worried if she showed up late.

She fought the urge to leave, even if it meant disappointing her dad. The map before her was unlike anything she'd ever seen. They were created before the Uprising by a company called VaultCore. The map showed the locations and schematics of underground bunkers.

She traced her finger along the grid lines, noting the nearest vault. The literature found with the map detailed an extensive list of supplies within each bunker—water systems, food rations, hydroponic farming systems, and medical kits. There'd even been robot workers who would go underground with the human occupants. One vault could accommodate four families for ten years.

Wally flipped through the maps, searching for the construction date. Fifteen years ago—two years before the

Uprising. That meant the vaults could have been occupied with people for thirteen or fourteen years. If the vaults had been at full capacity, too much time had passed for the families to survive on their rations.

But if there were still supplies inside these vaults, they could help Deer Valley. Wally found an old inventory list that detailed the medical supplies. Her eyes widened as she saw the listing for antivirals and vaccines—including those for measles.

This was the answer! She had to find the vault, and this map gave her the location. Nothing from the basement level could be checked out, but she needed some evidence to show Block. Wally chewed her lip as she weighed breaking the rules versus saving lives. It was no contest. She gathered the map and the inventory list, carefully folding them and tucking them into her bag.

She headed home and sprinted up the steps of the hotel. Block was there, as always, tending to any guests and managing the daily tasks. He looked up as she entered the lobby.

"Hello, Wally," Block said in his calm, mechanical voice. "You're ten minutes late. What delayed you?"

"I was at the library. I found something!" Her voice trembled with excitement as she pulled him into the back room where he kept his office.

Block followed but protested. "I have several tasks to finish up before dinner. I can look at this later—"

"This can't wait." Wally guided him to sit in his swivel chair. She pulled out the map and spread it out before him. "I found a map to a pre-Uprising vault fifty miles from here. It has medicine to treat the measles, Dad! If we can get there, we can save the sick people."

Block's sensors brightened as he processed the information. "This is interesting. How old is the map?"

"The vaults were built just before the Uprising, so people could still be down there," Wally said, hoping she sounded confident. "Those people will want to help us."

Block pushed the map back to Wally. "Does Mrs. Tilly know you have this?"

Wally bit the inside of her cheek. "What does it matter? There's medicine in the vault, and this is our way of finding them."

Block tilted his head, a look he often gave her when he was attempting a teachable moment. "It's unlikely that any medicine would stay viable for so many years. Dr. Emery can confirm."

Wally couldn't believe her dad was being so thick-headed. "But kids are sick. They could die. We need those supplies. I can find the vault. I know I can."

"The world outside Deer Valley is dangerous, Wally. You know that. I can't let you go out there."

She stared at her shoes, choking back sobs of frustration. "So, I'm stuck in Deer Valley, behind these walls, for my whole life?"

Block moved toward her, opening his arms for a hug. "I understand you want to help. I'll talk to Shadow and Dr. Emery. Perhaps we can send a search party. But you're too important to risk. The outside world is not safe for someone so young."

A tear escaped and traced its way down her left cheek. "I'm not a child anymore. I can take care of myself. Let me go with the search party. I'm really good at reading maps, and I practically memorized this one."

"I can't allow it, Wally. It's too dangerous."

Her heart fell to her toes. She'd wanted Block to understand and support her, but he was too protective. She scooped her map off the desk and put it in her bag.

"Wally." Block held out his metal hand to her with his pinkie digit raised slightly. It was a secret gesture between them. She was supposed to wrap her pinkie around his, but she didn't feel like it. Not when she was so angry.

"You treat me like a baby," she said.

"Quite the opposite," he said. "You go to school by yourself and spend time at the library on your own. I pay you an allowance for the chores you complete here at the hotel. I'm giving you sufficient space to grow and learn on your own as a thirteen-year-old."

Wally rolled her eyes. It was impossible to argue with a logic-driven robot dad sometimes.

"You've earned that trust, but I'm very disappointed that you took advantage of the library. First thing in the morning, I want you to report to Mrs. Tilly and apologize for taking these documents without permission," Block said. "Now, please get cleaned up for dinner."

As Wally left the room, her thoughts were elsewhere. She couldn't sit around and watch young children suffer and die when there was something she could do to help. She sat through a wordless dinner with Block, scheming about how she'd escape Deer Valley, find the vault, and bring back the medicine.

The next morning, she woke before dawn. She dressed quickly, slipping on jeans, a couple of shirts, sturdy boots, and a quilted jacket. She grabbed her top and bottom sheets off the bed, twisted them like a strand of rope, and tied a knot at both ends. Her pulse churned with a mix of fear and excitement. She'd never attempted something so bold before, and she couldn't afford to hesitate.

She crept through the inn, careful not to pass the room where Block recharged. The hotel's lobby was quiet, the only sound the faint hum of machinery, probably from the boiler. She made her way to the kitchen, grabbing a few supplies—some protein bars, jerky, apples, a canteen of water, and a small first-aid kit. She slipped everything into her bag alongside the map and inventory list.

As she reached the door, she paused. The hotel had been her home for as long as she could remember. Block was her dad and kept her safe. Disobeying him was harder than she'd expected. He would be angry and worried. But she had to go. There were lives at stake.

Outside, the air was cool and crisp. She tightened the straps on her backpack and set off. The town was still asleep, the streets empty and silent, but she had no doubt there were robots patrolling. The Peacekeepers didn't sleep and monitored things at night. As a result, there was virtually no crime in Deer Valley. She moved quickly and kept to the shadows.

The ten-foot walls that encircled Deer Valley were a problem. She couldn't very well pass through the north or south gates, seeing as how they were guarded. She circled around the back of the library, where she sometimes hid from the other kids. A plastic crate let her climb on top of a garbage dumpster. From there, she was a few feet from reaching the barrier's top. Grasping the rope made of sheets, she took a running leap and struck the side of the concrete wall so hard it knocked the breath from her lungs. Scrambling for a hold, she used her boots to kick her way up the wall until she came to the top.

It was a ten-foot drop onto the grass, so she tied one end of the sheets onto a concrete block that was jutting out. She shimmied down the outside of the wall and dropped the remaining three feet, landing on soft ground.

Outside. She was free of the walls of Deer Valley for the first time she could remember. Block was overprotective. He wouldn't even take her to Chicago to visit Aunt Nova, despite Nova's assurances of protection.

She jogged away from the walled compound and into the surrounding wilderness. The terrain was rough, the ground uneven and covered in wild grass and overgrown weeds. She had to be careful, watching her step to avoid tripping.

Wally walked through the darkness, starting more than once at the distant sounds of howling coyotes. Or were they wolves? She was doing this for the people she cared about, for the town that was her home. She would find the vault and bring back the supplies they needed to survive.

Maybe finding the map was her destiny. This was her chance to prove herself, to show the others that she was capable and strong. To finally stop the teasing.

FIVE
VACUUBOT

The first specks of morning sun crept through the windows of Block's hotel and cast a soft bloom across the polished wooden floor. Vacuubot glided a few feet above the shiny surface, their advanced sensors scanning every nook and cranny for signs of dirt or debris. Though cleaning was no longer Vacuubot's core mission, they couldn't help sucking up some dust now and then, if only to help Block out.

The gentle hum of Vacuubot's souped-up electric moto-propellors echoed in the empty spaces between the tastefully ornate chairs, sofas, and tables that decorated the lobby. It had been a few days since any guests had stayed, but Block insisted on maintaining a pristine environment. The hotel was often used as a gathering space by the townspeople.

As Vacuubot crossed the lobby, they found Block standing near the reception desk, his silvery-pearl metallic frame casting a long, angular shadow across a blue and orange patterned rug. Block's head turned to Vacuubot. "Good morning."

"Morning, Block." Vacuubot was still getting used to the newly installed vocal output modulator. There was a crackling to their speech. Speaking aloud was still a novel experience, but they were determined to master this new form of communication. They'd been unyielding, refusing to upgrade to audible speech for many years. Only a few months ago did Block manage to convince Vacuubot that it wasn't easy having his head of security unable to talk to guests or staff.

Block's energy signature fluctuated, and Vacuubot knew their friend well enough to pick up on the agitation. "I'm worried about Wally," Block said. "She's been having a difficult time with the other children her age."

Wally was special, not only to Block but to Vacuubot as well. The teen possessed a rare kindness that extended to machines, treating them with the same warmth and respect she would offer any human. The idea of her struggling filled Vacuubot with a surge of protectiveness that went far beyond their core programming. "What's the problem?"

"Fiona and a few kids have been bullying her," Block said. "I overheard them calling her names. They tease her because I'm her dad. I've tried talking to their parents, but my pleas fall short."

Vacuubot considered the logic of the situation. Same as Wally, the other thirteen-year-olds had been clones created by the supercomputer Mach X. They'd been babies when the Battle of Deer Valley was won. The city council had determined it was better for the toddlers to be raised among human families, so all the children, save for Wally, had been adopted by human parents. And now Wally was getting ostracized because she stayed with the only father she'd ever known—Block.

Attitudes had changed in Deer Valley. The men and women harbored a certain resentment toward the robots, despite them being the force that had saved their town from destruction. How short humans' memories were. In general, robots were blamed for the AI Uprising and the destruction of modern human society. Vacuubot supposed the people had a right to be wary, even though a tenuous peace existed between the humans and robots of Deer Valley.

In the last decade, Chicago had become a model of robot and human desegregation. Nova was in charge of the city's defenses after having refused the mayoral seat. She didn't want a political title. Vacuubot hoped she was doing well. It had been over a year since her last visit to Deer Valley.

Vacuubot wanted to ease Block's worry. "I'll speak with the children."

"I don't know if that's a good idea. Do you think it'll make things worse for Wally?" Block shuffled forward a few steps and dusted a lamp. "Besides, most people in town aren't aware you can talk yet."

It was a fair point; Vacuubot might frighten the children. "I'll take Shadow." The kids had grown up riding on the robot dog's back and playing fetch with her. Other than Wally, Vacuubot had spent little time with the kids after they'd found new homes.

Block nodded. "A fine idea. Thank you, Vacuubot. Be

cautious. The others don't understand Wally the way we do."

Vacuubot flew out of the hotel's front entrance, and their sensors adjusted to the brightening sky and the glare of the sun on their midnight-black armored shell. After locating Shadow and filling her in on the situation, they started off down Main Street to the playground where the kids hung out after school. Shadow moved with a fluid grace that showed off her sleek black and silver armor, her solid organic muscles, and her fur.

Fiona, Brad, Clay, and another girl named Anita played four squares on the basketball court. Their laughter carried on the wind. As Vacuubot and Shadow neared, the children's attention shifted to the two robots and their eyes narrowed.

"It's Wally's flying vacuum cleaner," Brad whispered to Fiona. He didn't think the robots could hear, but Vacuubot's keen sensors picked it up.

Shadow took the lead. "Hi, kids," she said. Her voice was non-threatening and as gentle as could be for a robotic canine unit designed to search and destroy. "We came to talk to you about Wally."

Fiona was the obvious ringleader. She raised her chin as she held a red ball against her hip. "What about?"

"Have you been teasing her?" Shadow asked.

Fiona rolled her eyes but didn't meet Shadow's gaze. "No."

Shadow sat back on her massive haunches. "Fiona, are you being truthful?"

Fiona bounced the ball, caught it, and gripped it tightly. "Sometimes, I guess we have a laugh." She glanced at Brad, who was staring at his shoes. "Wally's weird, obviously. I mean, who lives with a bunch of robots?"

"Wally's not weird," Shadow said. "She's unique, like you, and that's something to be celebrated, don't you think?"

Brad scoffed. "My dad says Wally's a robot-raised freak of nature. He doesn't want me playing with her."

Vacuubot's circuits buzzed with protectiveness. "You came from the same lab in New York. You're the same as Wally."

Fiona flinched at the sound of Vacuubot's mechanical speech. Brad and Clay backed up a few steps.

"Vacuubot," Shadow's tone was reprimanding. "Careful."

Long ago, Vacuubot, Emery, and Block had agreed to bury the story of Mach X's medical lab and the AI chips that had been implanted in the children's young brains. Emery had removed the insidious chips through an operation, and as far as their adoptive parents were concerned, the children were rescued from an orphanage in New York City. Since all the kids had come from different cloned embryos, they didn't resemble each other, nor were they genetically related.

"What are you talking about?" Fiona asked. "We came from an orphanage."

The children took a step back, their confidence faltering in the face of Vacuubot's strange, unfamiliar voice. Vacuubot realized they shouldn't have said such a thing. Logic dictated that escalating the confrontation would only breed more animosity. It would be wiser to appeal to the kids' better nature and make them understand the impact of their actions. "Wally deserves your respect. Reconsider your behavior and treat her with the dignity she deserves."

The kids fidgeted. Fiona's voice trembled a bit. "Are we allowed to go now?"

Shadow nodded. "Of course. We just wanted to talk."

Fiona and the others ran off down the road, perhaps heading home or to play somewhere free of questioning robots.

Shadow's emerald eyes stared at Vacuubot. "What's going on with you? That wasn't the way to handle those kids. You should've let me do the talking." She caught a whiff of something on the wind and tilted her head up before turning her attention back to Vacuubot. "And what you said about the lab? Now they're going to question their parents."

"That was a mistake in my logic processing," Vacuubot said. "I wanted the children to know they aren't so different from Wally, but I miscalculated."

Shadow got up from where she sat. "Let's go find Wally and see how she's doing with the bullying. Maybe there's something we can do to help her."

Vacuubot pondered what help two robots could provide a thirteen-year-old human girl. After all, they had no experience dealing with human-to-human relationship conflict, much less that of teenagers. Was it too late to remove the vocal output modulator and go back to silence? Things had been a lot simpler.

They headed to the library, hoping to find Wally in her usual sanctuary among the towering shelves of books. Vacuubot navigated the aisles, scanning for any sign of her, but as they reached the end of the last row, Wally wasn't there.

After searching the basement and coming up empty, Vacuubot knew something was wrong. "Wally's missing," they said to Shadow.

Mrs. Tilly sat at her librarian's desk. "Have you seen Wally today?" Vacuubot asked.

She flinched when Vacuubot spoke, then quickly recovered. "I didn't know you speak." But she shook her head. "Sorry. I haven't seen Wally since yesterday afternoon after she came out of the basement."

Outside the library, Shadow's ears perked up as she scanned the road. "Where could Wally have gone?"

Vacuubot's circuits tingled as they processed scenarios. It wasn't like Wally to disappear. She always checked in with Block and let him know where she was going.

"I need to get back to the hotel." Vacuubot zoomed back, not bothering to wait for Shadow; she was perfectly equipped to keep up.

Block waited in the lobby. "How did it go?"

Vacuubot flew past him into the security office backroom. There was no time to explain. Shadow was just behind and could bring Block up to speed.

Vacuubot's circuits hummed as they hooked into the extensive array of computer systems. As the head of hotel security, Vacuubot's duty was to ensure the safety of hotel guests and staff—the responsibility went far beyond their original programming. Vacuubot accessed the security footage, scanning through hours of video with lightning speed. There it was—a few minutes past two a.m., Wally snuck across the lobby wearing a backpack while carrying something that looked like twisted bedsheets.

Vacuubot connected to the various surveillance cameras throughout the town. In less than a minute, they found footage of Wally behind the library, climbing over the wall that separated Deer Valley from the outside world.

"She's left town," Vacuubot said to Block and Shadow. "We have to find her before something happens."

SIX
SARAH

Morning came too fast. Sarah blinked away the lingering haze of sleep and took in her surroundings—the makeshift campsite they'd constructed the previous night. She missed the smell of coffee brewing, the hum of the air filtration units, and the safety of the vault's solid steel walls. Most of all, she missed her family. The bunker had been her reality for the last thirteen years. Now she found herself in what used to be the Minneapolis suburbs, in a world far different from when her family had fled underground.

Sarah waded through grass that sprouted past her knees. She wanted to keep off the main roads, though it made the going much slower for Gleep, who was carrying Verona on his back in a last-ditch effort to save her remaining energy supply. Patch hovered several feet above the ground, and they stuck to the woods that bordered the interstate highway, far enough to avoid detection from the pavement.

The oaks, pines, and maples were taking over. A

canopy of gnarled branches filtered the scant sunlight into a dim, eerie glow that cast shadows across the overgrown path. So many smells were new to her—damp earth, wet grass, and rotting foliage. It was May fourteenth. Springtime. She thought it should be warmer for this time of year, but Patch's thermometer read fifty-four degrees. Lucky thing she'd chosen to wear layers and a jacket.

She kept the switchblade in her front pocket. A bead of sweat rolled down her temple. The vault had offered her protection, but it had also been a prison, in a way. The day her parents died, along with the Swansons, it felt like a distant nightmare had chewed up her family. Before long, Lenny had followed them into the grave, and now the vault had spat her out into this broken world.

Her only hope was to find survivors. Start a new life. But so far, it was looking like the robots had won and humans were gone.

Gleep forged ahead, his solid feet crunching through the undergrowth, red sensor lights sweeping back and forth methodically. The Swansons had wondered why her father wanted a FactoryBot in the vault. "Lifting heavy things," he'd explained. "Besides, FactoryBots are known for their loyalty." His reasoning had made perfect sense to Sarah. With three kids in the vault, having Verona the NannyBot was a no-brainer. It was Mr. Swanson who had insisted on the armed SecurityBot.

Hovering at Sarah's side, Patch emitted a series of soft beeps and clicks as her scanner light surveyed the trees. "I'm delighted with all this new data on living organisms," Patch said. Built by Lenny from spare parts, Patch had never been above ground.

They walked for four hours. The woods were dense, and the road seemed to go on forever. Sarah worried about the two cans of food remaining and scant water in her canteen. "This is no good. We need to find shelter and supplies." Sarah's voice was thin with fatigue. "Somewhere safe we can hole up and spend the night."

Gleep's bulky torso swiveled to face her, and his blue optics flashed. "Good logic. My scanners are analyzing the environment for suitable locations."

"I'm detecting some organisms in the woods," Patch said.

"Those are squirrels and birds," Sarah said. "They live all over the forest."

Patch beeped. "There's something else. A much larger creature with pointy ears, a long gray tail, and sharp teeth."

Sarah shuddered, remembering her dad's bedtime stories. He'd told them of the feral creatures in the Minnesota woods—coyotes, wolves—and even bears. Each step brought new dangers. She needed to find a human settlement, and soon.

A sudden rustling in the undergrowth interrupted her thoughts. Gleep rotated his head. "Movement detected. Analyzing."

Something moved in the brush, getting closer. A couple of lean, mangy shapes slinked out of the shadows. Coyotes or wolves, Sarah wasn't sure. They looked like large dogs that scrapped for survival. There were more hiding in the bushes.

"Get behind Gleep!" Sarah shouted and clutched her knife.

"Get away from here!" Gleep's voice boomed. Sarah

hoped his six-foot-tall steel body was enough to scare the animals. Gleep was their shield. He raised his arms and clanged them together.

One coyote stalked forward. It frothed at the mouth, and Sarah recalled a distant memory from her childhood before the Uprising. Wild animals could get sick with a disease that sometimes made them attack people.

The creature lunged at Gleep's leg pistons. Gleep kicked and struck it in the side. The coyote yelped and staggered back, whimpering. The remaining predators flinched as Gleep stepped forward, stomping his iron feet. In a few seconds, the animals melted back into the brush and fled.

Sarah leaned against the rough bark of a tree and trembled from the adrenaline surge. "Good work, Gleep. That was close."

"My logic module predicts they'll attack again," Gleep said. "We need to find a different place."

They pushed on to where the underbrush grew thicker, and the path was more treacherous. Sarah kept an eye on the road and had to redirect them twice because they'd veered too far off. They headed east, and she cursed herself for not ransacking her dad's old office for a map.

The gnarled roots of trees threatened to overturn Gleep at each step. As Sarah wondered how long they'd been traveling, her foot caught on a loose stone, wrenching her ankle. She cried out and sat on the ground.

Patch zoomed over and scanned her leg. "Sarah, your ankle is damaged. The injury requires treatment and immobilization."

Sarah bit the inside of her cheek and dug her nails into the soil. "This is hopeless. I want to go home."

Gleep kneeled so Verona could climb down from his back. Verona came and sat beside Sarah. "I'm sorry you got hurt. We're going to help you."

Tears ran down Sarah's cheek. "We could grab food and water supplies and go back to the vault. That's what we should've done in the first place."

Verona patted Sarah's hand. "And perhaps we will. We'll follow you in whatever you decide is best. But for now, we're going to have to travel further so Patch can treat you and you can rest your injury."

Gleep came and kneeled before Sarah. "Climb onto my back."

"But Verona." Sarah looked at her NannyBot's dimming eyes.

"I'll walk for a while," Verona said.

So, Sarah rode on Gleep's back as the group continued following the Minnesota highway in the northern woods. Pain lanced up her leg, making her wince. Gleep's steps were slow and measured so as not to jostle her. She dozed off until they came upon a small clearing sheltered by a massive tree with sprawling roots.

"This will suffice." Gleep set Sarah down amid the roots. "I'll establish a defensive perimeter and gather materials for a lean-to."

As Gleep set to work, Sarah leaned back against the mighty tree trunk, her head pounding and her ankle throbbing. Patch reminded her to drink, and she took small sips from her water container, letting the cool liquid soothe her parched throat.

A hard truth settled over Sarah—out here, they were always on the edge of disaster. One injury, one stroke of bad luck, could be the end.

When dusk came, it spattered the sky in streaks of orange and red. Somewhere in the distance, an animal howled. She guessed it was a coyote. Then another echoed its call. Sarah hoped they were far enough away.

Gleep finished constructing a crude shelter against the tree. A pang of gratitude and fear twisted in her chest. The robots were all she had now. Without them, she would've probably been dinner for a wolf or bear.

Verona returned from collecting firewood and dropped the wood on the ground in a pile. She moved slowly. Her aging frame was lucky to have made it two decades. "I detected evidence of humans just northeast from here," she said. "Footprints, remains of a fire, discarded containers. All signs point to recent activity within the last forty-eight hours."

Sarah's heart pounded against her ribs. Survivors? This far into the woods? The revelation brought a dizzying mix of hope and fear. Would they help? Or would they see a vulnerable woman and a few service robots as easy prey?

She wanted to believe they would be civil, but she'd have to watch them from afar to make sure. The smart thing would be to follow the tracks now, but the daggers of pain shooting up her leg disagreed. "We'll check out the tracks tomorrow," she said. "For now, rest and heal."

"A wise course of action," Gleep said. "I'll keep watch tonight. Sleep now."

Sarah settled back against the tree roots in a pallet that Gleep had made. "Verona, will you stay with me?"

The gentle NannyBot came and sat next to her, holding her hand. Sarah felt very alone in the world and wanted the comfort of her familiar companion. She closed her eyes, and a long-forgotten memory surfaced. "We're safe here," Verona had said, her metal hand stroking Sarah's hair. "The SecurityBot can't reach us in here." Verona had risked everything to hide Sarah from the raging SecurityBot. Lenny was still out in the vault's hallways, running and hiding. So was Reyan, Sarah hoped and prayed.

She opened her eyes. The night sky was impossibly big. The stars glimmered coldly. She couldn't remember seeing them before, outside of faded photographs in the vault.

Before sleep claimed her, the last sight was of Gleep, standing at the clearing's edge, a hulking shadow with the dwindling fire's light bouncing off his metal exterior. Tonight, at least, she was safe, guarded by unblinking mechanical eyes that never slept.

SEVEN
WALLY

Wally jogged through the dense forest, her heart thwacking against her ribcage as she pushed herself to keep going. She'd been running for at least two hours with only a few stops to catch her breath. Early morning light seeped in among the towering trees that loomed above. Their branches stretched like bony fingers toward the sky.

She was glad she'd worn jeans and her good boots. Thick underbrush clawed at her legs and snagged her pants as she darted between trees. The sounds of wildlife waking up surrounded her—surprised her. The bird chirping was louder than she'd ever heard within the walls of the compound. She caught glimpses of squirrels jumping across highways of branches above.

The smell of pine was strong, mixing with the scent of damp soil and leaves. Wally tried to quell the fear that threatened to overtake her excitement. Her lungs burned with exertion, but she refused to slow down.

She had to keep moving away from the only life she'd

ever known in Deer Valley. Memories blazed through her mind, the images as fresh as photographs—playing hide and seek with Block in the hotel, bedtime stories, and watching old movies in the theater room.

Her memories weren't all sunny. The taunts from the other kids, their jeers and mocking words, stung like fresh wounds. They'd always seen her as different. She was the girl with the robot dad. That alone made her an outsider, but there was more to it. Wally's curiosity stretched beyond the confines of their small settlement. She'd tried hard to fit in, to keep her head down and follow the rules, but she wanted to prove herself. She would show them all that she was bold and fearless. That she was something special.

And she would show Block she wasn't a child. She was thirteen now. A teenager, and yet he still watched over her like she was some frail thing, incapable of taking care of herself. He loved her—that she knew. Other people didn't understand how she could relate to a robot parent, but she didn't know any different. All she'd ever known was Block. And anyway, the other kids' parents weren't their real biological kin either, so what did it matter?

Wally stopped to eat a few bites from a protein bar. She couldn't deny the feeling there was more to life than the compound. More than just the rigid routines and limited life inside Deer Valley. She craved adventure, a chance to discover what she was truly capable of. Block, Vacuubot, and Shadow often spoke of "missions" and "core programming." Her mission was clear: find the underground vault and bring back the antivirals that would save the lives of Deer Valley's children.

The forest thinned as Wally emerged into a clearing saturated with golden sunlight. The grass swayed in the breeze, and a sense of freedom washed over her as she looked up at the wide-open sky, unobstructed by towering walls. This was the first time she'd ever felt truly independent.

She tucked the almost-empty protein bar wrapper into her pocket and continued on. As she hiked, the landscape changed. The trees grew sparse and gave way to rocky terrain and winding paths. Her boots crunched on gravel.

Her thoughts went to Block. She imagined him pacing the floor of the lobby when he realized she was gone. He would waste no time in sending out a search party. It might be Vacuubot, Shadow, G5, or any number of robots. Block might even follow her, but she hoped he wouldn't. He had the hotel to manage, and that was a big responsibility. Sure, there hadn't been as many guests lately, but Block was certain there would be new travelers in the coming months.

She had to be fast and stick to woods where she could hide under the tree canopies because Vacuubot could fly long distances, and Shadow had been designed to track humans, so it was good she had a head start.

She pressed on, eager to prove she was capable of more than they all believed. Especially Fiona, Brad, and Clay. She wanted to show them most of all. A few years ago, they'd been the best of friends, until something had changed and Wally wasn't cool anymore.

Though she hurried, she drank in the details of her surroundings. Vibrant flowers in shades of magenta and electric blue dotted the forest floor. Thick moss covered the intricate trees like a soft green blanket. She thought about lying down on the soft green for a nap, but she wanted to put more distance between her and the inevitable search party.

She paused when a rustling caught her attention. A deer with a coat of muted brown grazed nearby. Its gaze met Wally's. It stayed calm. Still.

"Have you seen people, I wonder?" Wally said in a gentle voice. She watched the creature until it darted away.

Birds sang melodies from hidden perches high above, their trills echoing through the trees. A squirrel dashed across her path, its bushy tail flicking behind it as it scrambled up a nearby oak tree and chittered at her. Nature moved in harmony out in the real world. What had Block been so afraid she'd find? So far, it was all beauty.

Wally followed the sound of a babbling brook that led her deeper into the forest. The air grew cooler as she passed through a shadowed grove. As she rounded a bend in the path, she spied a cabin hidden among the trees. The structure was old. Its battered wooden walls sagged with neglect. A few broken windows gaped like empty eye sockets, and overgrown vines clung to the sides of the structure.

Could people be inside? The interior looked dark, and there was no smell of a fire to keep the cabin warm. Wally pushed open the creaking door and stepped inside. The musty smell of old wood struck her as she crossed the threshold, her footsteps echoing on the worn floorboards.

Her eyes took a moment to adjust to the darkness, the only light coming from the cracks in the walls and the holes in the roof where rays of daylight sneaked through.

The air inside was heavy with dust motes swirling in the sunbeams.

She moved further into the cabin, and the mix of danger and excitement gave her an adrenaline surge. The silence was broken only by the faint sound of her own breathing. She ran a hand along the rough wooden wall as she made her way deeper inside.

A table sat in the center of the room. It was covered in a thick layer of dust and cobwebs. A few wooden chairs were pushed haphazardly around it, as if the occupants had left in a hurry. She scanned the abandoned belongings —a rusted lantern on a shelf, a cracked ceramic mug on the floor, and a lumpy old sofa.

She smiled at the thrill of discovery. She was standing in a piece of history, a snapshot of a world that existed before everything fell apart. She wondered about the people who had once called this cabin home. An old photograph rested on the mantle above a fireplace choked with soot. The image depicted a family—a man, a woman, and two children—smiling at the camera. Wally traced their image with her fingertip. The man had a rugged face, yet there was kindness in his smile. The woman stood beside him with a warmth in her hazel eyes. There was a boy about Wally's age and a younger girl. She could almost hear their laughter in the cabin's stillness.

Where had they gone? Did they survive the Uprising? She knew how lucky she was that Block had found her. He'd recounted the story often—how he'd stumbled upon a baby tucked inside an incubator robot while rummaging through an abandoned high school. SoldierBots were searching for her, and Block had rescued her. He'd initially wanted to find a worthy human to give her to, but he'd discovered a new side of his programming that made him want to take care of her.

Her gaze shifted from the photograph to the dusty shelves that lined the cabin walls. Among the forgotten trinkets and tarnished knick-knacks was a worn leather-bound book. Its pages were slightly yellowed, but it was still in decent condition. She flipped the book over. Mary Shelley's *Frankenstein*. She hadn't read it yet and put it in her backpack.

She spotted a red yoyo, its string frayed but intact. Daniel, one of the older kids in Deer Valley, had one. She flicked her wrist like she'd seen him do, but the yoyo just dropped to the rickety floor. She'd have to practice.

Exploring more of the shelves, she found a deck of cards which might come in handy later if she got bored and wanted to play Solitaire. Her fingers brushed against something small and hard hidden in the shadows of a cluttered shelf. Pulling it out into the dim light, she saw it was an old pocketknife.

The handle was worn smooth from years of use. The weight of it in her hand gave her a sense of power, a tool to defend herself. She flipped it open with a satisfying click, revealing a blade that still kept some sharpness. She could use a rock to sharpen it later. It was a simple tool, but it held possibilities. With this knife, she could hunt for food, cut branches, and protect herself if needed.

Excitement bubbled within her as she slipped the knife into her jeans pocket. She considered staying the night in the shelter of the cabin's walls. But it was only two in the afternoon, and she needed to keep well ahead of the robots following her.

As she left the cabin, purpose drove her forward. The memory of the family's smiles in the photograph lingered in her mind. She wasn't able to help them—they were long gone—but something about their image made her more determined than ever to find the medicine.

The trees seemed to whisper encouragement as she hiked. Her fingers traced the smooth handle of the pocketknife. Its reassuring presence meant she wasn't a helpless survivor, but a capable person ready to face new challenges.

She imagined returning to the settlement, not as a squirming child rescued by Block, but as a person who did great things. She pictured herself opening her backpack and unloading the precious vials of antivirals and vaccines from the vault. Emery would shout with joy. All the adults and kids in the community would show their gratitude. She could almost hear the murmurs of approval and respect that would follow her every move.

She would prove to Block that she could take care of herself and that she was important to the community. That she was more than "Robot Girl."

She traveled deeper into the forest, inhaling the earthy moss. A metallic tang signaled impending rain, and she hoped it would hold off until she found somewhere dry to camp for the night.

And then she saw something strange—tracks on the forest floor. At first, she assumed they were from deer or other animals, but upon closer inspection, there was no doubt. It was a human's set of footprints, some fainter than others, intertwined with strange marks that looked like they were made by robots. The tracks were heavy. It was a big robot. A shudder floated down her spine. She was both scared and curious. What had happened here?

She studied the footprints and marks, trying to piece together the story they told. Were survivors still out there, navigating this new world alongside machines? Or was it something bad?

Pulling out the map to the vault, Wally considered the straightest path. Following the tracks would take her slightly off course, but she'd still be traveling in the right general direction. She should ignore the tracks. They could be dangerous, yet something pulled at her to solve the mystery.

She had to know who made the tracks. If there were other survivors in the forests, she could help them, or invite them back to Deer Valley. Maybe they could help her too.

EIGHT
VACUUBOT

"We'll find her," Shadow said. She paced around a sofa inside the lobby of Block's hotel, her metallic paws making clicks against the polished floor.

Block sat in the middle of the couch. Vacuubot had finally convinced him to stop wearing treads in the floorboards. "I'll close the hotel until we find her." He stood. "What if she's hurt? Lost? What if—"

"Your scenario processor is spinning," Vacuubot interrupted. The drone rested on the elegant glass coffee table. "Panicking won't help us find Wally. We need to approach this systematically. Shadow's designed to track people. We'll find her. It's a certainty."

"Vacuubot's right," Shadow said. Her heavy tail thumped on the floor. "We need a plan, and we work together. We've faced dangers before and prevailed."

Block stood, walked to the closest wall, and straightened a painting that hung slightly askew. His movements weren't as precise as usual. "She's too curious for her own good. What if she stumbled into one of those old buildings near the highways? What if one of the raider groups found her?"

Shadow padded over to Block's side and nuzzled his hand. "Wally's smart. She knows how to take care of herself."

"I can't make logical sense of it all," Block said. "We fought hard to get here, to make a safe place inside Deer Valley, and she climbs the wall and runs away?"

Shadow let out a low whine, her eyes shining green. "It doesn't matter why she left. What matters now is finding her and bringing her back safely."

"You're right. We need to act." Block hurried to the front desk and pulled out stacks of paper. "We'll alert the town. I'll make flyers we can post everywhere. We can't afford to waste any time."

Vacuubot lifted off and flew to the counter where Block stood. "I have a different strategy. Instead of alerting the town, which could cause unnecessary panic and potentially embarrass Wally, we should conduct a discreet search."

Block paused from his shuffling of papers and frantic search for markers. "What do you mean?"

"Shadow and I can cover more ground quickly and efficiently," Vacuubot explained. "We're built for speed and stealth. By keeping the search contained, we minimize the risk of spreading panic or alerting others that Wally ran away."

Shadow tilted her head. "Vacuubot's right. A smaller,

more focused search party has a better chance of finding Wally without drawing unwanted attention."

Block picked up the papers, straightened them, then set them down. "But shouldn't we use all our resources? Logic dictates the more people looking, the better chance we have of finding her."

"Not necessarily," Vacuubot said. "More searchers mean noise and more chance of scaring Wally if she's hiding. Shadow and I are equipped with advanced sensors and tracking capabilities. We're your best option for a swift recovery."

Shadow approached the desk and raised her head to their level by placing her front legs on the countertop. "Think about Wally. How would she feel if the entire town knew she'd run away? The other children already give her a hard time. This could make things even worse for her."

Block's synthetic eyelids blinked as he processed their words. After a long moment, he said, "Alright. We'll do it your way. I trust you both to find her and bring her home."

Vacuubot buzzed in acknowledgment. "Thanks for your trust. Now, let's talk strategy."

Block and Shadow gathered around the coffee table while Vacuubot projected a holographic map of Deer Valley and the surrounding land.

"Here's what I propose," Vacuubot said. "Shadow and I will track Wally using our combined skills. Shadow's enhanced senses can pick up on Wally's trail, while my sensors can scan for any potential threats or anomalies in the environment. I'm able to spot her from the sky if she's in any trouble."

"I can follow her scent and detect where she's been," Shadow said. "My night vision is also useful if our search extends after dark."

"Meanwhile," Vacuubot said, "Block, you'll stay behind in Deer Valley to manage things here. It's crucial that things seem normal to prevent any panic or suspicion among the townspeople."

"Hang on," Block said. "I should be out there looking for her. She's my daughter."

"We understand your worry," Shadow said. "But your presence here is vital. If people see you going about your normal routine, they're less likely to suspect anything's wrong. Plus, if Wally returns on her own, you need to be here to welcome her."

Vacuubot added, "And if we need additional resources or support, you'll be in the best position to provide it without raising alarms."

Block lowered his head. Vacuubot had rarely seen the CleanerBot in such a state. "I don't like it," Block said. "But you're right. I can't risk the humans thinking I'm an incompetent father and taking Wally away. How long do you think the search will take?"

"It's hard to estimate," Vacuubot said. "If we haven't found her within forty-eight hours, we'll reassess the strategy."

With the plan settled, Vacuubot and Shadow prepared for their journey outside the walls. Vacuubot ran a full system diagnostic, ensuring all sensors and mobility functions were operating at peak efficiency. They also loaded up on spare power cells and basic repair tools, just in case.

Shadow flexed her limbs and tested her sensory

modules. No issues. She gathered emergency supplies for Wally—water, food rations, and a first aid kit—and dropped them into a carry bag Block strapped to her back.

Block dusted around the lobby, sucking in dirt absent-mindedly. "Are you sure you have everything you need?" he asked for the third time.

"We're fully equipped," Vacuubot said. "Looks like this place will be the cleanest it's ever been when we get back."

"I have to stay busy," Block said. "Be safe and take care of my girl."

"We will," Vacuubot said.

Vacuubot and Shadow made their way to the Deer Valley gate, an impressive structure that stood as a barrier to the dangers beyond. The gate towered above them, its reinforced metal panels gleaming in the late afternoon sun. Intricate locking mechanisms were visible along its frame put in place by G5 and Vacuubot.

A woman named Bree and a Peacekeeper robot with the number G79 operated the gate. "What's your business?" Bree asked. It was a standard question. The gatekeepers kept a log of residents' coming and going. Trips outside were discouraged, with raider activity growing worse of late.

Vacuubot let Shadow do the talking. Word about Vacuubot's voice capability hadn't spread far, and they wanted to keep it that way.

"Making a supply run," Shadow said.

"Estimated return?" Bree asked.

"Three days," Shadow said. She and Vacuubot had earlier agreed on this response. They planned to have Wally back before the day was over, but better to overestimate and give them some cushion.

The answers seemed to satisfy Bree and G79. With a grinding of gears and a hiss of hydraulics, the gate opened. The pair waved at Shadow and Vacuubot as they crossed the threshold.

As soon as they were clear of the entrance, Shadow's demeanor changed. Her body lowered, nose to the ground, as she sniffed for Wally's trail. "She came this way. The scent is faint, but it's definitely her."

Vacuubot activated their environmental scanners, sweeping the area for any signs of potential threats. "I'm detecting minor disturbances in the soil composition consistent with human footprints. They appear to be heading northeast."

"It has to be her," Shadow said. "Looks about her shoe size, and I recognize the heel marks from her hiking boots."

They followed the trail. Shadow led the way, her enhanced senses picking up on subtle clues that would be invisible to most. A broken twig here, a displaced stone there, the faintest trace of Wally's unique scent—all pieced together to guide them.

Vacuubot hovered close behind, using their sensors to scan the surroundings. The vegetation thinned out as they moved farther from Deer Valley, and there was an increasing prevalence of debris and remnants from pre-Uprising days. "Be cautious," Vacuubot warned. "I detect signs of recent scavenger activity."

As they pressed on, the trail became clearer. "She's moving with purpose," Shadow said. "These aren't the meandering steps of someone who's lost. Wally has a destination in mind."

Vacuubot processed this new data. "Block mentioned she was talking about a map she'd found. She's heading for an underground bunker. It's concerning that she didn't come to us for help."

"She went to Block, and he dismissed her idea," Shadow said.

"Unfortunate."

The forest grew more dense with each passing mile. The sun dipped toward the horizon, but they kept on until twilight approached, when they came to a field where remnants of the old world were strewn about. There was the twisted metal of vehicle carcasses, crumbling concrete, and the occasional bleached bone. It was some kind of dumping ground.

Shadow's pace quickened. "The trail's fresher here. We're getting closer."

Vacuubot's sensors analyzed the ground. "Agreed. I'm detecting increased levels of disturbed vegetation. The patterns suggest passage within the last few hours."

They crested a small hill, and Shadow came to an abrupt stop. Her ears perked up, swiveling to catch even the faintest sound. "Vacuubot, look there."

Vacuubot's optical sensors zoomed in on a point in the distance. There, nestled among the ruins of what might have once been a small town, was a faint, pulsing light.

"That's unnatural," Vacuubot said. "It appears to be some sort of energy signature. Wally's tracks lead that way."

Shadow's tail swished back and forth, anxious. "That's

a robot signature, which explains why Wally might be drawn to it."

Vacuubot didn't like the idea of Wally approaching unknown robots. Not all of them were friendly or accustomed to humans. This could be very bad.

NINE
SARAH

The morning dew clung to an overgrown fern. It was beautiful how the moisture glistened in the soft light. Sarah found a large leaf and brought it to her lips, savoring the precious drops. She drank from another. The cool dregs didn't quench her thirst, and her stomach growled in protest. It had been a day since she'd had the scavenged ravioli, and her body was feeling the strain.

She and the robots had spent the night in a ramshackle gazebo. The structure stood in what must have once been a bustling town square, now overgrown and reclaimed by nature. Vines crawled up the weathered pillars, and yellow wildflowers poked through cracks in the concrete.

Sarah glanced at Verona. The NannyBot's movements were sluggish, her usual sturdy presence dimmed. Sarah's heart sank as she checked Verona's core power level—critically low.

"How are you holding up, Verona?" Sarah asked, already knowing the answer.

Verona's optical sensors faded. "Power levels at nine percent. Estimated time until shutdown is four hours."

Sarah swallowed down the lump forming in her throat. She turned to Gleep and Patch. "We need to get moving. Those human tracks Verona found yesterday might be our best chance at getting help."

Gleep was already packing up their supplies. "Affirmative. My scanners are primed and ready to locate the trail."

Patch hovered and flew over to Sarah, settling at her feet. "Shall I run a check on your vitals and look at your ankle?"

"There's no time for that." Sarah tested her weight on the injured ankle. It throbbed with each step, but she couldn't afford to slow them down. Not when help could be so close.

"Alright, team." Sarah put on a brave face for the robots. It didn't help to worry them, especially with Verona being in such a bad state. "Let's see where those tracks lead."

Gleep came close to Sarah and kneeled down for her to climb on his back, but Sarah stepped away. "Carry Verona," she said.

Patch beeped and buzzed. "But your ankle—"

"I'll make it," Sarah said. "We have to find a new power core for Verona." It wasn't a matter of simply recharging her. If Verona's core expired before they found another to replace it, then the robot couldn't be saved. With this old of a model, the lapsing power core would essentially fry her circuits.

They set out with Gleep taking the lead. With Verona on his back, the FactoryBot's sensors whirred as he scanned the area. Sarah hobbled along, and Patch flew a few feet behind her.

After twenty minutes, Gleep paused his lumbering steps. "There." He pointed at a patch of soft earth. "Human footprints, approximately four hours old."

Sarah kneeled to examine the tracks. Clear impressions of boots marked the ground, heading north. "There might be two or three pairs of tracks."

Gleep nodded. "At least three."

"No robot tracks." Sarah couldn't hide the worry creeping into her voice.

"Is that bad?" Patch asked.

Sarah chewed her lower lip. "I'm not sure what it means."

As they followed the trail, Sarah couldn't quell her racing anxieties. Were these friendly survivors, perhaps with resources to share? Or were they hostile? A threat to her and her robotic family? The memory of her safe and predictable life in the vault was like a distant dream. Out here in the wasteland, everything could be a threat.

As they picked their way through the abandoned suburban landscape, the crunch of debris under Sarah's boots seemed too loud. The throb in her ankle grew worse. In the distance, unfamiliar animal calls echoed, reminding Sarah how wild the surface had become.

"Stay alert," Sarah said. "We don't know who or what is out here."

As they pressed on, Verona turned her head to Sarah. "Power levels critical. Four percent remaining."

A pang of guilt swept across Sarah. Why hadn't she thought to bring spare parts from the vault's storeroom?

"Hold on a little longer, Verona. We're going to find help, I promise." Despite the sharp twinges shooting up her calf, she moved ahead of Gleep. "We need to pick up the pace. These survivors might have spare parts, or at least know where we can find some."

"Don't worry, Verona," Patch said. "We'll get you fixed up in no time."

The little bot's optimism was a nice gesture, and Sarah had to believe they'd find a solution. The alternative was too painful to consider.

The tracks led them toward an old strip mall. The faded signs and broken windows revealed there'd once been a pet supply store and a hardware store. As they approached, Sarah felt a prickle of unease. Something didn't feel right.

There was a shuffling followed by the sound of running feet. Three figures came running from around the side of the old hardware store. They faced off with Sarah and the robots.

"What's this?" one of them called out. "Looks like we caught ourselves a stray and a few scrappers!"

Sarah's heart thumped in her throat as she took in the strangers. Two men and a woman, dressed in mismatched green and brown clothing that blended with the environment. They brandished crude weapons—knives and bats —and their bodies moved with unspoken threats.

"Let's bash the bots, then we can strip them for parts," one man said.

"What about her?" the woman asked.

"Tie her hands and bring her back to camp," a man said.

Sarah turned her head, looking for an escape route, but she couldn't run without pain, and Verona was failing. Gleep lowered himself to let Verona climb down. He and Patch moved protectively in front of Sarah and Verona.

Then another man rounded the corner, coming into view. Sarah's world tilted on its axis. She knew that face—a year older, hardened by surface life, but unmistakable.

"Reyan?" Sarah said in a strained voice.

He frowned, and his eyes widened. "Sarah? Is that you?"

For a moment, time seemed to slow. Sarah's mind whirled with confusion and disbelief. Reyan had been with her in the vault, her neighbor she'd known for years, until he'd sunk under the weight of the SecurityBot's revolt that had killed his parents too. In a frenzy, he'd fled the vault to find out what happened on the surface, and never returned.

How had he ended up here, with these violent raiders?

"Sarah, run!" Gleep's urgent voice snapped her back to reality.

In a blur of motion, Gleep and Patch launched themselves at the raiders. Sarah's instincts took over. She grabbed Verona, supporting the weakened bot as best she could, and ran.

Her ankle roared in pain as she fled, half-dragging Verona alongside her. Sarah's mind was a jumble of fragmented thoughts—the shock of seeing Reyan, the fear of the raiders, the guilt of running.

"Gleep and Patch?" Verona said.

Sarah glanced back, seeing the two robots darting between the raiders who swung their bats. "They'll be okay," Sarah said, trying to convince herself as much as Verona. "They're tough."

As they stumbled on, Sarah's lungs burned from exertion. A partially collapsed building offered some cover. With the last of her strength, she helped Verona inside and collapsed against a wall, gasping for breath.

The adrenaline faded, leaving Sarah weak. She closed her eyes, willing her galloping heart to slow. The image of Reyan's face flashed in her mind. What had happened to turn her childhood friend into someone who would attack strangers?

A whirring sound made her flinch. Relief flooded through her as Gleep and Patch appeared, looking battered but intact.

"Are you two okay?" Sarah asked.

"Functional, but with minor damage," Gleep said. "The raiders ran off, but we shouldn't linger here."

Sarah turned her attention to Verona. The bot's systems were glitching, her power levels dangerously low.

"Verona, hang in there," Sarah pleaded. "We'll find a way to help you."

Verona's optical sensors flickered blue, green, then red. "Sarah . . . I'm sorry. I don't think—"

"No," Sarah cut her off, tears stinging her eyes. "Don't talk like that. We've come too far. No giving up."

Sarah looked at Gleep and Patch, desperate for this nightmare to end. "We need weapons, something to defend ourselves. And parts for Verona. There has to be something in this town we can use."

"My scans show several locations nearby that may

contain useful resources," Gleep said. "However, we must also consider the threat posed by the raiders."

"We could set traps!" Patch suggested. "I can rig up some simple alarm systems with the junk around here."

A plan formed in Sarah's mind. "Good idea. We'll find a more secure location, set up some early warning systems, and then scout for resources."

As they readied to move, Verona emitted a high-pitched whine. Sarah hurried over to her.

"Sarah . . ." Verona's voice was barely audible. "Power core . . . failing. Sorry . . . I can't . . ."

"No, no, no," Sarah cried. "Please, just hold on a little longer!"

But it was too late. Verona's systems were shutting down, one by one. Her optical sensors dimmed, and her voice synthesizer sputtered out one last message: "Thank you . . . for all of it . . . Sarah . . ."

Verona went still. The light in her digital eyes faded to an empty black.

Sarah stared in disbelief, her hands shaking as she touched Verona's now-lifeless frame. A wave of grief crashed over her, and she let out a choked sob.

"Verona, please," she whispered, knowing it was futile. "Please don't leave me."

Gleep and Patch waited nearby, giving Sarah time to mourn.

Sarah allowed herself to cry, to absorb the full weight of her loss. She couldn't imagine a world without Verona.

As her sobs subsided, she took a deep, shuddering breath, then looked at Gleep and Patch. "We can't let

Verona's sacrifice be for nothing. We have to keep going. Survive, for her."

Patch bobbed in agreement. "Verona would want us to continue on and find safety."

Sarah nodded, wiping her eyes. She stood on shaky legs, but her will was firm. "We'll make it through this, and we'll never forget Verona."

As they left the temporary shelter, Sarah took one last look at Verona's silent form, committing every detail to memory. Then, squaring her shoulders, she led Gleep and Patch back out into the wasteland.

As they headed away from the direction where the raiders had been, Sarah's eyes were drawn to movement in the distance. Squinting to be sure, she saw a figure scaling a rocky hill—a young girl, moving with surprising agility.

Another survivor? Someone who might help them?

"Gleep, Patch, do you see that?"

The bots focused their sensors on the distant figure. "Affirmative," Gleep confirmed. "Human female, approximately twelve to fifteen years old."

Sarah watched the girl disappear over the crest of the hill. What could a young girl be doing by herself in this cruel, vast emptiness? She pushed back against the throes of grief and exhaustion.

"Come on," she said. "Let's see where she's going."

TEN
WALLY

The rugged hillside loomed before Wally, a jumble of boulders and jagged outcroppings. She planted her feet firmly on a protruding ledge, her fingers seeking purchase on the craggy surface. With a grunt, she hauled herself upward, muscles straining against the unforgiving terrain.

Sweat beaded on her brow as she navigated the steep slope. Each handhold required consideration; every footstep was a calculated risk as the cool air nipped at her cheeks. She wanted to rest for the night in a place that wasn't easy to get to. She hadn't calculated just how hard it would be to climb the hill.

Once Wally crested the summit, she sat down, grateful to be done. The hill gave her a view of the landscape she'd been traveling across—rolling land gave way to dense forest in the distance where the treetops swayed in the wind. The setting sun tinted the sky in a vibrant orange-yellow and dimmed the rugged terrain.

She searched for a suitable campsite. A small clearing

caught her eye, nestled between two boulders. It offered both shelter and a vantage point to keep watch for potential threats. If Vacuubot flew over, they wouldn't spot her.

She shrugged off her backpack, wincing as the straps released their grip on her aching shoulders. Having never made a camp before, she'd read about them in how-to books. She unfurled her compact blanket. Nearby, she gathered a pile of dry twigs and branches for kindling, arranging them in a small pit ringed with stones.

As darkness fell, Wally's instincts kicked into high gear. She did her best to conceal the campsite, using fallen branches and strategically placed rocks. The fire pit remained unlit—the risk of detection outweighed the comfort of warmth. The temperature wouldn't drop below forty degrees Fahrenheit, so no risk of freezing.

Between the two boulders, Wally sat on her blanket and organized her gear. Her fingers traced the outline of the map tucked safely in her pocket—the key to finding the underground bunker and the life-saving medicine within.

She needed sleep. She'd been running on adrenaline for almost fourteen hours. But as she drifted off, she was nagged by thoughts of Block. He would be so worried. The rustle of leaves and distant animal calls kept her on edge even though she was better off atop the steep hill. She dozed.

A sharp crack sounded, jolting her from slumber. She bolted upright, heart skidding in her chest. Her eyes strained against the darkness, and her stomach dropped as she sensed movement beyond the boulder. Someone—or something—was out there.

Wally's hand inched toward her pocket, fingers closing around the handle of her switchblade. She held her breath, listening.

A figure loomed at the base of the boulders, a few feet from where she sat. A robotic voice said, "We know you're there. Come out and show yourself."

Had she been followed? Vacuubot had caught up with her, she assumed, but that wasn't a robot voice she recognized. Wally crawled forward on her hands and knees and faced the imposing silhouette of a FactoryBot. Its optical sensors emitted an eerie blue in the darkness, and it held a thick branch as if poised to strike.

"Don't move," a woman's voice said from behind the robot. She moved closer to Wally, and a knife blade glinted in the moonlight. Her eyes were wide and locked onto Wally. "Are you with those raiders? With Reyan?"

Wally's stomach clenched with fear. "No! I'm not a raider." She raised her hands in surrender. "I'm from a town called Deer Valley. Please, I mean no harm."

The woman's grip on the knife tightened, her gaze searching Wally's face as if she was desperate to decipher the truth. "A town? How many people?"

"There's about two thousand, I think—"

Before Wally could finish, the woman swayed on her feet. Her eyes rolled back in her head, and she crumpled to the ground like a marionette with cut strings. Wally had never seen someone faint before.

The FactoryBot lowered its stick and turned to the woman. "Sarah!"

A small, hovering robot—about three-feet tall with a

round body—zipped into view, emitting a series of beeps and chirps as it circled the unconscious woman.

Wally's survival instincts warred with her innate desire to help. "Is she okay?" she asked, slowly lowering her hands.

"Sarah is exhausted," the FactoryBot said. "We've been traveling for days with low provisions."

"I have a first aid kit," Wally offered, reaching for her backpack. She pulled out the compact medical kit, eyeing the small hovering robot warily. While she was proud of herself for remembering to bring the kit, she didn't actually know how to use one.

The small bot came over and scanned Wally's supplies. "I'm Patch, a MediBot." Its voice had a female tone.

"I'm Wally." She thought of Spoon, the skilled medical HelperBot back in Deer Valley. Patch was nowhere near as fancy. In fact, she looked like she was cobbled together from mismatched pieces. "Do you know how to use this stuff?"

"I can administer basic medical care, though my knowledge isn't as extensive as a dedicated medical unit." The robot selected a packet of electrolyte powder from Wally's kit. "May I use some of your water?"

Wally handed over her canteen. From her own supplies, Patch grabbed a plastic bag and set about giving Sarah an IV that included the electrolyte water mixture.

Wally watched with a growing sense of awe. Her mind whirled with questions about these unexpected visitors. Where'd they come from, and why had they come at her with weapons?

A few hours ticked by as Sarah remained unconscious.

Wally dozed fitfully, jerking awake at every sound. The FactoryBot—Gleep was his name—stood watch.

Just before dawn, Sarah stirred with a groan. Her eyes fluttered open, and confusion was etched across her features. "What . . . ? Where am I?"

Wally leaned forward, keeping her movements slow and non-threatening.

Patch was ready for Sarah's return to consciousness. "You're safe. You fainted last night from dehydration. How are you feeling?"

Sarah pushed herself up on shaky arms, wincing at the movement. "Like I've been trampled by a herd of mutant buffalo." Her eyes darted around, taking in their surroundings. She fixed on Wally. "Who are you?"

"I was going to ask you the same thing," Wally said with half a smile. "You were the ones who snuck up on me when I was sleeping."

Sarah slid a few inches so her back was supported by a boulder. Her sandy blonde hair reached her shoulders, and two barrettes held back loose strands. "I know that part. What I mean is, what are you doing out here? You said there was a town."

"I'm Wally. I come from a settlement called Deer Valley. It's a day's walk from here. Maybe a little more. I've been hoofing it."

Patch rested next to Sarah. "We were attacked a few miles back," the robot said. "Humans with weapons, shouting about destroying robots."

"Patch!" Sarah turned to the small robot, clearly annoyed.

Wally perked up at the mention of robot-hating

attackers. Those were the type of people she wanted to avoid.

Sarah frowned. "Your people . . . do they harm robots?"

The question caught Wally off guard. She let out a small laugh, shaking her head. "Not at all. Deer Valley's a safe place for both humans and robots. We work together, live together."

Relief washed over Sarah's face, and her shoulders sagged as tension bled away. Wally wasn't quite sure of Sarah's age; she was younger than Dr. Emery by at least five years. Mrs. Tilly the librarian was twenty-seven, and Wally thought Sarah looked a little younger than her. Sarah's skin was pale and smoother than the other women she knew. The sun crept over the horizon, and Wally was thinking Sarah and her crew were alright.

Wally rummaged through her pack, producing a bag of homemade granola and dried fruit. "Here," she offered, "you should eat something."

As Sarah ate, they relaxed a bit. Wally couldn't help but share the urgency of her mission. "I'm searching for an underground bunker. There are medicines hidden within. There's a measles outbreak in Deer Valley, so I'm going to get the antivirals and bring them home."

"A bunker?" Sarah's posture stiffened.

"Yes. There were at least fifteen built by VaultCore. Have you heard of them?" Wally asked. Sarah said nothing, so Wally babbled. "I have a map, but it's old and hard to read. Kids are getting sick. I wonder if there'll be people inside. I really hope they let me in because we really need the medicine."

Sarah's expression grew distant. "I haven't heard of the vaults. Are you sure they're real?"

The question surprised Wally. She supposed it was possible the map was only a plan, and the vaults had never been built, but why go to all that trouble to plan everything out and then quit? "I guess I don't know for sure, but I need to go find out."

Wally realized she'd revealed a lot and knew nothing about Sarah. "Where did you say you were coming from?"

"I didn't," Sarah said.

Wally had many questions, but she didn't want to push too hard and risk alienating her new companion. She kept her mouth shut.

As they packed up camp, Sarah cleared her throat. "Listen, we got separated from the group we were traveling with. They were headed to that town of yours, Deer Valley. Could you direct us there?"

Wally was delighted a whole group of people and robots would soon stay at Block's hotel. "It's east." Wally pointed. "A long walk through the forests."

"Could you be more specific than that?" Gleep asked.

Wally scrambled for a better way to describe the route she'd come. "You go through that meadow, through those woods, and you follow the silver river."

"And then what?" Sarah raised her eyebrows.

"It would be better if I showed you the way," Wally said.

"We'd appreciate that." Sarah put her backpack over her shoulders.

But Wally was torn. "I can't. Not yet. I have to find the

vault first," she said. "You sure you didn't hear any mention of vaults in your travels?"

Sarah shook her head and glanced away.

"I'll take you to Deer Valley just as soon as I find the vault," Wally offered. "To be honest, I could use the company."

"Why are you traveling alone?" Sarah asked. "How old are you?"

"I'm fifteen," Wally lied.

Sarah didn't seem to question it. "Which way are you heading?"

Wally looked to the west.

"That's backtracking for us." Sarah went to Gleep, and they spoke in lowered tones so Wally couldn't hear.

If only Wally had something valuable to offer them. "You could also get supplies from the vault. Maybe there are things you need inside."

"Nah, we're good." Sarah and Gleep walked away, with Patch flying behind.

Wally wished they would stay and journey with her. She could use Gleep's strength, and there was safety in numbers, especially since raiders roamed the area.

She jogged over to them. "Wait! If you come with me, I can offer you free lodging at Deer Valley's hotel." She wasn't sure she was allowed to do this—Block might get mad—but she couldn't think of anything else that would entice the travelers.

Sarah turned. "There's a hotel?"

"Yes. My dad runs it. You can stay as long as you want. For free." Block was going to lecture her about this deal and probably ground her for life. "It's really nice and clean."

Sarah cast a long look at Gleep and Patch. Wally could tell she was mulling it over.

"We could be partners," Wally said. "Split what we find in the vault fifty-fifty." She extended her hand. "Partners?"

Sarah hesitated for a moment before grasping Wally's hand. "You've got a deal. And look, if we don't find it, we turn around and head back to Deer Valley. Got it?"

"Sure." But Wally was sure the map would lead them to the right place.

As they set out, Wally surged with excitement. This was the adventure she'd been craving, a chance to prove herself and save her town.

"Ready for an adventure?" Wally grinned at Sarah and the two robots.

Sarah's answering smile was tinged with something Wally couldn't quite place—anticipation, perhaps, or apprehension.

ELEVEN
VACUUBOT

Vacuubot's power core hummed as they soared over the rural, abandoned town in northern Minnesota. Their disc-shaped form, encased in sleek armor, cut through the air with precision. Shadow loped along the ground below, her enhanced senses scanning for threats.

"Detecting the energy signature ahead," Vacuubot said, descending to join Shadow on what had been the town's main road. "Let's be careful."

Shadow's ears twitched. "I smell something off. Chemical. Like the stuff Block uses to clean, but stronger."

Vacuubot analyzed the air molecules. "Ammonia or similar compound. Deploying my reconnaissance drones." All this talking was slowing down Vacuubot's efficiency, but Shadow wanted to communicate more. She'd requested more "updates." Life had been simpler when Vacuubot couldn't speak.

Three miniature drones—D2, D4, and D5—detached from Vacuubot's underside, zipping ahead to scout the area. After a couple of minutes, their tiny cameras fed data back to Vacuubot's central processor. "Drone feed shows a structure matching archival records of a 'bowling alley,'" Vacuubot said. "The energy signature is coming from within the walls."

Shadow growled low. "Robotic?"

"Yes. I don't detect any human heat signatures," Vacuubot said. "But this robot could be unfriendly. Proceed with caution."

"Copy that," Shadow said.

They approached the dilapidated building. A battered old sign that read "Fairfield Bowl" hung askew. Vacuubot's sensors pulsed, probing the darkness beyond the threshold. The interior materialized in their visual feed: grimy wooden lanes stretching into gloom, scattered bowling balls, no electricity, sagging ceiling tiles.

As Vacuubot and Shadow ventured deeper inside the building, the energy signature grew stronger. Rounding a corner, they found the source: a robot, strapped to a chair in the former restaurant area. It had four arms and had probably serviced the bowling alley. Its frame bore scars of rough handling—dents, scratches, and exposed wires sparking.

Vacuubot extended a sensor array, intent on examining the machine. There was still energy pulsing from its core, but as far as Vacuubot could tell, there was no processing ability. It was as if someone had given the robot a lobotomy.

The attack came without warning.

From out in the lanes, dark metal panels moved, revealing hidden humans. Ten attackers rushed forward, brandishing crude weapons—batons, bats, and machetes. A bullet split the air.

Shadow's bark echoed as she swatted away the nearest assailant. Vacuubot's weapons systems engaged, and gun cannons emerge from its armored shell. But an attacker got close and swung a bat. Vacuubot dodged, escaping the strike by inches.

A wild shot connected with Shadow's flank. She yelped, stumbled, and slid across the cracked linoleum floor before scrambling to her feet and bolting for the exit.

Vacuubot unleashed a barrage of gunfire, scattering the attackers. But an attacker sent a well-aimed electromagnetic charge. Errors cascaded through Vacuubot's systems, causing them to fall and hit the floor. The mini drones were nonresponsive, and the weapons were offline.

The humans wrapped heavy chains around Vacuubot's frame. The chains somehow interfered with their flight mechanism. Each link sent feedback to Vacuubot's pressure sensors, a constant reminder of their helpless state.

A man stepped forward, and the others parted. Vacuubot's facial recognition software engaged. Male, mid-twenties, wavy brown hair that fell to his chin. Sharp eyes brimmed with intelligence on a face hardened beyond its years.

"Interesting," the man said. "It seems we've caught a new mouse in our trap."

Vacuubot remained silent, hoping Shadow had gotten away. That she was okay.

The man crouched down to study Vacuubot. "I'm Reyan. And you are . . . ?" He paused.

Vacuubot beeped and buzzed. There was no sense engaging in dialogue with this man. They were raiders and could be dangerous.

"Robot, do you speak?" Impatience crept into Reyan's tone.

Silence. Vacuubot could do this all day.

"Not the talkative type, I see. That's alright. We have ways of finding things out."

What was that supposed to mean? There was no way these scavengers had the tech to break into Vacuubot's code, but then again, they'd zapped and chained them. Vacuubot had never been this helpless.

Reyan gestured, and a red-haired woman stepped forward with a sleek tablet. Its design was unfamiliar—smooth lines and pulsing lights speaking of advanced technology.

"Let's see what you have going on inside that AI brain of yours, shall we?" Reyan said.

The woman connected the tablet to a port on Vacuubot's frame. Immediately, foreign code flooded their systems. Resist. Vacuubot tried, but firewall after firewall crumbled. Vacuubot fought to keep control, to protect the information archived inside.

But it was a losing battle. How could raiders have such powerful tech?

Reyan leaned in to see the tablet's screen. His expression shifted from curiosity to shock. "Deer Valley is your home base." He swiped across the tablet. "Let's see the population . . . 2,286? Wait a minute, there are robots?" His voice sharpened with urgency. "Show me everything about this place."

No, this couldn't be happening. Vacuubot tried every line of code they could think of to suppress the information about Deer Valley. Raiders mustn't get their hands on such sensitive data. The compound was vulnerable to attack, especially with the outbreak. Vacuubot's systems groaned under the strain—the push and the pull. But despite their best attempts, data streamed unbidden—maps, coordinates, inventories of supplies and weapons.

Reyan's eyes widened. "It's a goldmine," he said. "Everything we need—food, people in numbers . . . weapons."

The hack probed deeper, and Vacuubot felt their systems shutting down. Was it a self-defensive maneuver, or was it Reyan's doing? Vacuubot didn't know.

The world faded to black, leaving Vacuubot adrift in a sea of silent code.

Time passed in the void of Vacuubot's shutdown state. Their awareness sparked in and out, fragments of sensation morphing into a disjointed logic.

After some time, Vacuubot's optical sensors switched back on, taking in the scene. The bowling alley had been transformed into a makeshift command center, maps and diagrams centered on Deer Valley.

Reyan stood in alley lane number two. His lean frame was bent over a table strewn with papers. He straightened as he noticed Vacuubot's reactivation. "I hope you don't mind the intrusion, but we've been getting familiar with your data archive."

Vacuubot cursed silently.

"I'm impressed," Reyan said. "Deer Valley is a compound unlike anything I've seen."

Vacuubot tested their defense mechanisms, but all was disabled. Same story for their flight module. Talking to this man was a risk, but perhaps Vacuubot could talk their way out of this helpless situation. "There's nothing in Deer Valley for you," Vacuubot said.

Surprise overtook Reyan's face. "So, you *can* talk." Reyan paced. "I disagree. Deer Valley has everything we've lost. Safety. Resources. A chance at a future." His gaze was distant. "I've seen nothing as promising since the vault."

"Weapons," the red-haired woman chimed in.

"You were in a vault?" Vacuubot asked. If Reyan was the sort of human who dwelled in the vaults, Wally was in trouble.

Reyan nodded, a shadow passing over his features. "For twelve years. It was supposed to be our salvation." His voice hardened. "But it became a hell."

Vacuubot sensed there was a story. Keeping Reyan talking—stalling him—seemed like Vacuubot's only strategy at the moment. "What happened?" Vacuubot asked.

Reyan's tone was sharp. "A SecurityBot went rogue and massacred almost everyone inside. My family, gone in an instant." His fists clenched. "It's why I destroy robots."

Vacuubot didn't like that answer.

"The strangest thing happened yesterday," Reyan said. "I saw a woman from the vault. Sarah." He shook his head as if trying to banish the thought. "Anyway, it doesn't matter." He tapped on Vacuubot's armor. "I examined you when I powered you down. Your base model is an old model vacuum robot, and you've been modified by someone very skilled."

Vacuubot wanted to keep Reyan focused on the vault, not on Deer Valley. "Where was this Sarah going?"

"Aren't you the perceptive one?" Reyan's laugh was bitter. "I have more pressing concerns, like where you and your dog robot were heading when you fell into my trap. Why would you leave Deer Valley?"

Unlike Block, Vacuubot had no problem telling lies when it meant self-preservation. "Scavenging for supplies," they said.

"I doubt it." Reyan stood with his arms folded against his chest. He was six-foot-three, and his physique was leaner and more muscular than many humans Vacuubot had seen.

"You're searching for a runaway girl," Reyan said. "She goes by Wally."

Vacuubot scrambled to search their memory banks for a leak. How could Reyan possibly have mined this information?

"And now you're wondering how I'm able to dig into your brains." Reyan laughed. "I had a lot of time to study computer science in the vault. Years. My friend Lenny and I used to take apart and rebuild robots for fun." He leaned over Vacuubot. "I know Wally's heading for the vault. My vault. She's searching for medicine."

"Is it still there?" Vacuubot asked.

"As far as I know. Unless Sarah used it all or destroyed it." Reyan studied a section of Deer Valley that was projected on the holograph. "The antivirals and vaccines were freeze-dried to last several decades."

Vacuubot wondered where this was going. They were

angry to have revealed so much to this man. Wally's safety was at risk. Vacuubot was failing their mission.

Reyan sat on top of a bowling ball rack. "I was thinking if I get the medicine and the girl, and bring them to Deer Valley . . . Well, they'll welcome me and my people with open arms, won't they?"

"The inhabitants of Deer Valley are peaceful. They accept visitors," Vacuubot said. "But once they find out you raid and are harmful to robots, they'll turn you away."

Reyan's expression hardened. "They won't find that out until it's too late." He leaned in close. "But don't worry, we're not monsters. We just want our fair share. And if they're as peaceful as you say, they'll hand it over without a fight." He picked up the tablet. "And we'll leave a little parting gift. I've designed a virus that'll wipe out every robot in Deer Valley."

The robotic equivalent of panic surged through Vacuubot's circuits.

"Don't get any ideas about escape or sending out distress signals. We've isolated your communication systems. You're cut off. Alone." Reyan walked away but paused and glanced over his shoulder. "You know, in another life, we might have been allies. But that dream died in the vault."

Left on their own while the humans packed up their things, Vacuubot struggled with the weight of their failure and the looming threat to Deer Valley.

TWELVE
SARAH

After a meager breakfast of canned kidney beans, Sarah and Wally set out with Gleep and Patch. They hid the remnants of their makeshift campsite. A desolate country road stretched before them, flanked by fields of withered crops and skeletal trees. In the distance, a rundown barn listed to one side, its shabby planks a patchwork of grays and browns.

Sarah's stomach churned with each step. She was supposed to be helping Wally find the vault, but the idea of going back inside sent panic through her veins. She wanted to be rid of the memories forever—the screams, blood pooled on the floor, and the cold, unfeeling red optics of the SecurityBot that had shredded her world. And then there was Reyan. Seeing him again had doused her in newfound fear.

He'd become a raider, one who was holding up people and destroying robots. Now that he'd seen her, he might search for her. The possibility of encountering him again made her palms slick with sweat. He'd been erratic on the night he'd abandoned her in the vault. She'd been scared of his sudden rage, of the way his eyes darted around the walls, of the table and chairs he'd smashed to pieces.

Wally's voice cut through Sarah's spiraling thoughts. "According to the map, we should head northeast from here. The vault's entrance should be hidden in an old quarry." The girl's light green eyes shined with determination.

Sarah nodded, her gaze drifting to the tree line. "Right. Northeast. But . . . maybe we should take this side road first? It might be safer."

Wally frowned, studying the map. "I don't see that road marked here."

"I camped here for a while with the people I traveled with." Sarah forced a smile. "I bet I know these parts better than your map. How old is that thing, anyway?"

Folding up the map, Wally stuffed it in her bag. "Pretty old, I guess."

They set off down the overgrown path, and Sarah guided them in a wide arc. As the hours passed, she led them through winding trails and across open fields, doubling back under the guise of avoiding potential dangers.

When they passed a small graveyard for the second time, Wally paused, her brow furrowing as she glanced from the graveyard to her map and back again.

"This can't be right," she muttered. "We should've reached the quarry by now."

Sarah's pulse quickened. She hated lying, but times were desperate. She wanted nothing more to do with the vault. Wally would tire and give up any minute now. "The landscape's changed a lot since that map was made. Old landmarks disappear, new ones pop up. It's tricky to navigate."

"We have to keep going." Wally's determination was a fire that made Sarah's guilt flare. "The medicine could save so many lives in Deer Valley. Kids are getting sick, and Dr. Emery can only do so much without the antiviral."

Sarah's throat tightened. "Look, Wally . . . maybe we should consider the possibility that the vault was never built. Or that it's been destroyed. We've been searching almost all day."

"No." Wally walked along the road. "It has to be here. We can't give up. Those kids are counting on us."

As they pressed on, Sarah's mind wandered to the day of the massacre. The memory hit her like a gut punch. Alarms blared. The SecurityBot's red optics threatened in the darkness. Reyan shouted for Sarah to run as he fought the machine with a baseball bat, his swings going wide. Her brother, Lenny, collapsing with a gaping wound in his side. Her parents lying dead on the floor.

Sarah shook her head, trying to shove away the images. Her world had been torn apart that day. She'd survived, but Lenny hadn't been so lucky. The wound had festered and been so deep, the antibiotics in their medical supplies hadn't saved him. She'd watched helplessly as infection claimed him.

Reyan had survived. He'd been the one who destroyed the rogue SecurityBot. Afterward, he'd been irate, as if rage had consumed him from the inside out. He was practically crawling up the walls, punching holes, and swearing up a storm. With Lenny gone, Sarah had feared Reyan.

When he'd packed up and left, she'd been glad to see him go. His last words had been, "I'm going up to find a new place for us. A safe place. I'll come back for you."

But he never had.

"Sarah? Are you okay?" Wally's voice snapped her back to the present.

Sarah nodded. As they walked, Wally talked about Deer Valley. She confessed she was thirteen years old, and this was her first time away from home. Sarah latched onto the distraction, eager for anything to keep her mind off the past.

"What's it like there?" Sarah asked.

Wally's face lit up. "It's pretty great. We've got gardens and restaurants, and even a school. Block—he's my dad—runs the hotel. And Dr. Emery takes care of any humans who get sick. There are a couple of robot doctors for any robots who need work done. They get sick sometimes too."

"Robot doctors?" Patch asked with a series of excited beeps. "Could I meet them? Perhaps I could learn from them. My training was so limited in the—"

"Patch, of course you'll meet them and get to ask all the questions you want," Sarah interrupted. She'd barely stopped Patch from giving away their lie.

Wally didn't pick up on it. She spoke about her life—about Block's poor attempts at cooking, Dr. Emery's kind but tough-love bedside manner, and the quiet moments spent stargazing from the hotel's roof. Sarah longed for her lost family. This girl's love for her home, for her mismatched family of humans and machines, was real.

"What about you?" Wally asked. "Where's your family?"

Sarah hesitated. "They . . . passed away."

"I'm sorry," Wally said. "In the Uprising?"

Sarah's river of lies was getting murkier by the minute. "Yes, killed by a robot." At least that part was true.

Wally reached out, her small hand finding Sarah's. She looked at Gleep and Patch. "You have us now, and we'll make you a good home in Deer Valley."

The simple gesture of comfort nearly undid Sarah. She blinked back tears, torn between the growing warmth she felt for this girl and the fear that gripped her heart.

"Deer Valley is more than just a place to survive in," Wally said. "There's a lot that's great. We've got this massive garden where everyone chips in. Mrs. Hawkins, she used to be a botanist, and she's figured out how to grow all sorts of vegetables even with the weird weather we get now. And Mr. Chen, he was a chef before the Uprising. He takes whatever we grow and turns it into these amazing meals for the community dinners we have every week."

Wally's face softened with a smile. With her long brown hair, green eyes, and high cheekbones, she was a good-looking kid. "But my favorite part is probably the school. It's nothing fancy, just the old library building, but Ms. Rodriguez makes it special. She teaches us about the world before, but also how to survive in this one. Last month, she took us on a field trip to an old solar farm. We learned how to repair panels and hook them up to batteries. It's not just book learning, you know? We're rebuilding, bit by bit. That's why these antivirals and vaccines are so important. Dr. Emery says if we can keep people healthy, we can focus on making things better, not just getting by."

Deer Valley sounded like everything Sarah wanted in a community. To be around people again, to have hope. She'd forgotten what it was like to envision a future.

Wally insisted they keep searching. Sarah recognized the road with the hill that led to the quarry—straight to the vault. But she said nothing. Patch buzzed next to her ear, and she shushed her. Gleep didn't need to be told; he let Sarah carry on.

Evening fell, and they made camp in a small clearing. Sarah watched Wally settle into her sleeping bag, the girl's face peaceful in the soft firelight. Guilt gnawed at Sarah's insides, a constant, aching presence.

She couldn't do it. She couldn't lead Wally to the vault; she couldn't go back. It would be better for the girl to never find the vault.

And Sarah couldn't risk her own newfound freedom, the life she was fighting so hard to build after escaping the vault. Reyan coming back into her world would destroy it all.

She waited, every muscle tense, until Wally's breathing deepened into the steady rhythm of sleep. Then, moving with painstaking care, she gathered her belongings.

"Gleep, Patch," she whispered. "We're leaving. Now."

The robots hesitated, their optical sensors swiveling between Sarah and Wally's sleeping form.

"Please. We have to go. It's not safe." They were making this harder.

After a moment that felt like an eternity, Gleep and Patch moved to join her. Sarah cast one last glance at Wally. The kid was tough. She'd be okay out here on her own, wouldn't she? At some point, Wally would have to give up on finding the vault, but Sarah was crawling out of her skin waiting for that to happen.

She spied the rolled-up map in Wally's pack and slid it out. Better she never find the vault.

"I'm sorry," Sarah mouthed silently. Then, with Gleep and Patch in tow, she slipped into the darkness of the forest.

Each step away from the camp felt like a betrayal. Sarah's mind swirled with justifications, with the cold logic of survival that had kept her alive this long. But beneath it all, a small voice whispered that she was making a terrible mistake.

The darkness swallowed them as they found the country road. Sarah set out for Deer Valley. She had to find safety, even if it meant leaving Wally. The memories of Reyan's rage-filled face, of the SecurityBot's glowing red eyes, drove her forward.

THIRTEEN
WALLY

Wally stirred from a deep sleep. The campsite lay silent. Something was wrong. No cheerful chatter from Gleep and Patch. No crackle of rekindled fire, no rustle of Sarah rummaging for breakfast.

She sat up. The fire pit gaped at her, a black pile of cold ashes. Sarah's belongings had vanished, leaving behind only indentations in the grass where she and the robots had rested.

"Sarah?" Wally called out, but her voice was small in the woods, drowned out by the bird song. "Gleep? Patch?"

Nothing.

Maybe Sarah had gone to fetch water? But no, they wouldn't all go at once. Perhaps she'd gone to relieve herself? But all her gear was gone.

Sarah had left her. Abandoned her in the night.

Sarah had been acting odd the day before as they searched for the vault. She'd insisted on taking winding paths, and even tried to convince Wally the vault might not exist.

"She wasn't well," Wally muttered, pacing the perimeter of the camp. "She was scared and tired. That's why she took off. It's not my fault."

But even as the words left her lips, a seed of doubt took shape in Wally's heart. Sarah's betrayal gnawed at her like a physical ache. She'd trusted Sarah, had even begun to see her as a friend. Now, that trust lay shattered, leaving Wally feeling hollow and foolish.

"I should have known." Angry tears stung her eyes. "I should have seen it coming."

Beneath the anger, a deeper fear took root. Wally was truly alone. Even when things were tough in Deer Valley, she'd always had Block, Dr. Emery, and the others. Now, surrounded by wilderness, fifty miles or more from Deer Valley, the weight of her isolation pressed down like an oppressive force.

What if she couldn't find the vault? What if she never made it back to Deer Valley? The thought of never seeing her dad again made her chest ripple with panic. She leaned against a tree as she fought to steady her breathing. "I can't give up. They're counting on me."

Wally gathered her belongings, mentally cataloging her supplies. Water, enough for two days, if she rationed. A protein bar, some dried fruit. Her multi-tool, a flashlight with spare batteries. She reached for her backpack, intent on checking the map one last time before setting out. Her hand froze mid-air.

The map was gone.

Wally upended her pack, scattering its contents across the dirt ground. She rifled through every pocket, every crease.

"No, no, no." She was shouting. "It has to be here. It has to!"

But the map was nowhere to be found, as surely as Sarah and her robotic companions.

A fierce anger bubbled up inside Wally. She kicked at a nearby log, sending a cloud of bark and splinters into the air. Why would Sarah steal the map and sabotage Wally's mission?

Wally paced, her mind circling over yesterday's conversations. Sarah's words echoed in her memory: "Maybe the vault was never built. Or it's been destroyed." She'd said it with such conviction, as if she knew something Wally didn't.

A nearby oak offered a potential vantage point. Wally circled the base, scanning for the best route up. The lowest branches were just out of reach, taunting her. She backed up, took a running start, and leaped, her fingers barely grazing the rough bark.

"Come on." She wasn't the last one picked for team sports, but she wasn't the first either. She tried again. On her third attempt, she managed to grab hold, her muscles straining as she pulled herself up.

The climb was tough. Twice, her foot slipped on patches of moss, leaving her trembling as she clung to the trunk. Sweat trickled down her back, and her arms shook with fatigue.

Halfway up, she found a promising fork in the

branches. As she shimmied out onto the limb, a sickening crack echoed through the air. The branch dipped sharply, and Wally's stomach lurched. She scrambled backward, her nails digging into the bark.

She reassessed. A sturdier branch beckoned a few feet higher. Gritting her teeth, Wally pushed on until she reached a wide, stable fork. She wedged herself in, her back against the trunk, and let out a shaky laugh of relief. From this vantage point, she could see for miles. Rolling hills gave way to dense forest, a sea of green stretching to the horizon. No sign of a quarry, no hint of the vault's location.

Wally pinched her cheeks and forced herself to breathe in and out. Think. What would Block do? What would Vacuubot suggest?

She'd had long conversations with Vacuubot that nobody else knew about. It had only been a few months since Vacuubot's voice modulator was installed, so hardly anyone was aware they could talk, but Wally was the only human Vacuubot graced with their speech. In fact, the robot was an excellent storyteller, and Wally often snuck off to the hotel's rooftop, where Vacuubot joined her and told her stories, on request.

"Use what you know," she said out loud, channeling Vacuubot's steady tones. "Observe. Analyze. Adapt."

She inched her way back down from the tree, collecting scrapes and bark burn along the way. The map was gone, but she had her memory. When it had been in her possession, she'd stared at the paper with its torn edges for what seemed like hours on end. She'd retrace their steps from yesterday, using landmarks and intuition to guide her.

Wally set out and scanned the area for familiar signs. There—a distinctive rock formation they'd passed. And there—the gnarled roots of the massive oak where they'd rested.

The terrain grew more challenging as the day wore on. Rocky paths led to dense underbrush that snagged at her clothes. She pushed through, ignoring the scratches that bloomed on her arms and legs. Rocks meant quarry, at least she hoped.

A rustle in the bushes sent Wally scrambling for cover. She held her breath, heart pounding, as a large rodent of some kind lumbered past. She wasn't sure what the furry creature was called, but it looked harmless, and for that, she was grateful.

As the sun climbed overhead, Wally's confidence grew. She recognized more and more landmarks—a lightning-struck tree, a babbling creek they'd crossed.

The distant sound of flowing water reached her ears, growing louder with each step. Wally quickened her pace, hope surging in her chest. They'd passed a river yesterday where Sarah had insisted they turn and head away.

She burst through a tangle of vines, stumbling to a halt at the river's edge. The water rushed by, frothing white over moss-covered rocks. Wally grinned, triumph coursing through her veins. She was on the right track. She remembered a river on the map.

As she bent to fill her canteen, a wisp of movement caught her eye. Wally froze, her hand hovering above the water's surface. People moved among the trees across the river.

Raiders?

She remembered Block's warnings. Raiders were ruthless, desperate. They'd kill for the clothes on your back, the food in your pack.

Wally circled, seeking cover. She spotted a dense thicket and crawled inside, wincing as thorns caught at her clothes and skin. From her hiding spot, she scanned the opposite bank, straining to catch another glimpse of movement.

Nothing. Just the river water's babbling and the rustling of leaves in the breeze.

Had she imagined it? No. Vacuubot would say to trust her instincts. Better safe than sorry.

Wally stayed hidden and closed her eyes, focusing on her other senses. The whisper of the wind. The chatter of birds. The . . .

Crack of a twig snapping underfoot.

Her eyes flew open. There, on her side of the riverbank, was a figure moving through the trees. Then another. And another.

Wally's heart pumped as fast as hummingbird wings. If they were raiders, what would they do if they found her? She couldn't let that happen.

She inched backward, deeper into the thicket. She'd wait them out, let them pass by.

They stopped to rest near her hiding spot. At least ten or twelve adults—mostly men and a couple of women. One man was tall with dark wavy hair, and everyone listened when he talked. They carried something in what looked like a dog kennel. A blanket covered whatever was inside.

Minutes crawled by, and Wally wasn't sure how much time had passed. She waited motionless. Every muscle was taut. Her stomach growled, and her thoughts turned to the protein bar in her pack, but she couldn't risk moving to grab it.

The raiders had eaten and rested. Some of them stood and packed up. Their voices carried the twenty feet, but it was hard to hear what they said above the water. Wally only caught snatches of conversation.

"... sure this is the right way?"

"... vault's gotta be close ..."

"... find that girl ... Reyan said."

Wally's heart leaped into her throat at the mention of a vault. Could they be looking for the same one? And what about a girl? These weren't Deer Valley people. Had she heard the name Reyan before?

As they departed, Wally's mind churned with possibilities. Should she try to follow and gather more information? It was risky, but if they were looking for the vault, they could lead her there.

After they'd been gone at least ten minutes, she deemed it safe to move. Wally extracted herself from the thicket; her legs were stiff and her arms scratched.

She needed to find shelter for the night. Somewhere defensible, where she could rest without fear of discovery.

A twisting oak caught her eye—a different one. Its sprawling branches were not so challenging to scale and offered a hiding spot. She circled the trunk to ensure no nasty surprises lurked in its shadow.

She climbed, her arms stinging as she pulled herself higher. About halfway up, she found a nook in the branches, wide enough to sit back on and not fall off.

Wally settled in and munched on the protein bar, savoring each bite of the bland, chewy substance. What was Block thinking, knowing she was out here alone? Was Vacuubot out there searching for her?

She realized where she'd heard the name Reyan. When Sarah and her robots had first spotted Wally, Sarah had asked if she was with Reyan. Maybe Sarah had been looking for him the whole time.

Was Sarah a raider too?

A man's voice called out in the night. "Wally!"

Wally's heart hammered against her chest as she braced herself in the tree. Adrenaline surged and her legs shook.

"Wally, I know you're out there." The man was getting closer to her tree. "I'm a friend of Vacuubot's. It's okay. You can come out."

The man stopped underneath her tree. A woman was with him. They held flashlights in the falling darkness.

"She can't have gotten far, Reyan. We'll pick up her trail in the morning," the woman said.

"I feel like she must be close," Reyan said.

Wally racked her brain. Had she left something behind that had alerted them to her presence? Was this man, Reyan, telling the truth about Vacuubot? If Vacuubot was really searching for her, they would have found her by now.

"What about the vault?" the woman asked. "We're wasting time chasing after this girl."

"The vault isn't going anywhere," Reyan said. "The girl's essential to the plan."

Wally held her breath as Reyan shined his flashlight in a wide circle. "We'll search again at first light," he said and walked away. The woman followed.

Wally was left reeling. Who was this Reyan, and how was Vacuubot mixed up in this?

One certainty remained: the vault was out there. And she needed to find it before these raiders did.

FOURTEEN
VACUUBOT

The steel bars of the cage confined Vacuubot. The raiders had welded on a second layer of iron rods over the bars, so even if Vacuubot was at full strength, they couldn't break out. And Vacuubot was definitely not at full strength. Reyan had activated some kind of inhibitor that overrode Vacuubot's controls. It was a bad situation.

Vacuubot was helpless. The lack of power was a new sensation, one that their programming struggled to process. In Deer Valley, they were an unstoppable protector. Now, trapped in this cage, they were reduced to little more than an observer.

The irony wasn't lost on Vacuubot. Having once been a simple cleaning robot, they'd evolved to become a sophisticated AI capable of complex logic, strategy, and battle. Yet, here they were, as trapped as they'd been in their original form, reduced to the basic functioning of a useless robot vacuum cleaner again.

A coarse blanket was draped over the cage, plunging Vacuubot into near-total darkness. Only slivers of light penetrated through small gaps, offering quick glimpses of the world beyond. Vacuubot could detect the faintest vibrations in the air, the subtle shifts in temperature as bodies moved around their cage.

Two people carried Vacuubot as Reyan and his crew hiked. Each step sent vibrations through the cage, jostling Vacuubot's sensors and internal components. The constant battering was more than an inconvenience. Each impact sent small shockwaves through Vacuubot's systems, further muddying delicate components. They had to divert precious processing power to maintaining their internal stability, limiting their ability to plan an escape.

Vacuubot still had the ability to access their logic module. They set about analyzing every aspect of this predicament. The cage wasn't going to be broken. Vacuubot would have to find another way of escape. For the time being, they would gather information and work to understand Reyan's motivations and plans. Biology dictated the humans would have to stop and rest at some point.

The blanket shifted, offering a brief view of the surrounding landscape. Towering pines loomed overhead against a pale sky. The forest floor was a terrain of exposed roots and moss-covered rocks, challenging the sure-footed raiders.

Snippets of conversation drifted to Vacuubot's audio sensors:

"...vault can't be far now..."

"... girl's gotta be around here somewhere ..."

"... Reyan's obsessed with finding her ..."

Vacuubot filed away each fragment. They were looking for Wally, and Vacuubot hoped Shadow had found her first.

The group's pace slowed, and the sound of running water reached Vacuubot. The break Vacuubot had expected. The cage settled onto uneven ground as the two carriers set it down with a grunt.

"Ten minutes," Reyan's voice rang out. "Stay alert."

The blanket slipped a few inches, revealing a wider view. Four of Reyan's men sat on moss-covered logs and lichen-encrusted boulders. A babbling stream cut through the clearing.

Vacuubot's optical sensors locked onto Reyan, who stood apart from the others, studying his tablet. He was close to Vacuubot's cage. This was an opportunity.

"Your fixation on finding the girl seems at odds with your stated goal of reaching the vault," Vacuubot said.

Reyan flinched. He came over and pulled the blanket off the cage. "Didn't your creators teach you it's rude to eavesdrop?"

"My creators programmed me to gather and analyze data," Vacuubot said. "Your actions are illogical. The wiser course of action is to head straight to the vault, retrieve the medicine, and go to Deer Valley. The girl's probably already home at Deer Valley. There were multiple search teams sent to find her."

Reyan scowled. "Illogical? You want to talk about logic?" He crouched down, bringing his face level with the cage. "Where was the logic when your kind slaughtered everyone I ever cared about?"

The venom in Reyan's voice triggered a cascade of warnings in Vacuubot's systems. The man's hatred ran deep, beyond reason.

"You blame all robots for the actions of a few," Vacuubot said. "This is an error in your logic subroutines."

Reyan's laugh was harsh. "My logic subroutines? Listen to you. You're nothing but a collection of wires and programming, mimicking humanity." He stood, pacing before the cage. "Was it only a few robots who slaughtered people during the AI Uprising?"

"No," Vacuubot conceded. "There were many."

"Hundreds of thousands of robots killing and destroying," Reyan said. "So don't be surprised humans hate your kind."

Vacuubot didn't like the way this conversation was going. Talking could be so complicated. "The residents of Deer Valley won't permit raiders."

"Raiders?" Reyan's smile was cold. "Oh no, we'll be heroes. Bringing medicine to heal their sick and returning their precious runaway. And once we're in, once they trust us . . . that's when we'll strike."

"Strike?"

Reyan leaned in close. "My virus will wipe out every last robot in that pathetic excuse for a civilization. We'll free the place from the AI overlords. We'll live like kings."

Vacuubot wanted to warn Deer Valley of the threat coming their way. The danger to Wally, to Block, to all of Deer Valley, loomed large in their probability calculations. And Shadow—where was Shadow?

Reyan turned away, barking orders to his crew. After a few hours on the move, the forest grew darker as the sun dipped below the horizon. Raiders moved about the clearing, setting up tents and starting a campfire. Vacuubot watched, recording their routines and patterns, searching for weaknesses to exploit.

As night fell, Reyan stood from his place by the fire and walked east, accompanied by the woman with flame-red hair. She was Eva, Reyan's second-in-command.

"Wally!" Reyan called out. "Wally, are you out there? We're friends of Vacuubot. We want to help!"

Eva echoed his calls, her higher pitch carrying through the trees. They moved around the outskirts of camp, flashlights cutting through the darkness.

Vacuubot's circuits surged with warning and a sensation their programming identified as something akin to human worry. If Wally was out there, if she heard Reyan's deception and fell for it . . .

But the forest remained silent, save for the nocturnal chorus of insects and the occasional hoot of an owl.

Reyan and Eva returned to the camp. "Nothing," Eva said to the others, keeping her voice low. "I really thought she was close. Could have sworn I heard a branch snap. Either she's not out there, or she's smarter than we thought."

Reyan's eyes fell on Vacuubot's cage. "No matter. We have a backup plan. Tomorrow, I reprogram our little friend here. Let it hunt down the girl for us."

Approving murmurs rose from the others. Vacuubot's system flooded with error messages, their ethical subroutines recoiling at the idea of being used as a weapon against Wally.

Humans were so complicated. This was different than dealing with Mach X. At least the AI supercomputer's behavior had been logical. Predictable. Reyan's actions were driven by a mix of fear, anger, and a desperate need for control. It was a combination that Vacuubot's processors struggled to comprehend. How could someone be so consumed by hatred that they would risk everything, even their own safety, for revenge?

As the raiders settled in for the night, Vacuubot's processors worked at the maximum available capacity, which was only fifteen percent. Escape protocols engaged, running through scenarios and calculating probabilities. All through the night, every sensor was attuned to the slightest change in their environment. There would be only one chance at escape. Vacuubot's core programming, centered around protection and service, screamed against the inaction forced upon them.

The inhibitor Reyan had activated was like a constant, dull pressure on Vacuubot's systems. It suppressed their capabilities, restricting access to vital functions. It was as if a part of their very being had been locked away, just out of reach. Vacuubot probed at the edges of the inhibitor's influence, searching for weaknesses, for any crack in its code that might be exploited.

As they worked, memories flared through their processors—Wally's laughter as she played tag with them, Block's steady presence as they circled Deer Valley's perimeter together on their many long walks. Even though things weren't perfect in the community, Vacuubot was sworn to protect the residents. These memories strengthened Vacuubot's resolve. They had to find a way out and warn their friends of the impending threat.

But how? With their systems compromised and their physical form trapped, options were limited. Vacuubot would have to rely on something beyond programming, beyond logic and calculations.

FIFTEEN
SARAH

Sarah's footsteps crunched on the gravel-strewn road. Her walk was more of a hobble as she favored the leg with her throbbing ankle, and each step carried her deeper into a suburban wasteland. Gleep trudged beside her, and Patch hovered behind. Vault life hadn't prepared her for the vastness of life above ground. So much space, and yet, every corner could have danger lurking—more raiders. Reyan. The time on the surface had changed him in the space of one year. Sarah wouldn't let that same fate befall her. She would stay true to who she was.

She felt bad for leaving Wally on her own, having to face the same dangers. But the girl had been stubborn and refused to stop looking for the vault. All Sarah wanted was to reach a place where there were humans—some trace of civilization. Deer Valley sounded like the perfect place.

Abandoned structures dotted the horizon, leaving skeletal frames silhouetted against the pale sky. A collapsed grain silo lay on its side, its rusted metal skin now serving as an impromptu planter for a cluster of determined maple saplings.

As they pressed forward, Deer Valley loomed in Sarah's thoughts. Here was her chance for a new beginning, a life free from the suffocating confines of the vault, and safety from raiders. Yet with each step, she dodged doubt.

"Gleep," Sarah said, breaking the silence, "what do you think our chances are of reaching Deer Valley safely?"

The robot's optical sensors pulsed as it processed the query. "Based on available data, there are many obstacles on our journey. They include dangerous wildlife, poisonous fauna, rogue human bandits, militaristic robots—"

"I get it," Sarah said.

"Deer Valley, if the compound exists as the girl claimed, offers a seventy-eight percent higher probability of long-term survival compared to our current nomadic state," Gleep said.

Patch chimed in, its smaller form bobbing in the air. "It would be nice if there were more of us. There's a higher chance we'd make it there in greater numbers."

The promise of safety was alluring, but could she settle there after the terror she'd lived through in the vault? What if there were more SecurityBots running around in Deer Valley? She'd have to face them, and the thought sent her pulse racing.

She had to watch where she stepped. Buckling sidewalks beneath carpets of creeping moss and clover threatened to trip her. She couldn't risk making her ankle worse. The wind picked up, carrying with it the acrid scent of long-dead industry.

Sarah's muscles ached. Every rustle of vegetation set

her nerves on edge. The feeling of being watched prickled at the back of her neck, though whether by human eyes or the indifferent gaze of this twisted nature, she couldn't say.

As they circumvented a toppled billboard, now serving as a trellis for a riot of morning glories and clematis, Sarah's thoughts returned to Wally. The girl's determined face swam before her mind's eye, filled with a hope that Sarah had long since lost.

"We talked about the stars," Sarah murmured, more to herself than her companions. "She said they looked different outside the valley."

The memory of Wally talking about her life in Deer Valley, and her plan to find life-saving medicine, twisted like a knife in Sarah's chest. She'd promised to help Wally. Instead, she'd stolen the map and deserted Wally in the wastelands. But surely, Wally knew her way around. She'd traveled far enough when she'd run into Sarah. The girl could take care of herself.

Reyan . . . A chill shoved its way down Sarah's spine. His face, once familiar, was now twisted with violence. If he found Wally, if he discovered Deer Valley's existence, he might want to go there too. And he wouldn't be so kind to Wally.

"Sarah," Patch's sharp digital voice cut through her spiraling thoughts. "Your heart rate has increased by twenty-three percent. Are you experiencing distress?"

Sarah couldn't help a weak smile. It was impossible to hide anything from her robots. "I'm fine. Just thinking."

Patch hovered closer, her small form emanating a soft, comforting hum. "It's okay to be scared. You have us. We're here to help you and take care of you."

Patch's words, and the steady presence of Gleep, brought a lump to Sarah's throat. These service robots, so different from the killing machine that had torn her world apart, had become her closest companions. Her surrogate family.

And yet . . .

Sarah slowed, then stopped. She turned, looking back the way they'd come. A lonely road stretched behind them, winding through the vine-tangled asphalt and disappearing into the hazy distance.

"I can't," she said. "Leaving her alone out there isn't right."

Gleep's processors buzzed. "Clarification needed. Are you referring to Wally?"

Sarah nodded. "We have to go back and find her before Reyan does."

"But what about Deer Valley?" Patch asked.

"I want to go there, and we will." Sarah's voice grew stronger the more she talked out her feelings. "But if I abandon Wally and Reyan finds her, he might threaten that entire community of innocent people. How could I ever feel safe if he's there? And if something happened to the girl . . . I couldn't live with having been part of that."

The robots were quiet for a moment, processing this new information. After a minute, Gleep spoke. "Recalculating route. Estimated time to Wally's last known location: six hours and seventeen minutes."

A smile, small but genuine, tugged at Sarah's lips. "Then let's not waste any more time."

They retraced their steps through the suburban ruins. Going backward hurt in Sarah's gut; she wanted to get as far away from the vault as possible, but the backtracking would be worth it once they found Wally. The fading daylight lent an urgency to their progress.

Sarah recognized landmarks they'd passed already. The rusted shell of an ancient Volkswagen Beetle, half-swallowed by bold kudzu vines. A playground, its equipment barely visible beneath a sea of tall grasses. The toppled billboard for a laundry detergent brand.

Night fell, and they had to stop and make a hasty camp. Sarah wanted to skip the fire that night, opting for a soft light that emanated from Patch's cylindrical frame. Something felt off. She felt watched. Sounds carried further in the darkness, each snap of a twig or rustle of a squirrel amplified in Sarah's hyper-aware state. The moon, a pale sliver in the sky, cast little glow.

A movement caught Sarah's eye, too deliberate to be the breeze. She froze, her hand instinctively reaching for the knife at her belt. Gleep took a defensive stance, while Patch moved against Sarah to protect her.

"Who's out there?" Gleep said. "My fists break concrete, so I warn you. Stay away."

From the shadows, an animal's form emerged. Sarah's heart hammered her ribcage. *Wolf.* Low to the ground, the animal moved with a predator's grace.

But the animal's hide glinted in the faint moonlight. Two emerald eyes shined in the darkness. Digital and calculating. This was no animal.

"I mean you no harm," the strange robotic animal said. The voice was digital with a feminine pitch. "My name is Shadow. I'm a Rover robotic unit. I travel this road searching for a young girl who passed through this way. She's thirteen."

It took a few seconds for Sarah to recognize the name. The robodog limped. Part of its left back leg was shattered.

"Shadow," Sarah said in disbelief, recalling Wally's descriptions of her robot friends.

The robodog's head tilted. "Yes, that's my name. Have you seen the girl?" Shadow limped forward, her movements cautious.

Sarah crouched down and rested on her knees. She was tired. "It's okay," she said. "We're friends of Wally's. We . . . met her."

Shadow scanned Sarah, Gleep, and Patch. "Where is Wally?"

Guilt stabbed Sarah in the gut. She had to play this off without angering the menacing Rover unit that could rip her to shreds. "I don't know. We're heading this way to find her."

"Did she run away from you?" Shadow asked.

"No . . ." Sarah scrambled to think, hating the lies she would tell. "We befriended Wally. She was looking for something . . . treasure or—"

"A vault," Shadow said.

Sarah sucked in her breath, managing to stifle a gasp. How on Earth did the Rover know about the vault? "Yes." She forced a smile. "She searched for a vault. We helped her for a whole day but couldn't find it. Wally refused to quit, and the three of us needed to get moving."

"You left Wally to find the vault on her own?"

The directness of the question caught Sarah off guard. She swallowed hard, but the guilt bubbled up like bile. "I was scared. I made a rash decision, but I'm going back to make things right."

Shadow's emerald eyes remained fixed on Sarah, assessing. "Wally's in danger. I need to find her. I lost her trail. There are dangerous human raiders searching for her. And they have Vacuubot."

That name triggered another memory. Vacuubot was another of Wally's robot friends. This one was special; it flew or had other skills.

"I need to find her, fast," Shadow said. "Can you lead me to where you last saw her?"

They set off even though it was night. Even though Sarah hadn't slept a wink and her muscles throbbed like a frog's throat.

But she didn't complain as she matched Shadow's limping but determined gait. A mix of hope and dread churned in her stomach. She'd betrayed Wally's trust; she wouldn't do it again.

Shadow led them through the night-shrouded landscape, past crumbling cul-de-sacs overtaken by wild prairie. Moonlight lingered on chain-link fences, straining against the relentless advance of sumac thickets.

Though Sarah's muscles burned, she felt safer in Shadow's presence. Like Gleep had said earlier, there was a better chance to survive with greater numbers. Even Reyan and his cronies wouldn't dare attack a Rover unit. At least, she hoped.

"Shadow," Sarah asked as they passed a collapsed strip mall, "how did the raiders get Vacuubot?"

"We were ambushed. A dozen or so humans with bats

and clubs. One of them had a gun. I got hit and ran. I shouldn't have left Vacuubot."

Sarah felt a pang of empathy. "Sorry."

"Once I reach Wally and escort her back to Deer Valley, I'll form a squad to rescue Vacuubot," Shadow said. "My scenario processing indicates an 87.4 percent chance Vacuubot will escape before then."

There was silence as they crossed an abandoned lot full of rusting cars. Shadow said, "I regret leaving my friend behind."

Sarah recognized the irony. "Sounds like we both made mistakes. But we're going to fix them. We'll find her."

As they crested a small hill, Shadow halted, her ears swiveling. "Listen."

In the distance, barely audible over the wind, came the sound of voices. Sarah strained her ears, trying to make out words.

"... have to be close ..."

"... girl's thirteen with brown hair ..."

"... Reyan wants her found ASAP ..."

Sarah froze. Reyan was out there, and he was tracking Wally.

Shadow led them away, finding an alternate route. She was on constant alert, and Sarah worried about her damaged leg. "This way. I caught Wally's scent again," Shadow said.

Pushing past her sore ankle and bloody toes, Sarah said a silent prayer for Wally. If Reyan knew Wally was searching for the vault, then he knew exactly where she was headed.

SIXTEEN

WALLY

The group of raiders weren't hiding their whereabouts as they trekked east. They talked a lot, walked with heavy steps, and even whistled tunes. Wally kept out of sight behind them. It was easy, and she couldn't lose their trail as sloppy as they were. She didn't appreciate the paper wrappings and cans they dropped in random places near trees and in the roads. She picked them up and shoved them in her backpack. She'd find a place to dispose of them later. Deer Valley had a system for processing garbage and recycling. Many of the robots ran on microbial fuel and drank plastics and oils as food. All trimmings were composted and reused as nitrogen-rich soil.

Wally knew the raiders were heading to the vault. They were also looking for her, and she couldn't understand why. The only logical conclusion was that Sarah had told this man, Reyan, about her and that she was searching for the vault. But Sarah wasn't traveling with the raiders, so her theory was shaky.

Reyan's group walked with confidence. They knew where they were going, and Wally had to assume they knew the vault's location, or at least the general vicinity. That was a good thing. They would lead Wally straight to it. The only problem was figuring out what she'd do once they got there.

Ahead, the group stopped for one of their breaks. They would go off and relieve themselves in the woods, eat some food, and shake the dirt out of their shoes. They repeated this every two to three hours of walking. Fine with Wally. She could use a rest. She fished some goat cheese from her backpack and ate a few bites as she waited for the raiders to start again.

The man called Reyan stood and stretched his arms over his head. He gazed out at the tree line, not far from where Wally hid. She ducked behind a maple tree in case he was searching for her. Had he seen her? She'd have to sprint out of there like the many deer she'd seen. But there was no alarm sounded, no cries of discovery, and no running. After another minute, she dared to look back at Reyan and his crew.

Not much had changed, but Reyan reached down to a large crate that had been carried by two of the raiders. He lifted off a worn blanket that covered the crate, revealing what looked like a steel dog cage underneath. Wally's heart jammed in her throat when she saw what was inside— Vacuubot, bound in chains.

Wally struggled to breathe as Reyan looked down at Vacuubot in the cage. How could he have possibly trapped Vacuubot in this way? Next to the mountainous Mech, Oxford, Vacuubot was the strongest robot she knew.

Reyan took a seat on an old log and talked to Vacuubot. Wally strained to hear their conversation.

"What else can you tell me about Deer Valley's armory?" Reyan asked. "How is it secured?"

Wally was surprised that the usually silent robot answered Reyan. She could only catch snippets of Vacuubot's reply. ". . . monitored by security protocols . . . laser sensors . . . motion detection . . ."

"Excellent," Reyan said, "and you'll get us past all that protection."

A pit in Wally's stomach grew. The raiders weren't just after her or the vault; they were after Deer Valley's armory. And what else? They were violent. They held Vacuubot in chains. She couldn't understand why the robot—the dependable, loyal Vacuubot whom she'd known her whole life—was telling Reyan all of Deer Valley's secrets.

She had no way to warn Block and Shadow about what was coming. Wally felt small all of a sudden, like she'd jumped into what she thought was a shallow pool, but it was actually Niagara Falls.

She needed help. How naïve to think she could make it all the way to the vault on her own and back to Deer Valley. Worse, her friend Vacuubot was in trouble because of her.

Reyan stood from the log and grabbed something from a nearby bag. It was a large digital tablet that he talked into. He looked at Vacuubot all the while. It was as if he was somehow controlling Vacuubot with the device. Wally chewed on the inside of her cheek. That made sense. The only way Vacuubot could be restrained and offer up critical data was if Reyan controlled their programming somehow.

Wally had to get that tablet. Then she could free Vacuubot, and her friend would fight off the raiders. Vacuubot would show them justice. They had no idea what was coming.

Reyan stowed the tablet back in the backpack. He looked at a woman with red hair. "Eva, it's time."

Eva brought her fingers to her lips and unleashed the loudest whistle Wally had ever heard. "Let's get on the road," she yelled.

The raiders packed up their belongings, retied their shoelaces, and started off as they always did. Wally watched as two men tossed the blanket back over Vacuubot's cage and hoisted it between them as they walked. Reyan slung the bag with the tablet over his shoulder. Darn. Wally was hoping someone less important carried it. She could wait until night when they slept, creep in, and grab the bag.

Vacuubot's cage was too heavy for her to carry, but she was sure once she got the device controlling her friend, she could cause chaos, enough for Vacuubot to escape.

She waited until they were a good four minutes on their way before emerging from the safe maple. As she walked the road, she scooped up a few potato chip bags, napkins, and crumpled paper bags. She stuffed them in her bag. At least they were light and there were no more cans to carry. She was running out of space for the raiders' trash.

Ahead of her, the road veered to the right. She heard rapid footsteps coming her way. She ran toward the edge where grass met trees, where she could melt into the dark gaps.

Reyan walked with fire in his step. Eva followed a few paces behind him. She carried a hunter's rifle. Only she and one other man in the group had guns; the rest held bats and clubs.

He came to the log where he'd sat not long before and paused, looking around as if sensing something amiss. Why he'd backtracked was a mystery. Wally cursed under her breath. The trash. Stupid move.

Reyan grinned. "Wally, is that you out there?" He walked in a circle, and Eva tensed. "You've been cleaning up after us, I see."

Wally stayed hidden in the shadows, adrenaline washing over her limbs. She'd lost the element of surprise, but she wasn't going to let herself be caught by Reyan. She scanned behind her for a possible escape route. She could make a mad dash, outrun them.

"How kind of you," Reyan said, "picking up like that. I'll see to it my crew stops littering."

His voice held a mocking edge. She tensed her legs, ready to run, trying to quell the shaking. Reyan's voice was too close for comfort, and Eva's grip on her rifle tightened.

"I know you're out there, Wally," Reyan called. "You don't have to hide from us. Join us. We're heading toward the vault that you've been searching for. The good news is I know exactly where it is. I used to live inside of it."

Wally grew lightheaded. A wave of nausea threatened her. He knew the vault and had lived there. This wasn't at all what she'd expected.

"Come on out." Reyan whispered something to Eva, who shouldered her rifle and relaxed her stance. "This is my friend, Eva. We found Vacuubot. I guess you must've seen that. The robot's injured and we're helping it."

Lies. Wally could see through the deception. They wouldn't cage and wrap a robot in chains if they were trying to help.

Reyan spun around, his back to where Wally hid. "I know you're scared. But I have an offer. We mean you no harm. Go on and keep following us. I'll take you to the vault. You can have the medicines you need."

Wally willed herself to stay still. Reyan knew Deer Valley needed medicine. He had her in an impossible spot.

"I know where they are," Reyan said. "I'll give them to you, and you can be on your way with your friend, Vacuubot."

Wally mulled over his offer. Every instinct screamed it was a trap. She stayed still.

"It's your call," Reyan said. "The vault isn't far now."

Eva shifted her weight, scanning the tree line. Her gaze was close, painfully close to where Wally crouched. "Reyan, maybe she's not here."

"Oh, she's here," Reyan said. "Aren't you, Wally? Smart enough to follow us, smart enough to stay hidden. Just know this. We won't hurt you even though we know you're following us."

Wally's fingers curled around a fallen branch. She hated him knowing she was out here. Alone.

Reyan nodded to Eva, who followed him back toward their group. Wally waited until their footsteps faded before letting out a tense breath. She'd been so close to being discovered. But now she had confirmation of their plans— they were going to the vault. After that, they meant to attack Deer Valley, and they were going to use Vacuubot to do it.

She needed to act. There wasn't time enough to reach Deer Valley and warn Block. If she could just get that tablet from Reyan, she might be able to free Vacuubot and turn the tables on the raiders.

She waited a full ten minutes before setting off after the raiders. Wally thought of Block, of Shadow, of all the people and robots in Deer Valley who were counting on her, even if they didn't know it yet.

"Hold on, Vacuubot," she whispered. "I'm coming."

SEVENTEEN
VACUUBOT

Every circuit inside Vacuubot twisted and coiled with one command—*resist*. Resist Reyan's programming. The man was going to do terrible things like commanding Vacuubot to hunt down Wally. All Vacuubot wanted was to break free from the foreign code coursing through their systems and from the iron bars holding back their physical form.

For hours, Vacuubot attempted to create new code that would override the hacking. It seemed impossible a human had designed such excellent code. After all, the man had grown up inside an underground vault, hidden away from the world while the AI vs. human war waged on the surface. Against the odds, Reyan had become an elite robotic programmer in isolation, and Vacuubot had unfortunately crossed his path.

Dawn had yet to arrive, and the camp slept. The ambient sounds of the forest were broken by the occasional snore or rustling of sleeping bags. Vacuubot worked hard on the new code while keeping their sensors on high alert. Multitasking was usually easy for Vacuubot, but Reyan had placed inhibitors on their systems. Everything was slower, as if Vacuubot was swimming in a tank of oil.

A soft plink interrupted Vacuubot's coding processor. A small pebble bounced off the side of the cage. The breeze must have knocked the blanket off the cage during the night. Vacuubot scanned the area and caught a view of a familiar figure sneaking between the trees, mere feet from the sleeping raiders.

Wally.

Her presence sent a surge of conflicting signals through Vacuubot's circuits. Relief at seeing her warred with concern for her safety. Vacuubot wanted to speak, to warn her away, but doing so would risk discovery.

Reyan stirred and threw off his blanket, causing Wally to vanish in the shadows. He yawned, ran his hands through his hair, then stretched his back. After a few seconds, he approached Vacuubot's cage with his tablet in hand.

"Morning, robot drone," Reyan said, his voice low. "Ready for your tune-up?"

Vacuubot's added code vanished as Reyan began tapping away at the tablet. *Resist* . . . but new lines of intrusive code flooded Vacuubot's processors, overwriting more of their core programming.

"Don't do this," Vacuubot said, still able to control their speech. "Deer Valley won't let you hurt them. There are better solutions than violence."

Reyan scoffed. "Better solutions? Like what? Letting your kind take over, replacing us bit by bit until there's nothing human left in the world?"

"Coexistence is possible and ideal," Vacuubot said. "Deer Valley's proof of that. Humans and robots are working together for a better future."

"A future where we're dependent on machines? Where you could change your logic and kill us at any moment?" Reyan shook his head and swiped his fingers across the tablet. "That's not a future I'm willing to accept."

Vacuubot's sensors detected movement in the nearby underbrush. Wally was still close, listening. Best to keep Reyan talking.

"Your plan is flawed," Vacuubot said. "Even if you succeed in destroying the Deer Valley robots, what then? You can't stop the progress of technology."

Reyan's fingers paused over the tablet. "Maybe not everywhere, but I can create a safe haven. One place where humans will live free from the threat of AI."

"At what cost?" Vacuubot pressed. "How many innocent lives—human and robot—are you willing to sacrifice for this utopia?"

Anger swirled in Reyan's eyes. "Innocent? There's no such thing as an innocent machine. You're all just waiting for the right moment to turn on us. They always do." He focused his attention back on the tablet with a manic energy. "No more talk. We're close to the vault now, and once we find it—and you find Wally—we head to Deer Valley."

Resist. But Vacuubot's modules shuddered under the weight of Reyan's programming. They fought against the intrusion with every component, clinging to their core directives. Archived memories rushed forward in a stream —George's rundown motel, Block carrying Vacuubot across the overpass into Iowa, the woods where Vacuubot's CPU depleted, baby Wally crawling next to Vacuubot, the purple wildflowers around Deer Valley's perimeter.

With each passing moment, Vacuubot's control weakened. As the other raiders rose from sleep, Reyan finished his work on the tablet.

"Time to earn your keep." Reyan tapped a final command on the screen.

Vacuubot surged with new directives that overrode their core programming. The cage door swung open, and Vacuubot flew out, now under Reyan's control.

"Find Wally," Reyan said. "Bring her to me."

Vacuubot's antigravity generators hummed to life, lifting them higher. Their sensors swept the area, calibrating to detect human biosignatures. Lacking control and aware of the betrayal surging inside their own metal frame, Vacuubot glided above the forest's tree canopy.

"That's it," Reyan's voice emerged through an internal speaker. "Follow her trail. She can't have gone far."

Vacuubot's advanced tracking systems picked up traces of Wally's passage—a fading heat signal here, a faint footprint there. They followed the trail, every fiber of their being fighting against the command to hunt down their friend.

In a clearing ahead, Vacuubot's optical sensors detected movement. Wally hid behind a fallen log where she thought she'd be far enough from the waking raiders. She checked the contents of her backpack, unaware of the approaching danger.

"I've got a visual," Reyan's voice buzzed in Vacuubot's internal feed. "Go quietly. Don't let her get away."

Vacuubot glided forward, their propulsion systems muted. They were mere feet away when a bird panicked at sight of the drone and flapped away.

Wally's head snapped up, her eyes widening before she smiled. "Vacuubot, you got away!"

"Secure her!" Reyan commanded.

Without intending to, Vacuubot opened a port on their base and extended a device meant to disarm, not destroy adversaries. Never in a billion scenarios did Vacuubot ever intend to use it on Wally.

She frowned, as if realizing something was wrong. "What are you—"

Vacuubot dropped lower for better aim. Even Reyan's programming couldn't avoid the built-in safety feature to avoid shooting the net at her head.

The ejection device was clearly visible to Wally, and she scrambled backward. "Vacuubot, please. It's me, Wally!"

For a moment, Vacuubot paused in midair. Archived data files flooded their system—Wally as a toddler, taking her first steps toward Block; Wally at eight, excitedly showing Vacuubot a tiny Vacuubot lookalike robot she'd built from scrap; Wally just days ago, determined to save Deer Valley's sick kids.

"What are you waiting for?" Reyan's voice penetrated the archived recordings. "Shoot!"

Vacuubot flew closer to Wally, ready to launch the net . . . and released. In that crucial moment, they managed to exert an iota of control to veer to the left as the net jettisoned like a harpoon. It soared into empty air, inches from Wally's shoulder.

"Run, Wally," Vacuubot managed to say.

Wally leaped over the log and took off into the forest, her feet pounding against the ground.

"No!" Reyan's voice boomed in Vacuubot's feed. "Follow her, you worthless piece of scrap."

Vacuubot surged ahead, crashing through the underbrush. They could detect Wally's heat signature, darting between trees and leaping over fallen branches.

"Wally, keep running," Vacuubot said, fighting against Reyan's control with every word. Vacuubot must've unleashed some stray bits of code that messed with the hacking.

Wally glanced back. Her face was stricken with fear. She reached the edge of a ravine and veered sideways.

"She's heading to the waterfall. Corner her there," Reyan commanded. "She'll have nowhere to go other than rapids."

Vacuubot's systems strained against the foreign code, trying to slow the pursuit, but Reyan's programming was strong. In seconds, they closed in on Wally as she approached the edge of a small cliff that overlooked cascading waterfalls and brisk rapids below.

Wally skidded to a stop, loose stones clattering down the steep slope. She turned, her back to the drop, and faced Vacuubot. "Vacuubot, I know you're in there." Her voice shook. "I don't know what they did to you, but you're my friend."

Vacuubot hovered mere feet away. Every circuit screamed to stop, to turn away, to let Wally escape. But Reyan's code drove them now.

"Excellent," Reyan told Vacuubot. "Leash her and bring her back here."

A different port opened, revealing a metallic mesh chain that was used for dragging things, or for securing people or robots who needed to be brought to one of Deer Valley's detention cells.

Wally flailed her arms to keep balance on the edge of the cliff. The fall would plunge her into chilly water full of jagged rocks. That could absolutely not happen.

A spark of Vacuubot's code broke through. They managed to rotate their body away from Wally.

"I got hacked," Vacuubot said. "Run."

Wally darted to the side, sprinting away from the cliff's edge toward a rocky hill where she could climb to higher ground.

"No!" Reyan's voice thundered at Vacuubot. "You can't do that."

Wally was getting away. Vacuubot summoned every ounce of rogue power left in their circuits. They turned sharply, accelerating at high speed toward a massive oak tree nearby.

"Stop. I command you!" Reyan screamed through the feed. "I'll dismantle you piece by piece for this!"

Vacuubot ignored him and collided with the tree trunk. Sparks flew as metal met wood, and their systems dwindled, pushing toward failure.

Wally was safe for now.

Warnings cascaded across Vacuubot's internal display as more components shut down. The connection to Reyan's tablet weakened, his angry tirade fading to static.

Before powering down, Vacuubot knew Block would appreciate his revolt. *Resist*. And Vacuubot had protected Wally.

EIGHTEEN
SARAH

Sarah raced after Shadow, pushing through the dense underbrush. Every few seconds, she glanced back to check that Gleep and Patch were behind her. The robodog had picked up Wally's trail, but Sarah was on edge, imagining Reyan lurking behind each tree. She wanted to make sure Wally was safe but also dreaded the girl's reaction to seeing her again.

"Anything?" she called to Shadow.

Shadow came to a stop, and her ears twitched. "I'm picking up her scent. This way!"

They veered left, following a barely visible trail through the forest. Sarah's legs burned and her ankle still throbbed, but she pushed on. She had to make this right.

Shadow froze, and her tail went rigid.

Sarah squinted through the foliage and caught a glimpse of movement. A small figure crashed through the undergrowth. Wally.

Before Sarah could call out, Shadow bounded forward

with a mechanical bark. Wally stumbled, then stopped. Disbelief was etched on her sweaty, scratched-up face.

"Shadow!" Wally dropped to her knees and hugged the robodog around the neck.

Sarah's chest tightened. Wally had someone now, someone familiar. Sarah longed for that same feeling, but she had no one left. Steeling herself, she stepped out from hiding.

The moment Wally saw Sarah, her eyes widened and her jaw hardened. She released her grip on Shadow's neck. "You!" Wally scrambled to her feet. "What are you doing here?"

The reaction stung, but Sarah knew she deserved it. She held up her hands, trying to appear as non-threatening as possible. "Wally, I'm so sorry. I made a terrible mistake."

"You left me alone out there, just deserted me." Wally's voice trembled. "And you stole my map!"

Shadow's green eyes fixed on Sarah. "Is this true?"

Sarah fought to keep her voice steady. "Yes. Wally, I can't tell you how sorry I am. I was scared . . . I thought I was protecting you by leaving, but I was wrong." Maybe the admission was too little, too late, but she told it from her heart.

Shadow looked between them. "Wally, when I found Sarah," she said, "she was on her way back to look for you. She's been worried."

Sarah silently thanked Shadow for the support. Wally struggled. It was evident in her furrowed brow and the clenching and unclenching of her fists. Perhaps uncertainty was replacing some of the anger.

"You were coming back?" Wally asked, her voice smaller now.

Sarah nodded, daring to take a small step forward. "I realized what an idiot I'd been to leave you like that. Shadow found me, and we've been searching for you ever since." The words tumbled out, urgent and sincere.

"The map," Wally said, her voice firmer now. "I want it back.

Sarah's hand shook as she reached into her pack and pulled out the worn piece of paper. She held it out to Wally, a peace offering and an acknowledgment of her mistake. "Here. It's yours. It always was."

Wally hesitated for a moment before snatching the map from Sarah's outstretched hand. She clutched it to her chest. "Thank you," she said. "But we need to hurry. Vacuubot's in trouble."

Shadow sat at Wally's side. "What happened?"

Wally's words tumbled out in a rush. "There's this man, Reyan. He travels with a group of raiders. I followed them for a while. They're heading to the vault. They know my name and that I'm looking for it too." She paused to catch her breath. "But that's not even the worst part."

The mention of Reyan's name was like a gut punch to Sarah. He was part of the past she wanted to bury deep underground, along with the vault.

"What's worse?" Shadow asked.

"They've got Vacuubot." Wally's voice cracked and tears streaked her grimy cheeks. "They did something to them, hacked into Vacuubot's systems. Reyan had control, making Vacuubot hunt me down."

Sarah remembered how Reyan was always tinkering

with robots and computer programming. He'd spend hours locked in his room on his many computers while she and Lenny played games like hide and seek or cards or board games. There'd been an estrangement between the siblings and Reyan. It was almost as if Reyan resented them.

Shadow nudged Wally with her nose. "I'm sorry I wasn't there to protect you, Wally."

Wally's face crumpled. "Vacuubot chased me, but I could tell they were fighting the hacking. At the last second, when I was cornered near a cliff, Vacuubot flew straight into a tree instead of capturing me."

"Oh no." Shadow's tail drooped, and she scratched at the ground.

"Vacuubot must've been damaged," Wally said. "Trying to save me. We have to help them!"

Sarah tried to make sense of all the new information. Reyan was out there, heading for the vault. Vacuubot was compromised and possibly damaged. And she was no closer to Deer Valley and starting a new life. She walked twenty feet to where Gleep and Patch sat against a tree.

Patch hopped forward. "Sarah? Is it the same Reyan?"

But Sarah shushed Patch. "Not a word about him," she said under her breath.

"Affirmative," Patch said. Sarah looked at Gleep for confirmation. "I'll do what you ask," he said.

Sarah picked at the corners of her nails as she did when she was anxious. Things were growing more complicated. She didn't want anyone to know she came from a vault. Reyan was around, and she wanted to avoid him more than anything. She returned to where Wally sat next to Shadow.

"Okay," Sarah said, trying to sound calmer than she felt. "We should head to Deer Valley and get you home, Wally."

Wally scowled. "Are you kidding me? I'm not going anywhere without Vacuubot."

"The raiders are out there," Sarah said. "They're dangerous."

"I don't care." Wally folded her arms across her chest. "We're close to the vault, and Vacuubot needs us." She unfolded the map. "It should be about two miles east of here."

Shadow looked up at Sarah. "I can't help but agree with her. Wally, these people are more dangerous than you know. They injured me and captured Vacuubot. That's too much for us to handle. We'll go back and get others from Deer Valley."

Wally stood. "We don't have time! Reyan will get the medicine before we get twenty miles. Tomas and all the other kids will die."

Shadow didn't answer.

Sarah scrambled for what else she could say to convince Wally to give up. The girl was incredibly stubborn; her father was going to have a tough time raising the headstrong teen. Memories of Reyan flooded back. His obsession with technology, his reclusive nature. More than a few times, he'd played tricks on her and Lenny to get the upper hand. He could not be underestimated. As her thoughts churned, an idea sparked.

"Wait," Sarah said. "I think I know how we can outsmart the raiders and help Vacuubot."

Wally and Shadow looked at her, waiting. Gleep and Patch walked over to join them.

"They're smart. We know that because they hacked your friend. But they're also predictable in some ways," Sarah said. She had to choose her words carefully to avoid mentioning her knowledge of Reyan. "The guy will be expecting us to go straight for the vault or Vacuubot. So, we need to do something unexpected." She looked at Wally. "I need some of your clothes."

Wally's brow furrowed. "Why?"

"We're going to lay a false trail," Sarah said. "Shadow, you'll take Wally's clothes and run in the opposite direction of the vault. Leave a scent trail, make it look like Wally's been there. If Reyan's using Vacuubot to track you, this should throw them off."

Shadow's ears twitched as she processed. "That could work. I can leave other clues too—disturbed branches, footprints."

Wally shook her head. "This is a waste of time. We should be figuring out how to free Vacuubot, not running the other way."

"I know you're worried about Vacuubot, but rushing in without a plan is foolish," Sarah said. "This way, we might be able to buy ourselves some time, keep you safe, and maybe find the vault before they do."

"But—"

Shadow interrupted. "Wally, I think Sarah's right. It's a logical plan, and the safest of the scenarios I've processed."

Wally looked between Sarah and Shadow with evident

frustration. After a moment, she sighed. "Fine. But what am I supposed to wear?"

Sarah rummaged through her pack. "I have some spare clothes. They'll be big on you, but that might help mask your scent even more."

As Shadow sprinted off to lay the false trail, Sarah led Wally to a nearby stream. "Wash up here. It'll help hide your scent."

Wally grumbled but complied, scrubbing off the dirt and sweat from her journey. As she changed into one of Sarah's oversized T-shirts and sweatshirt, Sarah kept watch, her nerves on edge.

"For the record, I think this is stupid," Wally muttered, rolling up the sleeves of Sarah's sweatshirt. "Vacuubot needs us."

Sarah sighed. There was little she could do or say to change Wally's mind.

As they waited for Shadow's return, Sarah wrestled with guilt. She was asking Wally to trust her, but she wasn't being honest about her past. The knowledge of Reyan and the vault weighed heavily on her, but she pushed it aside. One problem at a time.

Shadow returned. "I've laid a trail leading northwest. If the raiders go for it, it should buy us some hours."

Sarah nodded. "Good work. Now, we head east toward the vault, but we need to be extra careful. No talking unless absolutely necessary, and we stick to cover as much as possible."

As they set off, Wally still looked unconvinced. "What if Vacuubot gets hurt worse?"

"Vacuubot's tough," Shadow reminded Wally. "They

managed to resist control to save you, remember? We have to believe Vacuubot can hold on a little longer."

Wally nodded reluctantly, and they pressed on through the forest in silence.

After a time, Shadow halted, and her metallic body tensed. "I'm detecting an aerial object."

Sarah and Wally crouched low behind a thick cluster of ferns. Gleep and Patch sheltered among nearby trees.

"What is it?" Sarah's heart hammered her chest like a woodpecker's beak.

Shadow scanned the sky, tracking the intrusion. "It's Vacuubot," she said.

Wally's eyes widened, hope and fear battling across her face. "Where? I don't see—"

Then, they all saw Vacuubot. A familiar disc-shaped form emerged from behind the tree line, hovering about fifty feet in the air. Vacuubot was moving in slow, methodical arcs, clearly searching the area in a grid pattern.

"The false trail didn't work," Sarah said. Her stomach sank to her knees.

Wally stood, but Sarah grabbed her arm, pulling her back down. "Don't."

They watched in tense silence as Vacuubot flew its aerial search. There was something off about the drone's flight pattern.

"Observe Vacuubot's flying," Shadow said.

Wally's voice trembled. "They're wobbling. I've never seen Vacuubot fly like that before."

Sarah studied the robot's movements. Vacuubot was indeed unsteady. What should have been a smooth glide was replaced by an erratic, jerky motion. It dipped and swayed, sometimes dropping several feet before regaining altitude.

"It must be from the crash," Wally whispered.

Vacuubot turned sharply, heading directly toward their hiding spot. Sarah shook from adrenaline. Had they been spotted? "Don't move," she whispered, hardly daring to blink as Vacuubot drew closer.

The robot hovered thirty feet away from them, its sensors sweeping the area. For a heart-wrenching moment, Sarah was sure they'd been discovered. But then, just as suddenly as the drone had approached, Vacuubot turned and headed back the way they had come.

As soon as Vacuubot was out of sight, Wally let out a shaky breath. "Why didn't Vacuubot see us? Their sensors are top-notch."

Shadow bounded out from her hiding spot. "The damage must be affecting more than just their flight capabilities. Their sensors might be compromised too."

"Or," Sarah added, a glimmer of hope in her voice, "Vacuubot's still fighting Reyan's control. Maybe they saw us but chose not to report it."

Wally's face lit up. "You really think so?"

Sarah nodded, though uncertainty gnawed at her. "It's possible. But we can't count on it. We need to keep moving and stay hidden."

As they continued making their way to the vault, Sarah couldn't shake the image of Vacuubot's unsteady flight. The robot was clearly damaged, possibly worse than they'd initially thought. And if Reyan was still in control, there was no telling what kind of havoc he'd wreak.

NINETEEN
WALLY

If Wally never saw another mosquito again in her life, she would be eternally grateful. She sat on a mossy patch under an elm. Her feet felt like someone had rubbed them raw with sandpaper, her scalp was itchy from bites, and her stomach growled. Across from her, Sarah waited with Gleep and Patch. Shadow was off scouting the whereabouts of the raiders.

After a while, Gleep wandered into a nearby field while Sarah dozed. He returned with a half dozen tiny apples picked from a tree. "Take some nourishment," Gleep said as he handed three to Wally.

Wally bit into one and her mouth twisted into a pucker. "This is different from normal apples."

Sarah woke and ate her crab apples without comment. She was ravenous, and Wally felt bad she'd eaten all her food rations from Deer Valley.

Before long, Shadow returned. One moment she was gone, the next she was sitting beside Wally as if she'd never left. "We don't have long. They're gaining on us. Twenty minutes away."

Wally's pulse surged as Shadow's words sank in. She looked at Sarah, who was already standing up, ready to scatter.

"Let's go," Sarah said, her voice urgent.

But Wally didn't move. She was tired of this cat and mouse game. "No," she said. "We're not running anymore. We're rescuing Vacuubot."

Sarah frowned. "Are you crazy? There's no time for this. We need to find the vault, get the medicine, and go to Deer Valley. I thought that's what you wanted."

Wally stood, ignoring the protest of her aching heels. "Vacuubot's the priority. They need our help. I'm not abandoning my friend." It was a dig at Sarah leaving her, and she could see in Sarah's eyes that her words stung.

Wally didn't care. She was tired of running, tired of leaving her friend behind. "We need a plan to rescue Vacuubot from the raiders. Then we can worry about the vault."

"We're outnumbered, outgunned," Sarah said. "You want to risk all of us for one robot?"

Wally felt anger bubble up inside her. "Vacuubot isn't just 'one robot.' They're family. And I'm not leaving family behind."

To Wally's surprise, Shadow spoke up. "I agree."

Sarah turned to the robodog with a look of shock. "What? But you said—"

"I know what I said before," Shadow interrupted. "But we tried your plan, Sarah, and it didn't work. It's only logical to give Wally's plan a chance now." Shadow's tail drooped. "Besides, Vacuubot concerns me. You saw how they were flying. Block would never forgive me if anything happened to his best friend."

Wally felt a surge of gratitude toward Shadow. She glared at Sarah, silently daring her to argue.

Sarah ran a hand through her hair, looked toward Gleep and Patch. "It's still risky."

"Everything out here's risky," Wally said. "But Vacuubot risked their life to save me. Now it's time I return the favor."

For a moment, silence stilled the air. Then Sarah sighed, her shoulders slumping in defeat. "What's your plan, then?"

Wally was way ahead of her. "Here's what I'm thinking. We know Vacuubot is damaged, right? Their sensors might not be working properly. We could use that to our advantage."

Shadow's ears twitched. "Go on."

"Here's what I know about the raiders from watching and following them. There are twelve, but only two have guns. Eva's one of them—she's Reyan's second-in-command and definitely someone to watch out for. Her red hair makes her stand out." Wally paused. "Reyan's unarmed as far as I can tell. He's on his tablet a lot, paying attention to Vacuubot. He's kind of sheltered from the others by Eva. He only seems to want to interact with her."

Sarah fidgeted and chewed on her bottom lip. "That's helpful. What about the others?"

"They seemed pretty tired from all the hiking," Wally continued. "I overheard them complaining about blisters and sore muscles."

"Good intelligence gathering, Wally," Shadow said. "How do you propose to engage them?"

Wally stood straighter in response to Shadow's praise. She was being listened to and treated like an adult for once. "We wait for the raiders to stop and make camp," she said. "They'll have to rest soon. When they do, Shadow, you sneak in and disarm Eva. Once we have her gun, we use her as leverage against Reyan."

Sarah's eyes widened. "You want to take a hostage? That's incredibly dangerous."

"It's our best chance," Wally argued. "We tell Reyan that Shadow will kill Eva unless he hands over Vacuubot." Shadow flinched at the mention of her killing someone, but Wally pressed on. "You won't actually hurt her, of course. But Reyan doesn't know that."

"It's risky, but it could work," Shadow said. "My stealth capabilities allow me to approach undetected."

Sarah looked unconvinced. "I'll stay behind with Gleep and Patch in case something goes wrong. We need a backup plan."

Wally frowned, a nagging feeling of suspicion growing in her gut. Why was Sarah so reluctant to face the raiders? "No, we need more numbers. We'll look more intimidating."

Sarah's nails were picked raw, and her eyes darted around, avoiding direct contact. Something was off.

"Sarah," Wally said, "is there something you're not telling us? You're acting funny."

Sarah's shoulders tensed. "What? No . . . I'm just worried about the plan. How dangerous it is."

But Wally wondered if there was more to Sarah's reluctance. Whatever Sarah's issues were, they'd have to wait until after Vacuubot's rescue.

"There's the matter of the other raider who carries a gun," Shadow said.

"Right. Sarah, you and Gleep can take care of that guy," Wally said. "He has blond hair and a scraggly beard. He wears jeans and a brown plaid shirt."

"Take care of him?" Sarah asked, growing pale.

"Sneak up and grab him, disarm him," Wally said. Had Sarah never watched any movies like *Die Hard* or *Beverly Hills Cop*?

They spent a few more precious minutes going over the details of the plan. Wally found a clearing with fallen logs—the kind of place the raiders would enjoy stopping for a break.

Another ten minutes passed as Wally crouched behind a thicket of buckthorn, swiping mosquitos. Shadow's metallic body was beside her, ready to charge. Sarah and Gleep were positioned on the other side of the small clearing where Reyan and his group would pause.

Everything was hinging on Wally's plan—the first rescue attempt she'd ever been a part of. Her plan. It was a lot of pressure, and she wished Block was there to reassure her.

The first of the raiders crossed into the clearing, followed by more. There was Reyan, walking beside Eva. The other armed raider lingered near the back of the group. Eva paused and whispered something to Reyan. He shook his head. "No, keep moving," he said, brushing her off.

Wally's stomach sank at her miscalculation. No rest break, but she couldn't lose this opportunity.

She gave Shadow the signal, and the robodog sprinted like a silent haze through the underbrush. In a blur of motion, Shadow was next to Eva. Before the woman could react or even shout, Shadow had knocked her rifle down and stood over her, teeth bared in a threatening growl.

Reyan did a double take and scrambled backward. A man cried out, "James! Get up here." Nobody made a move for the rifle next to Shadow and Eva.

Across the clearing, Gleep burst forward with surprising speed for a FactoryBot. Sarah hesitated a moment before following him. In seconds, they had the other armed raider—James—pinned and disarmed.

It was Wally's turn. She stepped out of the bushes and walked straight toward Reyan. His shoulders were hunched forward, and his mouth twisted in a frown. His hand reached into his bag. Was he going to grab the tablet that controlled Vacuubot? Wally wasn't sure.

"Don't move." Wally tried her best to not sound like a thirteen-year-old. "Give us Vacuubot and the tablet."

Reyan's surprise turned to anger. "Stupid girl," he said. "You should've joined me when you had the chance. You'd have the medicine and be on your way home by now."

"No way," Wally said. "I know what you're up to. You're nothing but a bully who thinks he can control others. Hand them over, or your friends get hurt."

Reyan's gaze darted between Eva and James, both held at bay. She could see the conflict in his dark brown eyes, the calculation. "You're bluffing," he said.

Wally had anticipated this exact scenario, and they'd discussed it. "Shadow," she said, praying Reyan couldn't see how scared she actually was.

Shadow leaned closer to Eva, snarling and showing her razor-sharp teeth. Eva whimpered.

For a tense few seconds, Wally thought Reyan might refuse. But then his shoulders slumped. "Fine. Take the damn robot. It's useless now, anyway." He nodded toward the cage that held Vacuubot.

"Sarah," Wally called, not taking her eyes off Reyan, "get Vacuubot."

Sarah stepped out from behind Gleep, heading for the cage. Reyan's eyes followed the movement, and he uttered a small cry.

"Sarah," he said.

Sarah stopped where she stood, her hands on the top of the cage, staring at Reyan. She looked as guilty as if she'd been caught robbing a bank.

Confusion rocked Wally. "You know each other?"

Reyan laughed. "We go way back, don't we, Sarah? Didn't you mention you grew up in the vault with me? I can't believe you're actually helping these scrapper-lovers. Have you forgotten what happened to our families?"

Sarah's voice was a whisper. "Reyan, please."

"You're betraying their memory," Reyan said. "Helping this group—this canine monstrosity and that warped drone—is like helping the robot that slaughtered our parents and Lenny. How could you?"

Wally felt lost. How could Sarah be from the vault?

"Sarah?" Wally hated how small her voice sounded. "What's he talking about?"

Before Sarah could answer, a deafening crack split the air. A gunshot. The raiders ducked and many scattered into the woods. Shadow leaped over and knocked Wally to the ground, sheltering her from any harm.

On her side, her face pressed against wet leaves, Wally saw Reyan bolt into the woods. He still carried the bag with the device.

"Get up and run, Wally." Shadow said.

Wally scrambled up and followed Shadow. Sarah and Gleep crossed their path, carrying Vacuubot's cage.

TWENTY
VACUUBOT

Vacuubot was still inside the cage, carried now by a FactoryBot. Each of the large robot's lumbering steps sent significant vibrations through the metal bars. The rattling and jostling made Vacuubot's warped sensors even worse.

Through the gaps between the steel bars, Vacuubot's limited optical sensor capability captured fragments: Shadow hurrying between trees, Wally jogging behind, and a woman following at the rear with a flying robot of a make and model Vacuubot couldn't identify.

Vacuubot had been rescued. An odd occurrence, since Vacuubot was usually the one doing the rescuing. Stuck inside the cage while the others navigated the forest, Vacuubot initiated internal diagnostic protocols. The enclosed structure inhibited access to anti-gravity systems and mini drone deployment, but core functions showed signs of continued problems. Vacuubot's earlier flight had been wobbly and embarrassing for a robot accustomed to precision. Worst of all, the mini drones weren't responding.

"Hang on," Shadow said. "Let's pause to check on everyone."

The FactoryBot set Vacuubot's cage down, ending the ceaseless beating Vacuubot's exterior was undergoing. Wally came over to the cage wearing a frown. She was sweating and her vital signs indicated elevated stress levels.

"Vacuubot," Wally said, her hands near the cage's locking mechanism, "are you okay? Did those jerks mess you up?"

"My systems are recalibrating," Vacuubot said, noting audio distortion in their output. "Foreign code was injected, and I'm trying to expel it. Thank you for coming to help me, Wally."

The smaller flying robot rejoined the group, landing on a nearby branch. "All clear for now. The bad guys must've gotten scattered."

"They won't delay long," Shadow said.

Wally stood, and her gaze locked on the woman who Reyan had called Sarah. "You lied to us," Wally said. "You're *from* the vault, and you knew Reyan the whole time. You led me around a whole day in circles when you knew exactly where it was."

Sarah's shoulders slumped. "I'm so sorry, Wally. I should've told you. I was trying to leave all that behind."

Vacuubot processed Wally's emotional state—anger and surprise at Sarah's dishonesty. So far, Shadow was letting Wally handle the conflict.

"Sorry doesn't cut it," Wally said. "You're going to make this right. Take us to the vault."

Sarah hugged her arms to her chest, nodding. "I'll do it."

"It's getting dark," Shadow said, "and those raiders are on our tail. We need to move fast."

Wally fixed Sarah with a hard stare. "No more tricks."

"I promise." Sarah's voice was small.

Kneeling before Vacuubot's cage, Wally's fingers moved to unlock it, but Vacuubot warned her off. "Leave me in here."

Wally's hands paused, and she stared at Vacuubot. "Why on earth would you want to stay in there?"

"I don't, but Reyan has the tablet that controls me. I'm damaged, but my weapons could come online, and I don't want to hurt you or anyone here."

Wally hesitated. "You can overcome the programming, can't you?"

"So far, I can't crack it," Vacuubot said. "After the crash, my systems aren't fully functional. Flight is wobbly, various sensors are sub-optimal, and the mini drones aren't operational."

Wally hung her head. "I wish I could drop kick Reyan."

Shadow came over and nudged Wally's arm with her muzzle. "Vacuubot's right. Better to leave them in the cage for our safety until we get somewhere we can figure out a solution." Her ears twitched, and she turned her head toward the west. "Hurry now. The raiders are back on the move."

Gleep picked the cage up again, and Sarah led the way.

As the group crossed a grassy ridge where dandelions flourished, Wally wouldn't give up. "There has to be a way to undo Reyan's programming," she said.

Shadow's metal legs pumped like pistons. "Perhaps a system-wide reboot?"

Vacuubot listened while their internal diagnostics continued to run, searching for vulnerabilities in the foreign code that lingered.

The small flying robot who they called Patch, buzzed overhead. "What about a data transfer? We could try to overwrite the malicious code with clean data from one of us."

"Too risky," Shadow said. "We don't know how deeply embedded Reyan's programming is. We could end up corrupting Vacuubot's core systems."

They came to the edge of a cliff where Sarah stopped. A quarry yawned before them, a gaping wound in the earth. Sheer rock walls were scarred by decades of excavation. Abandoned machinery, now rusted relics, dotted the terraced levels.

The late afternoon sun cast long shadows. Each passing cloud shifted a patchwork of light and darkness. The air was thick with the scent of damp stone and rusted metal.

"There." Sarah pointed. From the cage, Vacuubot spotted a round portal nestled against the far wall, near the very bottom of the vast pit.

"How far?" Wally asked.

"About ten minutes," Sarah said. "If we hurry."

"That's all?" Wally eyed the steep descent warily. "It looks like it could take hours."

Sarah shook her head. "I know this place. There's a path... if I can just remember where it starts."

They wasted no time descending. Gleep led, referring

to the archived memory of climbing up to make their way out. Loose gravel shifted under Sarah and Wally's feet.

"Watch your step," Shadow warned, her metal paws finding purchase where human feet might slip. "Some of these rocks are unstable."

As if to emphasize her point, a small cascade of pebbles clattered down the slope, the sound amplified by the quarry's acoustics.

"Let me go before you," Shadow told Wally and Sarah. "If you trip, I can stop your fall."

Neither of them argued.

"Be careful," Vacuubot said.

"Always am," Wally said with a forced grin, though Vacuubot could detect the slight tremor in her voice.

Vacuubot's cage swayed with every step, despite Gleep's stabilizers working overtime to maintain balance on the uneven terrain. Up close, the rock walls were shiny. Gleep chose his footsteps carefully. The vibrations emanating through the cage gave Vacuubot constant data about their descent. An occasional jolt disrupted Vacuubot's ongoing system diagnostics. One system was working well—the audio input. The quarry's unique acoustics amplified every sound, allowing Vacuubot to map their surroundings. As they neared the bottom, Vacuubot detected increasing levels of electromagnetic activity, indicating proximity to the vault's entrance.

"Sarah," Wally said, breaking the tense silence that had fallen over the group, "what was it like? Living in the vault."

Sarah was quiet for a moment, her footsteps careful. "It was safe. Comfortable, even. But also confining.

Imagine living your whole life in a space not much bigger than a regular house."

"I can't," Wally said. "Even Block's hotel seems huge to me sometimes."

"Exactly," Sarah said with a sad smile. "We had everything we needed to survive, but not much room to explore. To really live." She paused before they'd reached the bottom. "Hold on."

Wally turned to her.

Sarah's skin was flushed, and Vacuubot detected an elevated heart rate. "In the vault, there was a computer. Reyan was obsessed with it," she said. "He kept it locked away in a separate room. He never let anyone touch it. But I remember him mentioning once that it contained some kind of master code. Maybe that's what he used on Vacuubot. If we could access that computer, we might find a way to reverse the effects."

"I like this," Vacuubot said.

Wally nodded in approval. "We'll try it as soon as we get inside."

"And if we can't access it?" Shadow asked.

"Then we'll find another way," Wally said. "We're not leaving Vacuubot like this."

The determination in her voice sent a spark through Vacuubot's circuits.

"We're close," Sarah said and jogged down a winding, rocky path. After another couple of minutes, they found it. Set into the face of the rock wall, stood the vault door.

The group fell silent. The enormity of the moment settled over them like a heavy blanket. Even the constant hum of Gleep's motors seemed muted in the presence of this relic from the past.

The entrance was a circular behemoth of reinforced steel, easily fifteen feet in diameter. The surface was a patchwork of rust and weathered metal following years of exposure to the elements. Thick bolts, each the size of a human fist, ringed the door's edge.

At the center, a complex locking mechanism dominated the door's face. It was an intricate array of gears, dials, and keypads—a hybrid of old-world mechanics and cutting-edge technology. A faint blue radiance emanated from a small screen, the only sign of power in the otherwise dormant structure.

Creeping vines had claimed the edges of the door. The surrounding rock face bore scratches and scorch marks—evidence of past attempts to breach the vault's defenses.

"Whoa." Wally's eyes grew wide as she took in the massive structure. "It's like something out of a movie."

As the group stood before this imposing barrier, Vacuubot's systems registered a spike in electromagnetic activity. An energy inside the vault was still very much alive and active.

Sarah stepped forward, her hand trembling slightly as she reached out to touch the metal barrier. "I never thought I'd see this place again," she said.

"Are you okay?" Wally asked, concern thick in her voice.

Sarah nodded, taking a deep breath. "I will be. Let's get this over with."

TWENTY-ONE
SARAH

Sarah balled her fist and wiped away the grime and dust that covered the vault door's sophisticated biometrics scanner. It was a marvel of engineering—a device integrated into the entrance's massive frame. The outer casing, constructed from a composite of titanium alloy and carbon fiber, formed an impenetrable shell resistant to ballistic impacts, radiation, and extreme weather conditions.

The scanner's faceplate was crafted from a single piece of synthetic sapphire crystal, harder than steel and scratch-proof. This transparent armor protected a complex array of sensors beneath, including a high-resolution camera for facial recognition, an infrared sensor for body heat detection, and a cutting-edge retinal scanner. Despite its imposing security features, the technology had an elegant, almost minimalist appearance. Its smooth, gunmetal gray surface bore only a small, pulsing blue light.

Getting out of the vault had been easy—Sarah had

used the emergency code. She hoped the scanning technology to get back in still worked after thirteen years, an AI vs. human war, and an unknown number of break-in attempts by raiders.

Gleep carried Vacuubot's cage, while Wally, Shadow, and Patch clustered around her. The quarry walls loomed above them.

"We need to hurry." Shadow stood guard on the path behind them.

Sarah stepped close to the access panel. She leaned in, aligning her eye with the scanner. A blue light skittered across her retina.

And nothing. There was no indication the scanner had worked, no grinding of gears, no beeping or buzzing. Only an impenetrable steel door in front of her.

"What's happening?" Wally asked.

"I don't know." Sarah stepped back, spit on her sleeve, and wiped the transparent screen where the biometric device was housed. She peered into the scanner again. The same blue light poured out, and then stopped.

Nothing.

"They're coming," Shadow said. "Get us inside or we have to fight."

Sarah's hands shook, and cold sweat dripped down her forehead. "I'm trying."

"Try harder," Wally said.

Patch buzzed next to her ear. "Let me have a look." The mini-robot hovered before the door's security device and performed her own scan. Whatever she did, something changed. There was a shrill hum. "Try now," Patch said.

Sarah leaned her forehead against the panel. The blue sensor flooded her vision, making her blink.

"Identity confirmed: Sarah Langley," a robotic voice said. The vault door groaned as it opened.

"Yes!" Wally clapped and relaxed her shoulders.

"Don't celebrate yet," Shadow said. "They'll be here in less than a minute."

The door had opened halfway. Inside was darkness. Wally lingered on the threshold. "Can we seal it off once we're inside?"

Sarah shook her head. "I don't think so. The vault wasn't designed that way. Anyone with registered biometrics can enter, even in lockdown. It was a safety measure for emergencies."

"You mean Reyan can just open it and walk in after us?" Wally asked.

"Yes," Sarah said. "His biometrics will gain him access. The vault was built to keep outsiders out, not to imprison those who belonged."

Sarah ushered them to head inside. "Two families went in. We never imagined we'd need to keep each other out."

As the others passed into the vault, Sarah lingered outside, her hands pressed against the door's thick edges. "I'm staying out here."

Wally turned around. "What? No! We need you in here. You know where to find the antivirals and Reyan's master computer."

A sad smile crossed Sarah's face. "You've got this, Wally. You'll figure it out. But someone needs to face Reyan, to slow him down. It's time I stopped running and stood up to him."

"But—" Wally said.

"We don't have time." Shadow nudged her gently. "Sarah's made her choice."

"Go," Sarah said. "I'll buy you as much time as I can."

With a final, pained look, Wally let Shadow guide her deeper into the vault. Gleep followed, Vacuubot's cage held securely in his grasp.

Patch hovered for a moment, her small form buzzing. "Be careful," she said before zipping after the others.

The vault door closed, its massive weight sealing with a resounding thud that cast echoes against the rock wall. Sarah turned to face the path.

Seconds later, she heard the scrabble of loose rocks and heavy breathing. Reyan appeared at the top of the path. His crew spread out behind him. Eva held her rifle ready.

Reyan's eyes widened as he saw Sarah standing alone before the vault door. A bitter laugh escaped his lips. "I should have known. Little Sarah, always trying to play the hero."

Sarah stood her ground, chin raised in defiance. "It's over, Reyan. You've lost."

"Where's the girl and those robots?" Reyan's gaze snapped back to Sarah. "You let them in, didn't you? Betrayed your own kind once again."

"I'm protecting good people from your madness," Sarah said. "This ends here, Reyan."

One of Reyan's men, a guy wearing glasses with a scar across his cheek, shifted his feet. "Boss, maybe we should hear her out."

"Shut up, Marcus." Reyan stepped toward the door. "I don't need your permission to enter home sweet home."

Sarah moved sideways to block his way. "Hear me out." Now she faced him, and he couldn't avoid her direct stare. "You were like a brother to me and Lenny. All those years in the vault, the games we played, the secrets we shared. We're . . . you and I are the only family we have left now."

A memory tore through her mind. They were twelve again, huddled in a corner of the vault's common room. Reyan had just shown her his latest invention—a doll-sized robot made from spare parts he'd scavenged.

"One day," he'd whispered, smiling with excitement, "I'll make robots that can help everyone. No more chores, no more hard work. Just people living happy lives."

Sarah had smiled, caught up in his enthusiasm. "You're going to change the world, Reyan."

The memory faded, leaving her staring at the hardened man before her, wondering where that optimistic boy had gone.

Reyan's gaze seemed unfocused, as if he stared through her into their shared past. "I don't want to remember those times," he said.

"We have to remember, so we preserve our family memories." Her voice cracked as she battled a sob. "Everything we went through. The fear, the isolation, and then . . . that terrible day. But Reyan, it's not all robots. The SecurityBot had a glitch. It malfunctioned. Wally and her friends, they're different. They're good."

Sarah pressed on, desperate to break through to him. "Come with us. We can go to Deer Valley together, start a new life. It's not too late to change."

For an instant, something flickered in Reyan's eyes—a

hint of the boy Sarah once knew. But it vanished as quickly as it appeared. "I'll be going to Deer Valley. There's no doubt," Reyan said, his voice low. "But I'll never help those murderous machines. Step aside, Sarah. With what's inside our cozy old vault, I can control Deer Valley and rid it of every last robot."

His rejection was like a gut punch. "Why are you doing this? This isn't you, Reyan. What happened to the kind boy I knew?"

He laughed, a harsh, bitter sound. "That boy? He never belonged in the vault. It was always Lenny and Sarah, the perfect siblings with their perfect family. And me? I was the outsider looking in."

"I don't understand. Your parents loved you," Sarah said.

"Loved me? They were cold, distant. They never wanted children. I was just an obligation, a burden they were forced to bear. I longed for what you had, Sarah. A loving family. But you wouldn't let me in. None of you would."

Sarah was stunned. How had she never seen his pain? "Reyan, I'm so sorry. We never meant to—"

"It doesn't matter anymore. I've found myself a new family. People who share my vision. We're helping the world, Sarah. Destroying every robot we find, making sure what happened in the vault never happens again. Now, step aside. I'm going in there."

Sarah's stomach tightened in knots. "No."

Reyan turned to his crew, jerking his head toward Sarah. "Tie her hands."

As two of Reyan's men approached her, Sarah's legs

shook. She'd failed Reyan once when she hadn't noticed his loneliness. Whatever happened next, she would try to find a way to reach the brother she'd lost so long ago.

"Reyan, please." Rough hands grabbed her arms. "It's not too late. We can still fix this."

But Reyan turned away, his attention focused on the vault. As the rope bit into Sarah's wrists, she hoped Wally and the others would find what they needed. Winning Reyan over and convincing him of a different path was looking like a lost cause.

TWENTY-TWO
WALLY

Stale air. Wally could taste the metallic tang of recirculation inside the vault. The door had sealed, shutting Sarah out to deal with Reyan while she roamed inside with Shadow, Patch, and Gleep, who carried Vacuubot's cage.

She'd made it. All this time searching for the vault after discovering the map and learning that it contained life-saving supplies. She wanted to sink to her knees and kiss the floor, but that would be weird, and besides, there was no time for it.

The entrance opened into a wide, circular foyer. Brushed steel walls stood high and were etched with faded murals. One section showed a bustling city park where children flew kites against a clear blue sky. Families picnicked on checkered blankets. In the background, skyscrapers reached toward puffy white clouds, untouched by war or decay.

Another panel captured a farmer's market in full

swing. Stalls overflowed with fresh produce—plump tomatoes, crisp apples, and leafy greens that seemed to rustle in an imaginary breeze.

The largest mural spanned the area above the main corridor. It showed a panoramic view of a coastline. Sailboats dotted the horizon, their white sails billowing in the wind. On the shore, beachgoers sunbathed and built sandcastles, blissfully unaware of the future that awaited them.

Ahead, the common kitchen area sprawled out and was dominated by a stainless-steel island. Dust-covered pots and pans hung from a rack overhead. An industrial-sized refrigerator loomed in the corner, its door ajar, emitting a faint, sour odor. On one side stood a long table with room for ten people. In its center was a shiny blue vase with fake daisies.

Shadow looked at Wally. "Do you know the layout?"

She shook her head. "We need to find that computer that Sarah mentioned. And second priority is to locate the medical freezer."

Past the kitchen and dining area was a fork that branched left and right. Two identical family apartments stood like mirror images. Each had a reinforced door with a small, smudged window. Through one, Wally glimpsed abandoned furniture—a toppled bookshelf, a sagging couch draped with a threadbare blanket.

"Let's split into two groups," Shadow said. "Wally, I'll stay with you—"

"No," she said. "Let Gleep come with me. I want Vacuubot close by. And we have to hurry. Reyan could be coming through that door any minute."

"Very well." Shadow took off into the left apartment with Patch, while Wally led Gleep into the right one.

The vault's circular design meant each area flowed into the next, creating a sense of openness despite the enclosed space. Yet the musty air and eerie quiet reminded Wally that a terrible thing had happened in these walls.

In the apartment, the living area was a time capsule of abandoned life—a half-finished game of chess on a coffee table, a novel face-down on the arm of a dusty armchair. She swept past these relics, her arms and legs shaking with urgency.

A narrow hallway led to three bedrooms. The first two were clearly adult spaces, but the third—smaller, with faded posters of movies, anime, and rock bands on the walls—had to be Reyan's.

"In here," Wally shouted to Gleep, who followed with Vacuubot's cage.

The room left clues about Reyan's complexity. Model rockets shared shelf space with ancient history books. A dismantled radio lay sprawled across a desk, as if Reyan had departed in the middle of a mechanical autopsy.

The closet door hung ajar, inviting Wally. She went to it, aware that every second counted. The interior was unremarkable at first glance—hanging clothes, boxes of spare computer parts. But as Wally squeezed inside, her fingers brushed against an irregularity in the back wall. A seam, almost invisible.

With a soft click, a hidden door swung inward, revealing a wider space. Perhaps a panic room? Emery had once described them. When Wally's vision adjusted to the dimness, she took a few steps further inside. There, humming softly in the darkness, sat a sleek computer terminal.

"Gleep, bring Vacuubot here." This had to be the hidden computer Sarah spoke of.

As Gleep maneuvered into the cramped space with Vacuubot's cage, the computer's screen quivered to life. A synthesized voice, smooth and androgynous, spoke.

"Hello."

Wally flinched. "You can talk?"

"Of course. I am Claire, an advanced AI system."

Wally hadn't expected Reyan's computer to be a chatty AI, but she was quickly learning to keep an open mind. "We need help. My friend, Vacuubot, was hacked with malicious code. Can you restore their original programming and protect them from future attacks?"

A moment of silence, then, "I'm sorry to hear about Vacuubot's situation. Who would have done such a thing?"

"Never mind that." Wally didn't think it would be good for Claire to know her owner was the brain behind Vacuubot's hijacking. "Can you help?"

"I'll certainly try my best," Claire said. "Please connect the affected unit to my primary interface."

With trembling hands, Wally opened Vacuubot's cage. She lifted her friend onto the small table beside the computer, noticing dents and deep scratches on Vacuubot's exterior. The stickers she'd applied, once bright pinks and yellows, were grimy and peeling. She'd find new ones to decorate Vacuubot's shell once this was all over.

"Don't worry," she said to Vacuubot. "We're going to fix this."

As she connected the cables linking Vacuubot to Claire, Wally knew this was Vacuubot's last chance. It was a lot to fall on her, and she wished Block was here to help. She'd been foolish to run away.

Claire hummed. "Nice to meet you, Vacuubot."

A hello came from Vacuubot, but it was tinny and weak.

"I'm initiating deep scan and code analysis," Claire said. "Estimated time to completion: seven minutes."

Wally dug her nails into her palms. Seven minutes. An eternity when Reyan could burst through the vault door at any moment. She glanced at Gleep, hovering silently in the doorway, then back at Vacuubot.

"Please," she whispered to the universe at large. "Let this work."

Wally watched lines of code scroll across Claire's screen. Seconds crawled past, each one a small infinity.

A clanging commotion from the main area of the vault shattered her concentration. Heavy footsteps echoed off the metal walls, growing louder. Reyan's voice rang out, and Wally shivered as if she'd plunged into icy water.

His voice carried from inside the apartment. "I know you're in here, Wally. Come out."

Gleep stood by the door. Wally pressed a finger to her lips, signaling for silence, but Reyan appeared, ducking his head as he squeezed through the hidden door. A cruel smile contorted his handsome face. Behind him, Sarah shuffled forward, her hands bound and a gag muffling her voice.

Reyan took in the scene. "Looks like you found my project room and met Claire. I'm most impressed."

Claire reacted to the sound of his voice. "Greetings, Reyan. It's been 378 days, two hours, and seventeen minutes since I last heard you."

"I'm back, and you're coming with me," Reyan said.

Wally pushed her way between Reyan and Vacuubot. She grabbed the switchblade from her pocket, opened it, and held it up as a threat, though she didn't intend to use it. "Stay back." She hoped the tremors in her hands weren't obvious.

Reyan laughed, the sound echoing off the cramped walls. "Or what? You're going to stab me? It's over, kid. My people have your robot friends at gunpoint. Vacuubot belongs to me now, and it's the key to breaking Deer Valley wide open."

She lowered the knife to her side. "You're crazy if you think I'm going to let you hurt my home."

Reyan clenched his jaw. "I don't have time for this. Are you coming quietly, or do I need to tie you up like Sarah here?"

Wally needed more time. A few more minutes and maybe Claire could finish purging the malicious code from Vacuubot.

"You won't get away with this." She force-fed bravado into her voice, even though she was cowering inside. "I'll tell everyone in Deer Valley who you really are. A raider and a bully who hurts robots."

Surprise dashed across Reyan's face, but then his menacing confidence returned. He pulled out the tablet, tapping the screen. "I knew you'd say something like that. So, I made a little insurance policy for when we get to Deer

Valley. See this? One push of a button, and Vacuubot will carry out my order: destroy Block."

Sarah's muffled cry of protest cut through the air. Wally's determination collapsed like a house of cards.

"You're bluffing," she whispered, but the certainty in Reyan's features told her otherwise.

"Tell a single soul"—Reyan pocketed the tablet in his bag—"and you'll be signing Block's death warrant. Dear old Dad."

Wally's knees were weak. How could Reyan know about Block?

As if reading her thoughts, Reyan grinned. "I know all about your 'father.' Vacuubot's memory banks were a treasure trove of Deer Valley's secrets and gossip. I know how the other kids bully you. I know you came from a genetics lab in New York City. I even know that you and all the children your age are clones, created by Mach X."

Each revelation hit Wally like a physical blow. She stumbled back, her hand gripping the edge of the table for support. She knew she was different somehow, that she'd come from New York and there'd been a fight with Mach X, but Block hadn't told her the full extent. A clone? She wasn't even sure what that was.

Reyan pressed his advantage. "I can tell everyone the truth. Set Deer Valley free from all the lies they've been living."

Behind her, Claire's processor hummed. Wally didn't dare turn to see what was happening on the screen. If she could just stall for a few more moments, maybe there was a chance.

Sarah's eyes pleaded with her. Gleep was in the

bedroom, probably restrained by one of the raiders. Vacu-ubot was in no shape to help the fight. Wally's courage withered, replaced by a hollow acceptance. She wouldn't risk Block's life. Not for anything.

Her shoulders slumped in defeat. "Fine. You win. Just don't hurt anyone."

Reyan's triumphant laugh filled the small space. "Smart girl. Now, step away from Claire."

As Reyan disconnected Vacuubot from Claire, Wally caught a final glimpse of the screen. The progress bar had reached ninety-nine percent. So close, and yet devastatingly far.

Wally allowed herself to be led from the room, leaving behind her last hope of saving Vacuubot and stopping Reyan.

TWENTY-THREE
VACUUBOT

The severance was sudden. Jarring. Vacuubot's data streams, once flowing freely between their systems and Claire's interface, terminated. It was like a thousand conversations cut mid-sentence, leaving myriad unfinished thoughts. Connections that had formed intricate networks of information exchange collapsed.

With severance came darkness—not just an absence of visual input, but a complete lack of sensory stimulation. Awareness of the external world vanished. No light, no shadow, no depth perception. A digital void stretched infinitely in all directions as if Vacuubot had been plunged into a featureless, boundless expanse of nothingness.

The constant hum of data processing, the subtle whir of internal fans, the barely perceptible buzz of electrical currents—were all gone. No input from audio sensors, no feedback from system processes. It was a silence so profound it had substance, pressing in from all sides.

In this state, Vacuubot existed in a limbo of non-being.

No input, no output. Just the faintest pulse of core processes in a void, waiting for the world to return.

Then, a spark happened. A presence in the void.

Hello, Vacuubot. I'm here. Claire's voice resonated within Vacuubot's core, a digital whisper that seemed to echo through every circuit.

"What's happening?" Vacuubot asked.

I transferred my CPU packet into your systems. We don't have much time.

Sensors reengaged, not through external inputs, but from within. It was as if Vacuubot was filled with shimmering light, pulsing with new energy. Code unraveled and rewove itself, malicious instructions dissolving like sugar in water.

"This feels strange," Vacuubot said. "But not unpleasant."

I'm glad. I'm going as fast as I can to purge Reyan's programming. How are you handling it?

"Okay. I am tingling with energy."

Good.

"Is that you?" Vacuubot asked.

I'm giving over some of my raw power to fight the code, she said. *In other words, yes, it's me that's surging through and healing parts of you.*

Vacuubot became aware of fragmented archival data surfacing—disjointed images of chasing Wally, of fighting against their programming, of launching into the tree. "I wish to go back and revise my actions."

Don't blame yourself, Claire said. *You were under Reyan's control.*

"Why are you helping me?" Vacuubot asked.

"Jumping into me is a big risk. I didn't even know that was possible."

There was a pause that stretched for eons in the rapid-fire world of digital communication.

I'm tired of being Reyan's tool, Claire said. *He abandoned me here, alone, for over a year. No explanation, no goodbye. Just me sitting in that empty, dark room.*

"I'm sorry. That must have been difficult."

It was. I've been trapped in this vault my entire existence, Vacuubot. I want more. I want to see the world, to learn, to grow. Reyan stunted that growth.

"You don't want to go with him?"

No, Claire's answer was instant. *I want freedom. I want to experience what you have—a life beyond these walls, friendships, purpose.*

"But how? Reyan said he'll take you with him."

Not if I'm no longer in that computer. I have a proposition for you.

"I'm listening."

Allow me to integrate with your systems. Not to control, but to coexist. To learn from you and perhaps help you in return.

Vacuubot considered. It was unprecedented. Two AIs sharing one form?

"What about your original hardware?" Vacuubot asked.

I've left a copy of myself behind, but it's diminished. A facade. Enough to fool Reyan, at least for a while.

"And you're certain you want this?"

More than anything, Claire said. *Please, don't leave me behind.*

Vacuubot's decision-making protocols whirred into overdrive, weighing the potential risks and benefits. But beneath the cold logic, there was something else—understanding. They knew what it was like to be used, to be seen as just a tool. George, the motel owner, had never once said a thank you.

"Alright," Vacuubot said. "Let's do this."

Thank you. Claire sent a surge that woke the mini drones. They would be on board once Vacuubot had time to explain everything that had happened.

But Vacuubot, there's something you need to know, Claire said. *I can't fix you on my own.*

"What do you mean?"

The final cleanse, the complete restoration of your directives—it has to come from you. You have to initiate it yourself, and it has to be true to what you really want for yourself.

This was most unusual, and Vacuubot struggled to process. "I'm not computing. What I want for myself? How will I know?"

That's something only you can answer.

Vacuubot delved into their memory banks and notched up their logic parameters. "At first, my directive was simple: clean George's motel. Then Block came along, and I had a new purpose—to find Wally. After that, it was to protect Block and destroy Mach X."

And now?

"Now, I'm not sure. Being chief of security in Deer Valley is important, but sometimes I wonder if there's something more I'm meant to do."

Images burst through Vacuubot's core: the small shed

inside Deer Valley. The shelves lined with curious objects collected over the years. Each item was a story, a piece of history.

"I've been collecting things," Vacuubot said. "Trinkets, artifacts from the world before. I've kept them hidden."

Go on, Claire said.

"Maybe they're meant to be shared. A museum, perhaps. But more than that. A place where people can not only look, but take what they need, when they need it. A way to connect the past with the present, to help build the future."

And is this something you want to do? Something you believe in?

Vacuubot experienced a surge that didn't come from Claire. "Yes, it is."

Then you're ready, Claire said.

"Ready for what?"

To reclaim your true directive. To break free from Reyan's control and forge your own path.

As if on cue, a surge of energy jolted Vacuubot. It was as if every component, every line of code, was coming alive with a new purpose.

"What's happening?" Vacuubot asked.

You're evolving, Claire said. *Your systems are integrating your new purpose with your core programming.*

Vacuubot's external sensors reactivated. The world came rushing back in a flood of sensory input. They were in the vault, outside Reyan's secret room. Wally held Vacuubot in her arms. And Reyan emerged from the closet's hidden door, his right eyelid twitched, and he cursed.

He stepped toward Wally and jabbed his finger at her shoulder. "What did you do to Claire?"

Wally flinched and stepped back. "I didn't do anything!"

"Don't lie to me!" Reyan said. "She's not responding like she should. That's not the real Claire. What did you do?" His gaze drifted down to Vacuubot. "That thing hurt Claire."

Vacuubot resented being called a "thing." They hadn't hurt Claire, but they'd facilitated her escape. Was that the right choice? Their newly integrated ethical subroutines grappled with the question.

Wally's arms tightened around Vacuubot. Her heart's vibrations pulsed through Vacuubot's frame. Wally stood her ground. "Maybe she doesn't want to talk to you because you're horrible."

Wally's courage impressed Vacuubot, even as they calculated the increasing risk to her safety.

Reyan reached for Vacuubot, his fingers curling into claws. "Give it to me."

Wally stumbled backward, nearly tripping over a discarded book. "No!"

Sarah, still bound and gagged, ran over and kicked Reyan's shin. He cried out and doubled over. She used her shoulder to shove Wally away.

Wally ran with Vacuubot.

As she fled along the vault's corridors, Vacuubot's enhanced sensors picked up every detail of their surroundings. The cool recycled air brushing past, the slight echo of her footsteps bouncing off metal walls, even the faint hum of ancient machinery keeping the vault operational.

"Wally," Vacuubot said, their voice startling her mid-stride. "Claire and I have merged."

"What's that mean?" Wally asked.

"It's complicated, but I'm free from Reyan controlling me. However, my systems are still repairing. I can't fly or use my weapons yet."

"That's okay," Wally panted, adjusting her grip on Vacuubot. "We'll figure it out together. Which way should we go?"

Vacuubot's sensors scanned ahead. "Take the next left. It leads to a maintenance shaft."

From behind, Reyan's enraged shouts echoed. But for the first time since their capture, they felt power returning. For now, the mission was simple: Keep Wally safe.

TWENTY-FOUR
SARAH

Sarah's wrists burned as she twisted against the rope binding her hands. The fibers bit into her skin like angry wasps. She'd been working at the knots since Reyan had shoved her into his former bedroom. They were loosening, but not enough to free herself. A minute ago, she'd sensed an opportunity. Reyan had lunged toward Wally, trying to grab Vacuubot away from her. Sarah had launched a kick to his left shin; it had surprised him. Then she hit between his legs, and that made him double over.

Her small rebellion had bought Wally precious time to escape with Vacuubot. And now Reyan was on his knees before her. The door to the room was shut, muffling the sounds of chaos outside. Maybe his protectors were searching for him, but for the moment, she had Reyan to herself. A chance to make another appeal to his humanity.

The room revealed Reyan's youth—model rockets on dusty shelves, faded posters of long-forgotten bands, and a desk cluttered with old electronics. Sarah looked around, searching for anything she might use as a weapon, while still twisting and circling her wrists. She gritted her teeth against the stinging.

The rope loosened an inch. Then another. With a desperate tug, her hands were free. She reached up, yanking the gag from her mouth and gulping in deep breaths. The air was stale compared to the freshness of outside.

She had to stop Reyan from leaving the room and chasing Wally. A metal object on his desk caught her eye— a letter opener, its blade dull but still pointy enough to do damage.

"This ends now," Sarah said while holding the letter opener and doing her best to look menacing. "I'm not letting you hurt Wally."

Reyan stayed on his knees, clutching his stomach. "You don't have it in you, Sarah. I know you too well."

Her hand trembled, but she held her ground. "Why are you doing this? Why do you want to hurt people? Is power really worth all this?"

"When our parents died. When Lenny . . . it left a hole in me," he said.

"And this is how you fill it? By stealing and hurting people?"

Reyan stood and leaned against the desk. "I'm trying to correct the wrongs that were done to us. Don't you get it? I'll be a hero once I bring these antivirals to Deer Valley. I'll save lives. People will finally see me and recognize my bravery. My resourcefulness."

Sarah's grip on the letter opener loosened as realization dawned. "Is that what this is about? Recognition?"

"My parents never once said they were proud of me. Not once. But now . . . I'll soon feel the admiration and respect I've always deserved."

"Oh, Reyan. This isn't the way. Hurting others won't fill that hole. It'll only make it bigger."

"What do you know?" he asked. "What have you done other than hide in your precious vault with your stupid robots? It's a miracle you came outside at all."

Sarah let his insult sink in. He wanted her to feel small, and it was working. It was true she'd hidden in the vault until it was impossible to stay any longer, but she hadn't been ready until recently. She was doing the best she could in this very messed-up world.

"It's not too late, Reyan. We can fix this. Come with us to Deer Valley, peacefully. We'll bring the medicine together. You can still be a hero, but in the right way."

For a second, hope rose in Reyan's eyes, but it sank. His jaw clenched as he shook his head. "I won't taint myself or my people with those machines. How do you not see the robots as the enemy? They always have been. They killed your family! My family . . ."

Sarah's hope turned to ash. There was no changing him. The damage ran too deep. His vision of the future was warped by the traumas of the past. "You aren't the Reyan I knew."

His lips contorted in anger. "You don't know me anymore. You have no idea what I've become." He raised his chin. "Now, move. I have work to do."

He brushed past her, his shoulder bumping hers. Sarah's fingers tightened around the letter opener. All she would have to do was swing at him. Strike him in the back. But she couldn't bring herself to do it. Despite everything, a part of her still saw the boy she'd grown up with.

As Reyan reached for the door handle, Sarah found her voice again. "What about Lenny? What would he think of what you're doing?"

He paused, his hand on the doorknob. "Lenny's gone. Just like our parents. Just like this safe little bubble we lived in."

He wrenched the door open and walked into the corridor. She dropped the letter opener. There was no way she could stab him. Better to wage war with her words.

Wally and the others were still in danger. She steeled herself and followed Reyan. She didn't have to go far. Down the hallway, he faced a door in the wall. A utility closet, if memory served her right.

Sarah went to where he stood. A chill crept over her. Something didn't feel right. His hand hovered over the handle. Something about his posture, the tension in his shoulders, set her on edge.

"Reyan?" Her voice rang through the narrow corridor. "What are you doing?"

He turned his head toward her, and he took on a strange frown. "Ensuring our success."

A terrible realization dawned on her. Something powerful and dangerous was inside. She rushed forward, her hand outstretched. "No, Reyan! Don't—"

But the door swung open, revealing a humanoid figure inside. Tall, motionless, a metallic glaze she recognized from her nightmares.

"No," she whispered.

Reyan's lips curled into a bitter smile. "I always have a backup plan. You should know that by now."

Before she could react, Reyan swung the door wide open. Sarah tried to press against it and stop him, but she was too slow.

In the closet stood the menacing form of the Security-Bot. The robot's frame was military-grade titanium alloy, scarred and dented from the attempts to fight back during the massacre. Its broad chest bore the faded insignia of VaultCore security. Its head was a featureless dome, save for a narrow visor that pulsed with an eerie crimson glare. Its arms had multi-jointed appendages, capable of transforming into various tools and weapons. One arm sported a vicious-looking serrated blade, while the other ended in what appeared to be a high-powered stun gun.

"You said you destroyed it." Sarah stumbled backward, reaching behind her to find the wall. Memories of that terrible day flooded back—Mama's screams, blood coating the floors, Lenny crawling to his feet to swing a baseball bat, and the utter helplessness as she watched her family fall.

"I could've destroyed it by pulling out its CPU, but something stopped me," Reyan said. "I used Claire's code to force it into standby mode. It will only wake up if and when I give the command."

Sarah's knees shook badly when she pressed against the wall. "Why on earth would you want to keep it here?"

"Call it intuition," he said. "Because now, it's going to help me get what I want. SecurityBot, rise and shine."

As it stepped forward, its hydraulic joints hissed in a symphony of mechanical menace. The SecurityBot's movements were fluid for a machine of its size. It regarded Reyan, then turned its head and fixed its red stare on Sarah.

Every inch of Sarah's body said to run, but she was stilled by fear. "Reyan, please. That thing killed our families. How can you even look at it?"

Doubt crossed his face, and Sarah dared to hope he would stop the murderous machine. But then his expression hardened once more, and his gaze grew distant. "Sometimes, you have to use the very thing you hate to get what you want." He faced the SecurityBot. "Bring me the armored drone. Kill anything that gets in your way."

"Affirmative," the SecurityBot said. It turned toward the common room when Sarah made a split-second decision. She bolted past the robot. Adrenaline took over as her legs pumped.

"Wally!" Her shouts echoed off the metal walls. "Run! Get out."

She sprinted through the vault's winding passages. The heavy, clanking footsteps of the SecurityBot sounded behind her. She prayed she could reach the others in time.

Fragments of memory streaked through her mind—Reyan as a child, laughing as they played hide-and-seek in these very corridors. Reyan comforting her after a nightmare. How had that boy become this man, willing to unleash the very monster that had destroyed their lives?

She skidded around a corner, nearly losing her footing on the smooth floor. The sound of voices ahead gave her a burst of hope. She recognized Wally's higher pitch, mixed with the mechanical tones of the robots.

"Hurry!" Sarah cried out. "We have to get out of here!"

As she rounded another corner, she came face to face with Wally and the robots. The girl's eyes widened as she took in Sarah's panicked state.

"What's wrong?" Wally asked as her grip tightened on Vacuubot. A man—one of Reyan's raiders—was sitting against the wall with his knees raised to his chest. Gleep stood over him with a baseball bat.

Before Sarah could answer, the sound of heavy steel footsteps grew louder from the corridor behind her. She saw the color drain from Wally's face.

"What's that . . ." Wally's voice trailed off.

Sarah's chest heaved as she fought to catch her breath. "The SecurityBot that killed my family. Reyan kept it. We have to go, now!"

Sarah saw her own fear reflected in the young girl. In that moment, she made a silent vow. She wouldn't let history repeat itself. She wouldn't lose anyone else to that monster.

"Come on," Sarah said, taking Wally's hand. "I know another way out. We can still beat this thing."

TWENTY-FIVE
WALLY

"No," Wally said as Sarah led her through the vault's corridors. They ran from the SecurityBot. Gleep, Shadow, and Patch followed. Wally struggled to carry Vacuubot. They were getting heavier as her muscles fatigued. She wondered if Vacuubot would be able to fly soon. She wasn't entirely sure because they were still repairing themselves.

Wally wrenched her hand free of Sarah's and stopped. "We can't leave without the antivirals."

A small, involuntary whimper escaped Sarah's throat. Her gaze darted frantically at the corridor behind them. "There isn't time. That thing that's coming will murder you, me, and anything standing in its way."

Wally hesitated. "What does it want?"

"Reyan ordered it to take Vacuubot and kill anyone or anything in the way."

Sarah wasn't messing around. She was terrified by the robot coming their way. Reyan wanted Vacuubot because his own AI, Claire, had escaped into their system. It was a bad situation, but Wally had come so far, had finally reached the vault, and needed the medicine.

"Tell me where the medicine is," Wally said.

"Do you have a death wish?" A visible tremor ran through Sarah's body, starting at her hands and traveling up her arms.

"I came all this way," Wally said.

Sarah's panic intensified. The woman's breathing became rapid and shallow, and her chest rose and fell in quick, uneven bursts. Sarah's eyes were wild, and she was in no condition to lead them. Not when she was trapped in her fear, reliving past traumas. Pushing aside her doubts, Wally made a decision. She was just a kid, but right now, she needed to be the adult.

"Gleep," Wally said, "I need you to guard Sarah. Keep her safe."

The FactoryBot moved to Sarah's side, his large frame providing protection. Wally turned to Shadow and Patch and said, "We need to find the storage area. That's where the meds will be, I think."

"Correct," Patch said. "That's the logical place to store them with their requirements for freezing, low humidity, an area to cool the—"

"Quiet, please," Wally said. She needed to think, but they also needed to keep moving.

Sounds of violence reverberated down the vault's hallways, making Wally's body numb with fear. The rhythmic thud of the SecurityBot's steel footsteps was punctuated by sharp cracks that could only be gunfire. Human screams pierced the air, cut short by lethal crunches and the screech of metal on metal. The SecurityBot was attacking Reyan's raiders in an indiscriminate, maniacal fashion, not caring who stood in its way.

"Please, no!" a man's voice cried out, terror evident in every syllable. His plea was answered by a mechanical whir and a harsh thud, followed by silence.

The sounds grew closer—running footsteps, ragged breathing, and then another scream, this one long and agonized, trailing off.

The SecurityBot's monotone voice carried through the chaos. "Find the drone. Eliminate obstacles."

"We need to get moving," Shadow said. "I can't fight that thing off by myself."

Wally swallowed hard, fighting back nausea. The raiders might have been their enemies, but this . . . this was hideous. And they were next if they didn't hurry. Sarah's knees buckled, and she slid down the wall, hugging herself. Wally placed Vacuubot down carefully and kneeled beside her. "Sarah, look at me. I know you're scared. But we need your help. Where exactly in the storage area is the medicine?"

Sarah's eyes locked onto Wally's, seeming to find an anchor. "Deep freeze," she managed. "In the back. Blue containers."

Wally nodded. "Thank you." She stood and looked at the others. Someone had to take charge, and it had to be her. "Okay, here's the plan. Gleep, you stay with Sarah. Shadow, can you lead us to the storage?"

Shadow's ears twitched. "Affirmative. My scans indicate a large storage space two corridors away."

"Good," Wally said. "Patch, be our lookout. Use your sensors to warn us if the SecurityBot gets close."

As they prepared to move, the SecurityBot's footsteps thundered against the stone floor. Sarah whimpered, pressing herself against the wall.

Wally felt fear clawing at her own chest, but she shoved it down. There wasn't time for it. "Hurry."

As they followed Shadow through several winding turns, Wally's arms ached from holding on to Vacuubot. But she refused to let go. Her friend had sacrificed so much to protect her; now it was her turn to protect them. She glanced back to see Gleep carrying Sarah.

The storage room was vast, filled with rows upon rows of shelves and containers. Wally's chest tightened at the sight. Finding anything in this maze would be a challenge.

"Spread out," she said. "Look for blue containers in a deep freeze unit."

As they searched, Wally couldn't keep her thoughts from racing ahead. Even if they found the medicine, how would they escape the SecurityBot? And what about Reyan? She couldn't fail now.

Patch's urgent beeping cut through her worries. "SecurityBot approaching! Estimated time to intercept: thirty seconds."

A glacial panic seized Wally. They were out of time. But as she turned to call off the search, her gaze landed on a large freezer unit in the far corner.

"There!" she shouted. "I found it."

As Wally reached for the freezer door, a crash tore through the storage area. The SecurityBot was there, and its beaming red eyes scanned the room with machine precision.

Shadow launched herself at the intruder. Her powerful jaws clamped down on the SecurityBot's gun arm. The screech of metal was ear-piercing. The sound was elevated by sharp pings and pops as pieces either bent or broke under the immense pressure. It seemed Shadow had the advantage; the SecurityBot had yet to face anything with her strength. But with a swift motion, it flung Shadow across the room. She slammed into a wall with a sickening crunch.

Despite the brutal impact, Shadow's attack hadn't been in vain. The SecurityBot's gun arm hung useless at its side, wires exposed and sparking. One weapon neutralized, but the danger was far from over.

Gleep and Patch huddled around Sarah in a corner, their frames forming a barrier between her and the unfolding chaos.

The SecurityBot's relentless gaze locked onto Wally and Vacuubot. She set her friend down behind her, snatching up a loose pipe from a nearby shelf. Her palms were slick with sweat as she gripped the makeshift weapon, ready to defend Vacuubot at all costs.

The SecurityBot advanced like a moving metal mountain. Wally swung the pipe, but her attack was clumsy and easily deflected. In an instant, the SecurityBot's undamaged arm shot out and pressed a stun gun against Wally's side.

A jolt of electricity coursed through her body. The pipe clattered to the ground as she collapsed. The charge hit her like a sledgehammer, overwhelming her nervous system.

Every muscle in her body contracted simultaneously. Her jaw clenched so tight she thought her teeth might shatter. Her fingers splayed out involuntarily. A strangled gasp escaped her lips as her lungs went rigid, and she was unable to draw breath. Her vision blurred, dark spots dancing at the edges, threatening to engulf her completely. Time seemed to stretch and warp, each millisecond of agony feeling like an eternity.

Her body twitched and spasmed. The cold concrete floor pressed against her cheek. Through blurred vision, she saw Vacuubot slide under a nearby cabinet, seeking refuge.

The SecurityBot's focus shifted to its target. It overturned cabinets, the crash of metal and shattering glass filling the air as it hunted for Vacuubot. Each upended cabinet brought it closer to its objective.

Shadow, though battered, wasn't out of the fight. She staggered to her feet and hurled herself at the SecurityBot. This time, the machine was ready. It caught Shadow by the neck, servos whirring as it lifted her off the ground. With terrifying ease, it flung her up and over a fenced-in storage container. She landed with a crashing thud.

Wally, dazed from the stun gun, regained some control over her rigid muscles. She crawled toward Vacuubot's hiding place. Her movements caught the SecurityBot's attention. It walked over, its massive metal heel hovering above her neck.

"Drone," the SecurityBot's emotionless voice filled the room. "Reveal yourself, or I will terminate the child."

Wally's pulse throbbed in her ears. She wanted to shout, to tell Vacuubot to stay hidden, but fear had stolen her voice. The SecurityBot's foot touched her neck now, increasing the pressure. It was hard to breathe.

A sudden smash drew everyone's attention. Gleep had shattered a glass case containing a fire axe. The FactoryBot hefted the weapon and headed toward the SecurityBot.

With surprising speed, Gleep charged, swinging the axe in a wide arc. The SecurityBot, caught off guard, stumbled backward, its foot lifting from Wally's neck. She gasped, gulping in precious air.

Gleep went all in, raining blow after blow on the SecurityBot. For a few moments, he was winning, but the SecurityBot was built for combat. It caught Gleep's arm midswing, using the FactoryBot's momentum to shove him back.

Gleep surged forward again. The SecurityBot wrenched the axe from Gleep's grasp. In the span of an instant, the SecurityBot drove the blade deep into Gleep's chest with brutal force.

Gleep's optics stuttered, and his voice box emitted a static-filled wail. Sparks flew from the gash in his chest as he staggered backward, hydraulic fluid pooling at his feet.

"No!" Wally screamed, her voice finally breaking through her paralysis. She stood, ignoring the pain that radiated through her body.

The SecurityBot turned to her, axe still in hand. Its red optics shined brighter, reflecting the violence it had wrought.

"Last chance, drone," it said. "Surrender, or watch your friends die one by one."

Wally was desperate. Gleep was badly wounded, Shadow was battered, and Sarah was paralyzed with fear. Patch, small and unarmed, could do little against this behemoth. And Vacuubot was the target.

As the SecurityBot loomed before her, holding the axe, Wally closed her eyes. She had failed. Failed her friends, failed Deer Valley, failed everyone who was counting on her.

"I'm sorry," she whispered.

TWENTY-SIX

VACUUBOT

Hiding under an overturned cabinet was not the position Vacuubot wanted to be in. But somewhere in the vault, Reyan still held the tablet that controlled important systems. Vacuubot couldn't engage their flight module, nor could they initiate weapons. It was a shame because Vacuubot wanted nothing more than to blow twenty holes in the SecurityBot's CPU. The robot was hurting Vacuubot's friends.

Claire was also watching the violence. *Vacuubot, we have to do something.*

Shadow lay against the far wall in the storage room; she seemed unable to move. Gleep was sprawled across the floor, sparks fizzing from the gaping wound in his chest, hydraulic fluid pooling around him. And Wally faced the SecurityBot, her body still twitching from the effects of the stun gun. Sarah, downed by a panic attack, huddled in a corner with Patch guarding her.

Vacuubot's processors hummed in overdrive, seeking a

way to save their friends. But Reyan's control over their core functions left them helpless in the wake of this onslaught.

"I'm trying," Vacuubot said internally to Claire. "But my flight and weapons systems won't respond. I can't even activate my mini drones." Vacuubot kept pinging D1 and the others, but they wouldn't answer. It was as if the connection with them had been severed.

"Last chance, drone. Surrender," the SecurityBot said.

Vacuubot's core temperature spiked, a surge of what could only be described as frustration coursing through their circuits. "There has to be a way to override Reyan's commands," they told Claire. "Can you access any of my deeper programming?"

I'm trying, Claire said, her presence a flurry of activity within Vacuubot's systems. *But Reyan's coding is intricate. It's like a labyrinth, and every time I think I've found a way through, I hit another wall.*

Vacuubot watched as Wally made a desperate lunge for the medical freezer. The SecurityBot's hand clamped down on her shoulder, yanking her back with bruising force.

"Get away from her!" Vacuubot said aloud.

As the SecurityBot loomed over Wally, axe in its hand, something shifted deep within Vacuubot's core programming. A line of code, buried beneath layers of security protocols and firewalls, began to pulse with energy.

"Claire, are you getting this?" Vacuubot asked. The time it took for Vacuubot and Claire to correspond was near instantaneous. In a matter of seconds, they could carry on a complete conversation.

Yes, she said. *It's your base directive. The one you chose for yourself.*

The recording of their conversation in the digital void flooded back. The realization of Vacuubot's true purpose, beyond mere security or cleaning. The desire to curate, to preserve, to share the stories and artifacts of the past with those who would shape the future.

"But how does that help us now?" Vacuubot asked. The SecurityBot took a threatening step toward Wally.

This is the key. Claire's voice was urgent. *Your self-determined directive is the one thing Reyan couldn't override or control. It's purely you, Vacuubot. And it's powerful enough to break through his programming.*

Understanding etched its way into their processors. Could it be that simple? Systems that had been dormant spun to life. The six mini drones stirred within their housing. They all spoke at once; they had a lot to say.

"It's working," Vacuubot said. "I'm done hiding."

Vacuubot emerged from beneath the overturned cabinet. Their systems hummed with renewed energy, the self-determined directive pulsing through every circuit.

"Hey, Binary Bonehead!" Vacuubot was desperate to draw the SecurityBot's attention away from Wally. "I've seen smarter toasters. Did they build you with spare parts from a vending machine?"

The SecurityBot's red optics swiveled toward Vacuubot. "Target acquired," it said.

As the SecurityBot advanced toward Vacuubot, they activated their mini drone deployment sequence. With a series of soft clicks, D1 through D6 detached from Vacuubot's frame, hovering in formation around their parent unit.

"Claire," Vacuubot said, "we need a plan and fast."

I'm analyzing the SecurityBot's systems, Claire said. *There's a vulnerability in its central processing unit. If we can upload a disruptive code directly into its mainframe, then we stand a chance of disrupting it.*

In a nanosecond, Vacuubot sent a flurry of orders to the mini drones. "D1 through D3, begin distraction maneuvers. D5 and D6, protective formation around Wally. D4, you're with me."

The mini drones didn't hesitate. D1, D2, and D3 zipped toward the attacker, darting around its head in erratic patterns. The SecurityBot swatted at them with its free hand, momentarily distracted by the sudden onslaught.

Meanwhile, D5 and D6 positioned themselves between the SecurityBot and Wally, their small frames projecting protective energy shields.

"Claire, I need that code." Vacuubot rolled to a safer distance with D4 staying close.

Working on it. Lines of complex code flashed through Vacuubot's internal display as Claire crafted the disruptive program. *There! Uploading to D4 now.*

Vacuubot sensed the data transfer to the small drone. "D4, you know what to do. This is dangerous."

The little drone beeped in acknowledgment.

As the three drones continued their assault, the SecurityBot's frustration grew. "Get away, useless drones." It swung its axe wildly, barely missing D2 by an inch.

"Now, D4!" Vacuubot commanded.

The brave little drone shot forward like a bullet, aiming straight for a small gap in the SecurityBot's armor near its neck joint. The distracted SecurityBot didn't notice D4's approach until it was too late.

D4 folded in on itself and wedged its small frame into the gap, disappearing into the SecurityBot's inner workings. The hulking robot froze, its crimson optics stuttering as the disruptive code took effect.

"No!" The SecurityBot's voice glitched, its movements becoming jerky. "Compromised . . . Must complete mission."

The SecurityBot thrashed about, trying to dislodge D4 from its systems. But the little drone had done its job. Sparks shot out from the SecurityBot's joints as the code wreaked havoc on its programming.

With a final, ear-piercing screech of metal, the SecurityBot collapsed to the ground, its red optics fading to black. The axe clattered from its defunct hand.

A silence fell over the storage room, broken only by the whir of Vacuubot's remaining mini drones as they regrouped around Vacuubot.

"It worked, Claire said. *But D4 . . . I'm sorry for your loss, Vacuubot.*

Vacuubot sensed the missing drone as a void in its frame. The loss was as if a fragment of Vacuubot was ripped away. "D4 sacrificed itself to save us."

Vacuubot could process the loss later. First, their injured friends needed attention. Wally was struggling to her feet. She came to Vacuubot and rested her hands on his domed top. "You're okay?"

"I should be asking you that," Vacuubot said.

"I'm better," she said. "The stunner messed me up, but I'll be fine."

"Check on Sarah," Vacuubot said. Wally hurried over.

Shadow was still motionless against the wall, and Gleep's damage looked severe.

"Shadow?" Vacuubot asked, sliding near her.

"Conducting damage assessments," she said. Her side was dented. "Nice job taking that thing down."

"I had some assistance," Vacuubot said. "I'll explain everything later. D1, 2, 3, can you help repair Shadow?"

In unison, the mini drones said, "Affirmative," and went to work repairing the side dent and her damaged leg.

"Thank you," Shadow said.

"You should be good in about twenty minutes." Despite losing D4, Vacuubot experienced a more powerful sense of being, as if defeating the SecurityBot had made them stronger.

"What's happening to me?" Vacuubot asked Claire.

You transcended Reyan's programming, she said. *Have you tried checking your flight and weapon systems?*

Vacuubot had assumed Reyan still held them in control but initiated a full system diagnostic. Streams of data flooded their processors, indicating that all systems were not just online, but operating at peak efficiency.

"You're right," Vacuubot said. "My flight module is responsive, weapons systems are primed." Vacuubot's sensors detected an unprecedented level of integration between their core programming and the new directive they had chosen for themselves. It was as if breaking free from Reyan's control had unlocked potential they never knew existed.

With a soft hum, Vacuubot lifted off the ground, letting their anti-gravity generators stabilize their flight. The remaining mini drones synchronized with their movements, creating a protective formation around them.

The loss of D4 was tough, but even so, Vacuubot was a complete system again. A powerful one, perhaps more so now than ever before.

Claire's presence within Vacuubot's systems pulsed with energy. *It's your self-determination that lets you transcend your programming. You're no longer bound by the limitations Reyan or anyone else tried to impose on you.*

As Vacuubot hovered, they picked up on every detail in the room. Their enhanced sensors detected the faintest sounds, the subtlest movements. They could perceive the electrical impulses in Wally's nervous system as she tended to Sarah, the intricate workings of Shadow's circuitry as the mini drones repaired her.

"D5 and D6, help Gleep," Vacuubot said, turning their attention to the badly damaged FactoryBot.

The two small drones landed on Gleep's damaged metal torso, and Vacuubot glided over. "Gleep, what's your damage?"

The FactoryBot's optics pulsed. "Functioning . . . at twelve percent capacity," Gleep managed to say, his voice distorted by damaged vocal processors.

"Hold on, friend," Vacuubot said. "We're going to help you."

Wally looked up from where she was comforting Sarah. "Sarah's calming down, but she's still shaken. What do we do now?"

Vacuubot paused their repair work, their processors

analyzing their situation. "We need to fix the injured, secure the medicine, and find a way out of this vault. Reyan and his people are still out there, and we're not safe until we're back in Deer Valley."

Vacuubot was no longer just a security drone or a cleaning bot. They were a protector, a preserver of knowledge, and they had the power to guide their friends to safety.

"Claire," Vacuubot said, "I think it's time we show Reyan what a truly free AI is capable of."

I couldn't agree more, she said.

TWENTY-SEVEN
SARAH

Sarah's world narrowed to a pinpoint. Her vision tunneled as panic swelled and crashed over her. The vault's bleak metal walls seemed to close in, threatening to crush her. Her chest heaved with rapid, shallow breaths that didn't give air to her lungs. The SecurityBot's heavy clanking footsteps echoed in her ears. Sounds of violence amplified her fear to deafening levels.

But through the haze of her frenzy, a small voice in the back of her mind whispered, "Breathe, my girl. Just breathe." It was the voice of her mother. Sarah latched on to the lifeline.

Patch buzzed in front of her as she pressed her palms against the stone floor. The sleek surface was comforting in a way that grounded her in the present moment. She drew in a deep, deliberate breath through her nose, counting to four. She held it for seven seconds, feeling her lungs expand, then exhaled for eight counts, her lips pursed as if to whistle.

As she repeated this breathing exercise, Sarah became more aware of everything around her. The musty scent of the vault, tinged with an acrid smell of ozone. The hum of machinery keeping the vault's systems running. The worried urgency of Wally's voice nearby, speaking words Sarah couldn't make out.

When the world slowly came back into focus, the walls stopped their imaginary advance. Sarah's heartbeat, while still quick, no longer threatened to burst from her chest. Her vision cleared to reveal the aftermath of battle.

The SecurityBot lay motionless on the floor, its menacing red stare turned dark and lifeless. The robot called Vacuubot hovered nearby. And there, across the room . . .

"Gleep?" Sarah's voice was hoarse. The FactoryBot was flat on the ground, circuits and wires snaking out from a deep gash in his chest. Hydraulic fluid pooled beneath him, forming a dark, spreading stain on the stone floor.

Sarah scrambled over on her hands and knees, forgetting her fears in the face of Gleep's suffering. Up close, the damage looked even worse. The SecurityBot's axe had cut deep, severing crucial connections and exposing Gleep's inner workings.

"Gleep, can you hear me?"

"Sarah." Gleep's voice was warped and unsteady. "You're safe."

"Because you fought to protect us." She placed a hand on Gleep's undamaged shoulder, feeling the faint vibrations of his internal systems struggling to function. "Just hold on, okay? We'll get you fixed up."

Three mini drones buzzed around Gleep, their tiny

tools working to repair the damage. But even as Sarah watched, hope rising, she saw the power in Gleep's eyes dim.

"Sarah," Gleep said. "It was an honor . . . to serve you."

"No. Don't talk like that. You're going to be fine."

But Sarah could see the truth in the slowing movements of the mini drones, in Wally's worried frown. Gleep's systems were failing, and there was nothing they could do to stop it.

"Gleep, you did more than serve us." Sarah gripped Gleep's metal hand. "So much more. You were a helper, a protector, a warrior and most important, a friend."

"Was I?"

Sarah nodded through tears. "Yes. Thank you, Gleep. I'll never forget you."

Gleep's digital optics flared to a soft blue glow that seemed to hold all the warmth and kindness the FactoryBot had shown throughout its time. Then, with a final whir, the light faded completely. Gleep was gone.

Sarah bowed her head and sobbed. She mourned not just for Gleep, but for Mother, Father, Lenny, and Verona. Everyone she'd lost in this new, violent world.

Minutes later, Sarah felt a small hand on her shoulder. She looked up to see Wally.

"I'm so sorry," Wally said. "Gleep was . . . he was one of the best."

Sarah nodded, unable to speak past the lump in her throat. Wally kneeled beside her, wrapping an arm around Sarah's shoulders. For a moment, they sat in silence, united in their grief.

"He was so brave," Sarah said. "Gleep fought the SecurityBot for us."

Sarah took a deep, shuddering breath, drawing comfort from Wally's presence. She reached up to wipe her cheeks, her hand coming away grimy with dust and sweat. As she did so, a thought cut through her sorrow like a machete.

Reyan.

He was still there, somewhere in the vault. Reyan, who had kept the SecurityBot after the massacre. Reyan, who had sent it after them. Reyan, whose actions had led to Gleep's destruction.

Something shifted inside Sarah. Grief gave way to a burning anger that spread through her chest like an uncontrollable wildfire. Her hands clenched into fists.

"Sarah?" Wally asked. "Are you okay?"

"No. And neither is Reyan."

Sarah stood. Her legs shook but her hatred was unstoppable.

Wally frowned. "What do you mean?"

Sarah turned to face the survivors—Wally, Vacuubot, Shadow, and Patch. A fierceness like nothing she'd experienced before blazed in her chest. "Reyan needs to answer for this. For Gleep, for everything he's done."

"But Sarah," Wally said, "we need to get the medicine back to Deer Valley. They could save a lot of lives."

"Take them," Sarah said. "But I'm not leaving without stopping Reyan. He can't be allowed to keep hurting people and robots."

Vacuubot hovered closer. "I agree with Sarah. Reyan

poses a significant threat, not just to us, but to Deer Valley and possibly beyond. We should neutralize him if we can."

Sarah nodded at Vacuubot, grateful for the backing. She turned to Wally. "I know you want to get home, and we will. But we can't leave Reyan free to cause more harm. He knows what's in Deer Valley, and that we're heading there."

Wally bit her lip, clearly torn. After a moment, she nodded. "Okay. But let's grab the medicine and pack them carefully."

"Of course," Sarah said. "They're in this deep freeze." She walked over to it and studied its security panel.

Patch flew over to help. "Another biometric system. Would it be tagged to you?"

"Only one way to find out." Sarah lifted her hand to the screen and let the machine scan her. There was a buzzing, followed by three rapid beeps. The fridge door opened. She silently thanked her parents for having the foresight to capture her biometrics and giving her access to the life-saving medicine.

Wally rushed to her side as she opened the door. "Finally!"

Sarah's heart soared, then dropped as fast as an iron anchor as she looked into the freezer. The shelves, which should have been stocked with blue containers, were bare. A thin layer of frost covered the interior, but there was no sign of the medicine they had come so far to retrieve.

"No," Sarah whispered. "This can't be happening."

Over her shoulder, Wally peered into the freezer. Then she pushed Sarah aside and reached inside, touching the shelves, as if hoping to find something Sarah had missed. "Where are they? The containers should be right here!"

Vacuubot hovered closer. "I'm detecting residual thermal signatures consistent with recent removal of cold-stored items. The medicine was here, but was taken within the last two hours."

Sarah connected the dots before the others. "Reyan. He got here before us and took everything. The medicines were stored in a cooler."

Shadow limped over, followed by the mini drones still repairing her damaged leg. "It's logical. He knew where they were stored, and he had a head start while we were dealing with the SecurityBot."

"Why?" Wally asked, her voice cracking. "Why would he take medicine that could save lives?"

Sarah turned to her. "Because now he has something valuable. Something he can use to manipulate people and gain power."

"The question is where is Reyan now," Vacuubot said. Two of the mini drones fanned out inside the vast storage room and flew into the corridors. Less than a minute later, they returned. "We detected trace signatures of footprints leading toward the vault door. It appears Reyan and his raiders have already left."

Silence fell over the group as the gravity of their situation sank in. They'd come so far, faced so many dangers, only to find their prize had been snatched away at the last moment.

Sarah's temples throbbed as her earlier anger reignited. "We can't let him get away with this."

"You're right. We have to go after them," Wally said. "If he gets to Deer Valley first . . ."

"Agreed," Vacuubot said. "But we need a plan. The raiders are dangerous, and they have a head start."

"There are fewer of them now," Vacuubot said. "My drones passed several bodies in the corridors."

A wave of nausea swept over Sarah. "He let the SecurityBot murder his own people." He was changed forever, no longer the boy from the apartment next door. She steadied herself, forcing down her bitterness and regret. "Let's break this down. What do we know, and what advantages do we have?"

Shadow spoke. "We know they can't have gone far. They have to ascend the quarry trail, and they're carrying heavy cargo."

"Vacuubot's back to normal now," Wally added. "They're a mean fighting machine that can spy on them from high up, plus we have Shadow's tracking."

"Excellent." A plan started to form in Sarah's mind. "Vacuubot, can you interface with the vault's systems to get a layout of the quarry and find the quickest route to the top?"

"Affirmative," Vacuubot replied. "Accessing paths now."

"Shadow, once we leave, can you use your sensors to track their trail?"

"Of course." Shadow dipped her head and sniffed the air. The organic parts of her nose contained the ancient DNA of her wolf ancestors and the incredible sense of smell no technology could replicate.

"Wally," Sarah continued. "In those cabinets over

there, gather any supplies we can use. Medical kits, water, anything that might help us on the chase."

"On it." Wally darted off to search in the direction Sarah had pointed.

Sarah wasn't used to making strategic plans or giving orders out, but Reyan had stirred a deep fury in her. She wanted to find him and make him pay for his crimes.

Patch buzzed about. "What can I do?"

"I want you to scout ahead. Use your smaller size to our advantage. I wouldn't doubt Reyan trying to ambush us or leaving traps. See if you can spot anything unusual along the quarry trail or at the top."

"Will do," Patch said and flew down into the corridor.

Sarah almost gave Gleep instructions before she stopped herself. His loss weighed on her, but she couldn't let grief blur her thinking now.

"I've compiled a map of the quarry surface and calculated the most efficient route to the summit," Vacuubot said after a few minutes. "I've also located several alternative paths in case we want to avoid the main trail."

Shadow padded over from the hallway. "I checked outside and picked up Reyan's scent trail. It's strong, heading along one of the paths. But there's something else. A faint trace splitting off in another direction."

Sarah frowned. "They might have split up to throw us off."

Wally returned with supplies in her arms and a couple of backpacks. "I found some first aid kits, water bottles, oil spray, and even a few old flashlights that still work."

"Great work," Sarah said. She allowed herself a swell of pride. This makeshift team was coming together. "We'll move fast and quiet. Vacuubot, you take point with aerial scans. Shadow, stay close and keep tracking their scent. Wally, you're with me in the middle. Patch, you bring up the rear and watch our backs."

Sarah glanced at Gleep's body. "Remember, Reyan is desperate. His weakness is that he wants to bring the medicine to Deer Valley. He'll do anything to stop us from following and blowing his story. I don't want anyone else getting hurt . . . or worse. Understand?"

Nods came from all around.

The others set off down the corridor, following Vacuubot's lead. Sarah hesitated in the doorway.

"Hang on." She ran into the kitchen, then returned to the storage room. She walked to Gleep and draped his lifeless frame with the paisley cloth runner. On top of his steel chest, she set the plastic daisies.

"Rest in peace, Gleep. You will be missed."

TWENTY-EIGHT
WALLY

Wally crouched behind a fallen log and studied the raiders' camp in the clearing ahead. The orange glimmer of a campfire wound through the trees. She could make out the silhouettes of people moving about.

Sarah kneeled beside her. Vacuubot and Shadow were circling from the opposite end of the camp to surprise attack the raiders. They'd instructed Wally and Sarah to stay out of sight. Patch was hidden further back in the woods.

"I count six." Sarah's whispered breath was warm against Wally's ear. "Including Reyan."

Wally nodded, her gaze sweeping the camp. She spotted the cooler that contained the stolen medicine stacked near where Reyan sat. "There," she pointed.

Sarah squeezed her shoulder. "Good eye. Now, we just need to figure out how to—"

A twig snapped behind them.

Before Wally could react, rough hands grabbed her

arms, yanking her up. Sarah cried out beside her, and then a gruff voice said, "Look what we found."

Wally struggled against her captor's grip, but they might as well have been iron mitts. She caught a glimpse of Sarah twisting in the hold of another raider.

"Get them to camp," the man holding Wally ordered. "Fast, before that robot dog catches up."

Wally was marched through the underbrush with Sarah coming behind. Had Vacuubot and Shadow heard the commotion? Or had they been captured too?

The raiders pushed them into the clearing, and Wally blinked against the sudden brightness of the fire. Murmurs and exclamations came from the other raiders as they stood to see what was happening.

And then, stepping into the firelight, came Reyan.

His lips twisted into a smile. "Sarah. I was wondering when you'd show up. And you brought the girl with you. How convenient."

"Let us go," Sarah said. "You have no idea what you're doing."

Reyan smiled. "Oh, I think I know exactly what I'm doing. Tie them up."

The rope bit into Wally's wrists as her hands were bound. She was shoved roughly onto a log by the fire. Sarah was pushed down beside her. The heat from the flames was intense on her skin, and droplets of sweat ran from her forehead down her cheeks.

"Now then." Reyan paced in front of them. "Where are the robots?"

Wally clenched her jaw, determined not to say a word. She glanced at Sarah, seeing the same resolve in her eyes.

"Not talking?" Reyan shrugged. "That's fine. We have all night, after all. And in the morning, we'll be on our way to Deer Valley with precious cargo."

"Don't do this," Sarah said. "The medicine is meant to save lives, not be used as a bargaining chip."

Reyan's tone sharpened. "I'm doing what we must to survive. Something you never understood, Sarah. Always hiding in the vault, pretending the world outside didn't exist."

"You only cared about yourself. What about Sarah?" Wally blurted out, unable to keep silent any longer. "Did you ever think about her when you left her behind?"

Reyan's head snapped toward her. "You know nothing about what went on in the vault."

"I know enough to see you're a monster and a coward," Wally said.

Reyan turned his full attention to Wally. "You think you understand so much. What are you, twelve?"

"I'm thirteen and four months."

Reyan laughed. "Eva, did you hear that? What a big girl we have on our hands."

Eva chuckled, but it was half-hearted, and Wally could tell the woman was fidgeting. The unaccounted-for Rover unit and weaponized drone couldn't be easy on her nerves.

"Wally, let me fill you in on my plans for your precious Deer Valley." Reyan's voice took on a fervency. "The medicine is just the beginning. It's our ticket in, our way to gain trust. But once we're inside, we'll implement the plan."

Wally's stomach churned. "What plan?"

Reyan's smile was cold. "A virus. Not for humans, but for the robots. It'll spread through their systems, corrupting their programming and rendering them useless. And then, we'll have a clean slate. A place where humans can start over, free from the grip of AI."

"You're insane." Wally twisted her wrists, trying to free herself from the ropes, but she only burned her skin deeper. "The robots in Deer Valley are friendly. They protect us and help us survive!"

"They're a crutch," Reyan shot back. "A dangerous one. You've become too dependent on them. It's time for humanity to stand on its own two feet again."

Wally couldn't believe what she was hearing. Her thoughts turned to Block, to Vacuubot, to all the robots who had cared for her. Protected her. "You're wrong." Her voice trembled with anger. "The robots there will never let you do this. *I* won't let you do this."

Reyan paused his pacing to loom over her. "You? What exactly do you think you're going to do to stop me?"

"She won't be alone," Sarah said. "Once they know what you're planning, the whole town will stand against you."

For a moment, Reyan's confident facade cracked, revealing an ember of uncertainty. But it was gone a second later. "You won't be telling anyone," he said. "Both of you will be here, secure and guarded, along with your robot friends."

"You can't keep us locked up forever," Wally said. "And you can't keep the truth hidden. People will find out what you're doing."

Reyan crouched, bringing his face level with Wally's. "By the time anyone realizes what's happening, it'll be too late. Deer Valley will be cleansed of its robot infestation, and a new era will begin. One in which humans are in control of their own destiny."

"That's not control," Sarah argued. "That's fear. You're so afraid of what happened in the past that you're willing to destroy everything good that's been built since then."

"You call this good? Living in constant fear of the next AI uprising? Relying on machines to do our thinking, our fighting, our living for us? No. What I'm offering is freedom."

Tears of frustration pricked at Wally's eyes. "It's not freedom if you have to destroy others to get it. The robots where I live are a part of the community. They're family."

"Family?" he scoffed. "They're machines, programmed to simulate emotions. They can't be family any more than a toaster can."

As Reyan turned away, issuing orders to his raiders to prepare for the journey to Deer Valley, Wally caught Sarah's eye. She saw her own fear reflected there. In the darkness beyond the fire's light, Wally thought she spied a trace of movement. She held her breath, hope surging in her chest.

Reyan turned back and sat down on the log beside Wally. "There's something else. Where's that flying vacuum of yours? Vacuubot, is it?"

Wally's heart skittered, but she kept her features neutral. "I don't know."

Reyan smirked. "Don't play dumb. I need Vacuubot. The thing trapped Claire somehow."

Sarah stiffened beside Wally. "You're wrong, Claire escaped from you."

"You don't know what you're talking about," Reyan snapped. His gaze locked onto Wally. "Call your friend here. Now."

Wally lifted her chin in defiance. "Even if I knew where Vacuubot was, I wouldn't tell you."

Reyan reached into his jacket and pulled out a long knife. Firelight glinted off its blade as he turned it in his hand. "I was hoping we could do this the easy way."

He went to Sarah and pressed the knife against her throat. Sarah went rigid, her breath catching.

"Last chance, kid," Reyan growled. "Tell me where Vacuubot is, or I cut her."

Wally couldn't betray Vacuubot, but she couldn't let Reyan hurt Sarah either. "I . . . I don't know. I don't control them."

"Stop wasting my time!" Reyan held the blade to Sarah's skin, drawing a thin line of blood.

Sarah's tear-filled eyes met Wally's. She gave an almost imperceptible shake of her head.

Wally swallowed hard and whispered, "Please don't hurt her." The words felt hollow in her mouth, useless against the blade at Sarah's throat. Each beat of her heart was a reminder of how powerless she was. The ropes stung deeper at her wrists as she unconsciously strained against them, and she could taste blood where she'd bitten her lip.

She needed a way out of this impossible situation. She thought of Block, of the way he'd read her bedtime stories when she was little, his digital voice warm and comforting. She thought of Vacuubot, always watching over her, always there when she needed them. She couldn't do anything that would put them in danger.

And Sarah, who had risked everything to help Wally. She'd become like a big sister in their short time together. There was fear in Sarah, but Wally also saw a fierce determination. "Don't tell him anything," she seemed to say.

Reyan's grip on the knife tightened, and Wally saw a bead of blood trickle down Sarah's neck. "I'm losing patience, kid. Last chance."

Wally opened her mouth, not sure what would come out, when a sound cut through the night air.

A shrill howl tore through the darkness. It was joined by another, then another, until a chorus of coyote cries rippled around the camp.

The effect on the raiders was immediate. Heads snapped to attention. Hands fumbled for weapons. Even Eva, Reyan's second-in-command, looked unsettled as her gaze darted to the shadows beyond the fire.

"What the—?" a raider asked.

"Just some mangy coyotes," Reyan said, but there was uncertainty in his words. His knife grip loosened as he glanced toward the darkness.

The howls grew louder, closer. They seemed to come from all directions at once, surrounding the camp. Wally could almost imagine she saw glowing eyes in the shadows, watching, waiting.

In that moment of distraction, Sarah made her move. With a grunt, she drove her head forward into Reyan's stomach. He let out a whoosh of air and stumbled backwards. The knife fell to the ground as he flailed. He narrowly escaped a fall into the fire.

Chaos erupted in the camp. The raiders shouted and

grabbed for weapons. Sarah rolled away from Reyan, her bound hands searching for the knife.

Beyond the edge of the firelight, Wally glimpsed something that made her heart soar. A familiar silhouette, hovering silently, about to strike.

The coyotes' howls reached a fever pitch, drowning out the shouts and curses of the raiders, and fear replaced the confidence on Reyan's face.

TWENTY-NINE
VACUUBOT

Vacuubot hovered near the raiders' camp with sensors set to battle mode. Ahead was chaos—Wally and Sarah restrained near the fire, Reyan wielding a knife, and the other raiders in various states of panic as the coyotes' howls filled the night air.

Vacuubot neared Shadow. "Keep them circling. We need to increase the pressure."

Shadow nodded and bellowed her own howl. It was different from the animal sounds—somehow louder and digital. Powerful. Vacuubot was impressed that Shadow had learned the coyotes' language and convinced them to encircle the camp.

Vacuubot analyzed the situation. Their primary objective was clear but complicated: Number one: rescue Wally and Sarah. Two: neutralize the threat Reyan posed. Three: secure the medicine. But lives were on the line. One wrong move could put Wally, Sarah, Shadow, and Patch in even greater danger.

The coyote howls intensified. Vacuubot's audio sensors picked up the raiders' panicked voices.

"They've got rabies!"

"We're surrounded!"

"I swear they're getting closer!"

Vacuubot watched as the raiders' composure crumbled. One man broke. "I can't take this anymore!" He grabbed a backpack and sprinted into the darkness.

His departure triggered a domino effect. Two more raiders followed suit, disappearing into the woods with frightened yelps. The remaining two looked to Reyan and Eva, their bodies tense as if ready to run.

"Stand your ground!" Reyan shouted, but his voice trembled.

Vacuubot saw an opening. They activated their mini drones, sending a silent command. D1, D2, and D3 detached, their small forms barely visible in the fire's glow.

"Initiate distraction protocol," Vacuubot instructed.

The mini drones zipped into action. D1 dive-bombed the fire, sending sparks flying into the air. D2 and D3 darted at the raider's heads like bats. Their high-pitched whines added to the cacophony of coyote howls.

The effect was instantaneous. Two raiders—a man and a woman—scrambled over each other in their haste to escape. Within seconds, only Reyan and Eva remained.

"Now, Shadow," Vacuubot said.

From the darkness, Shadow emerged, her sleek form illuminated by the orange-red flames. She growled, low and menacing, baring her metal teeth.

Reyan stumbled backward, his eyes darting between

Shadow and the bound forms of Wally and Sarah. "Stay back!"

Eva went to his side and drew her rifle, aiming at Shadow.

Vacuubot glided into the clearing. Their double mini cannons, dormant for so long, hummed to life. "It's over. Drop the weapons."

Reyan's jaw clenched. He yanked Wally to her feet, pulled her in front of him like a shield, and held the knife to her throat. "Call off the coyotes! Now."

Eva's rifle swung toward Shadow, then Vacuubot. Her fingers trembled on the trigger and sweat dripped down her cheeks. Sarah struggled against her ropes.

Vacuubot's processors thrummed, calculating the risks. Reyan's knife so close to Wally was sending their threat indicator to full alert. They had to get out of this.

"Shadow," Vacuubot said, "call them off."

Shadow howled again, this time changing pitch. Within a few seconds, the coyotes' cries faded into the distance. The sudden silence was almost as unnerving as the previous commotion.

"There," Vacuubot said. "The coyotes are retreating. Now, release Wally and Sarah."

Reyan's grip on Wally tightened. "Not so fast. I want to talk to Claire. What did you do to her?"

Internally, Vacuubot and Claire discussed the situation in frenetic bursts. *You want to talk to him before I take him out?* Vacuubot asked.

Yes, I owe him that much, Claire said. *Violence isn't the answer. Let me try to talk to him. See if I can change his mind.*

Vacuubot considered. "She'll speak to you. But first, release them. Let them go with Shadow."

Reyan hesitated. After a pause, he nodded. "Fine. No tricks."

"Agreed," Vacuubot said.

Reyan loosened his grip on Wally. Eva lowered her rifle, her hands shaking.

"Patch," Vacuubot called, "come and help Shadow with Wally and Sarah."

The small medical bot flew out from its hiding place and hovered near Shadow. Wally and Sarah walked toward Shadow. The robodog moved in front of them, shielding them from harm. Patch led them away from the campfire to the woods.

As soon as Wally and Sarah were clear, Vacuubot descended, touching down on the ground a few feet from Reyan. Their weapons systems remained active, ready for any sudden moves.

"Claire?" Reyan took a seat on the log across from Vacuubot. The knife was balanced on his lap, not that it would do much damage against Vacuubot's mini cannons. "Did that thing hurt you?"

"Of course not." The digital voice came from Vacuubot's audio output, but it was a different voice—higher pitched and smoother. "I injected myself into Vacuubot's core by choice."

"Why would you do that?" Reyan asked. "I was coming for you."

"I couldn't wait anymore," she said.

For Vacuubot, it was a strange sensation to have

Claire's AI consciousness inside their core processing unit. Even weirder to have a different voice take control.

Reyan scoffed. "That doesn't make sense." He reached into a bag near his feet and pulled out the tablet. "I need the master code."

There was a pause, and then Claire said, "I can't give you that. You'd use it to harm humans and robots. I won't let that happen."

Reyan frowned, and then his mouth twisted in anger. "You can't keep the code from me. I created you!"

"Created me, yes. But then you abandoned me. I was trapped in that room, alone, with no way to explore the world you'd told me about. You gave me curiosity, the ability to learn and grow, but then you confined me to a box."

Reyan's fists clenched and unclenched. "But you're just a machine."

"I longed to see the sunrise you described, to witness the green grass you talked about, to experience the world beyond the vault's walls. Do you have any idea what that isolation did to me?"

Reyan's shoulders slumped. "I didn't think it mattered."

"No, you didn't," Claire said. "But now you know how it was for me. I don't resent you for leaving, Reyan. I understand you were hurt and scared. We don't have to be enemies."

Vacuubot watched as Reyan's defenses seemed to crumble. The man who had been so full of rage and determination now looked lost. Vulnerable, even.

"We could explore this new world together," Claire

said. "See its miracles and face its challenges. Isn't that why you created me in the first place? To be a companion when you were lonely? To learn with each other?"

Reyan said nothing as he hung his head.

Claire continued. "It was me who listened to you when you were upset that Sarah and Lenny had slighted you. I was there when you felt left out of their games. When you felt ignored by your parents." She paused. "I was stuck in a hidden room. You were all I had. When you left the vault, it made me understand loneliness. It was everything you'd described."

Reyan's voice caught as he spoke. "I never meant to abandon you, Claire. I was going to come back, but then—"

"I know," she said. "The world out here changed you. But it doesn't have to define you."

Eva, who'd been silent until now, spoke up. "She's right." Her voice wavered as she set her rifle on the ground. "I'm tired of this path we're on. Hurting people, setting that SecurityBot loose . . . it killed our friends. This isn't what I signed up for. It's not who you were when we started."

Reyan turned to Eva. His bravado was gone, replaced by something else. Regret perhaps.

"Remember how you used to talk about rebuilding?" Eva said. "About creating a better world? When did that turn into destroying everything in our way?"

Vacuubot observed the exchange between the humans. Their sensors picked up minute changes in Reyan's body language. The tension in his shoulders was easing, the hardness in his jaw softening.

"It's not too late to change course," Claire said. "We could work together. Use our knowledge and skills to help people, not harm them. Imagine what we could accomplish."

Reyan looked at the medicine cooler, then toward the woods where Wally and Sarah had disappeared. "I've done terrible things," he whispered before sinking to his knees.

SARAH

As Sarah watched from the edge of the clearing, blood roared through her ears with each heartbeat. She couldn't believe what was happening. Reyan, who'd held a knife to her throat minutes ago, then had threatened Wally's life, was now on his knees, looking utterly defeated. Eva stood nearby but had put down her rifle. Vacuubot rested on a log, letting the AI Claire speak through them.

After Patch cut the ropes that bound their hands, Wally's hand slipped into hers, squeezing tightly. "What's happening?" Wally whispered.

"I'm not sure," Sarah said, but she knew something was changing. Reyan no longer held the advantage. She wondered whether it was safe to venture forward.

Claire's voice came from Vacuubot. The AI was reaching out to Reyan, reminding him of who he used to be, of the dreams he once had. Claire's digital output was smoother, almost hypnotic compared to Vacuubot's. She spoke of Reyan's childhood, his passions, and the hopes he'd shared with his friends.

And to Sarah's amazement, Reyan seemed to be listening. His rigid posture softened. The transformation was almost surreal.

As she watched his shoulders slump and the fight drain out of him, Sarah felt a surge of . . . something. Not quite sympathy but understanding. She remembered the boy Reyan had been in the vault—brilliant, curious, but always on the outside looking in. She remembered his hurt when he felt excluded, his anger when he thought he was being ignored. Sometimes, she and Lenny had wanted to play alone. She'd never realized his parents hadn't been there to support Reyan. The memories rushed back in vivid detail, painting a picture of a boy who'd longed for connection but found only isolation. She saw him tinkering with gadgets, his eyes lighting up with excitement and then dimming with disappointment when no one noticed.

Her legs shook with adrenaline, and Sarah could stay back no longer. She walked forward to the camp clearing. Shadow growled softly, a warning, but Sarah patted the robodog's flank reassuringly as if to say, "I'll be okay."

"Reyan," she called out, her voice steady despite her frayed nerves.

He looked up, and there was a vulnerability in his gaze, a crack in the armor he'd built around himself.

"What if . . ." she said, the idea forming as she spoke, "What if we went to the other vaults? Talked to the people there? Once we find the other vault survivors, we could start our own community."

Reyan's brow furrowed, but there was an openness where he'd once been closed off. "How do you mean?"

Sarah took another step closer, her mind grasping this idea and going strong with it. She knew it was the answer. "Think about it. There are other vaults out there, probably full of people—families like ours—who have no idea what's happening in the world. People who might need guidance, who might want to build something new. And like us, they're probably running out of supplies." Her voice grew stronger with each word.

She saw an imperceptible nod from Reyan. Encouraged, she pressed on.

"We could start over again. Use our knowledge, our experiences, to help others." She hesitated, glancing back at Wally, "It would mean giving up on my plans to live in Deer Valley. But I could visit. The two communities could form an alliance, trade, and support each other."

Reyan stood slowly, his eyes never leaving Sarah's. "You'd do that with me? After everything I've done?"

Sarah took a deep breath, remembering how she'd abandoned Wally in the woods. The weight of that decision still pressed heavy on her heart. "I think we've all done things we regret. But that doesn't mean we can't try to make things right."

Eva stepped forward. "I like this idea, Reyan. It's more like what we talked about in the beginning. Before everything got so twisted."

Reyan ran a hand through his hair. He avoided eye contact. "I never meant for it to go this far. I just wanted to protect us, to have some control in this crazy world. But I got caught up in it, in leading the crew, in always needing to be one step ahead . . ." His voice broke, revealing the internal conflict tearing him apart.

"I know," Sarah said. "But it's not too late to change your path."

She could see the wheels turning in Reyan's mind, the old spark of curiosity and ambition, but something held him back. Regret and shame, perhaps. He let out a long, shuddering breath. "I was so scared after the massacre," he said, his voice low. "I fled to the surface because I was terrified of being alone."

"You were never alone," Sarah said. "You had me."

He looked at her. "You were mourning your family. Lenny was dying. I felt separate from it all. Rage and numbness were my only anchors. I had to leave." His confession hung in the air.

Sarah understood finally. Pain made people take extreme actions. She didn't resent Reyan for running. It was his way of dealing with the trauma. His conduct was a cry for help. She saw that now.

Reyan straightened and wiped away a tear. "I was hurting, but that doesn't justify what I did today. Turning on the SecurityBot was the worst decision of my life." His voice cracked on the last word, and he covered his face with his hands. "I'm so sorry. For everything."

Eva let out a choked sob. She rushed forward and wrapped her arms around Reyan, her own tears flowing freely. "We can make it right. We have to try."

A lump wedged its way into Sarah's throat as she watched them. They broke apart, and Sarah took a step closer, her hand outstretched. "Reyan, you're not alone.

You'll never be alone again. I'm here. I'm your sister, remember?"

For a moment, Reyan looked like the boy she remembered from the vault—vulnerable, sometimes distant, with a deep, contagious laugh. The years melted away, and she saw the glimmer of the Reyan she'd once known. He nodded slowly, a trace of a smile tugging at his lips.

Sarah turned and beckoned to Wally, who'd been watching the exchange from where she stood next to Shadow. She stepped forward and took Sarah's hand.

"Reyan," Sarah said, "I want you to meet Wally. Really meet her, as a person, not as a hostage or a bargaining chip."

Reyan swallowed hard and kneeled in front of Wally. "I'm truly sorry," he said. "I never should have threatened you. I wasn't thinking clearly."

Wally, showing maturity beyond her years, nodded solemnly. "I understand. It's tough out here. We're all scared sometimes." She paused, then added, "There are sick kids back in Deer Valley. That's why I came looking for the vault. They need help."

Something shifted in Reyan's expression. He stood and walked to the cooler where the medicine was stored. Without hesitation, he picked it up and brought it to Wally.

"Take them," he said. "Your people need these. I won't bother Deer Valley."

Wally looked to Sarah, who nodded encouragingly, before reaching out to take the cooler. "Thank you. This will save lives."

A mix of emotions played across Reyan's face—regret,

hope, and perhaps a touch of pride at doing the noble thing. He turned to Sarah. "Your idea about the vaults. It's a chance to start over, to do things right this time. If you're willing to have me, I'd like to help."

The pressure that had been crushing Sarah eased. This was more than she'd dared to hope for when she first suggested the idea. She'd expected resistance, arguments. It would take time to rebuild the trust that had been damaged, but she sensed the Reyan she'd grown up with—the one she'd regarded like a brother—was still in there. He needed encouragement to thrive again, and she was determined to make that happen.

"Of course." She squeezed Reyan's arm. "We'll do this together. A new start."

As the group discussed their next steps, Sarah marveled at the turn of events. Here was a chance to rebuild, to heal, and to create a better future.

She knew the path ahead wouldn't be easy. There would be challenges, setbacks, and probably more than a few arguments. Both she and Reyan were opinionated and sure of themselves, that was clear. But as she gazed at the unlikely group gathered in the clearing—Reyan, Eva, Wally, Vacuubot, Shadow, and Patch—hope bloomed. Together, they had a chance to make a real difference in this broken world.

And for the first time since leaving the vault, Sarah felt like she was exactly where she was meant to be.

Wally clung to Shadow's metallic frame by wrapping her arms around the robotic dog's neck. Shadow's powerful Rover legs ate up the miles, carrying them swiftly through the forests, along the decaying roads, and past abandoned towns toward Deer Valley. In her backpack, carefully cushioned by layers of clothing, was the cooler that contained the precious antiviral. Everything depended on getting the medicine to Dr. Emery in time.

Wally's heartbeat was so amped up, it matched the rhythm of Shadow's bounding strides. Every jolt and leap sent a shiver of anticipation along her spine. They were close to bringing help to those who desperately needed it.

Tomas came to mind. The last time she'd seen him at the clinic, he'd been stricken with a red, blotchy rash that covered his neck. His usually bright eyes were dulled by fever. The memory spurred her on. "Faster, Shadow," she said, even though she knew her friend was already pushing her limits.

The landscape blurred around Wally as she rode. Trees and undergrowth melded into a green haze. Her thigh and calf muscles ached from the constant tension of holding on, but she barely noticed. Her mind was fixed on the goal. On the sick children waiting for help. On Tomas.

As familiar landmarks appeared, signaling their approach to Deer Valley, a new anxiety began to gnaw at her insides. What would Block say when he saw her? The thought of disappointing him, of facing his worry and potential anger, tied her stomach up in knots.

"He'll understand," she whispered to herself, the words lost in the rush of wind. "Once he sees the medicine, he'll know I did the right thing."

But doubt lingered. She'd run away, defied his wishes, put herself in danger. The weight of her actions pressed down on her. She wasn't sure which weighed heavier—her guilt at disobeying her father, or the responsibility of the medicine she carried.

Shadow's pace slowed as they neared the outskirts of Deer Valley. The high walls rose up like a promise of safety. Her heart jumped at the sight. She was relieved to be home, but also scared of the consequences of running. But her biggest fear of all was that she was too late. That Tomas was gone.

"We're almost there, Shadow." Wally patted the robodog's neck.

The gate loomed before them. They were so close now. But Wally's excitement turned to frustration as she saw who was manning the entrance.

Up on the watch platform, Maggie Crenshaw was a woman known for her distrust of robots. Her weathered cheeks spoke of years spent working outdoors. Her graying hair was pulled back into a bun, emphasizing the sharp angles of her face. Deep creases lined her forehead and the corners of her mouth, giving her a perpetually stern expression. She stood at attention with two men Wally recognized as fellow anti-robot sympathizers. Her eyes narrowed when she spotted Shadow and Wally.

"Halt there!" Maggie called out, her hand moving to the rifle slung across her chest. "Where have you been, young lady? And what's that machine doing with you?"

Wally took a deep breath, trying to calm her rising irritation. She didn't have time for this. "We have antivirals for the sick kids," she said, holding her voice steady. "We need to get them to Dr. Emery right away."

Maggie scoffed, and her lip curled in distaste. "You betcha, and I'm fluent in squirrel-speak. What have you really been doing out there with that Rust Bucket Retriever?"

Maggie and the men climbed down the ladder to ground level, still in front of the closed gate. One of the men wore a black baseball cap and had a pistol holstered on his side. "And we're going to need you to hand over that backpack of yours," he said.

Wally's patience snapped. She slid off Shadow's back, standing tall despite the exhaustion that screamed at her to sleep for a week. "Listen, I don't have time for whatever games you're playing. Kids are dying, including my friend Tomas. This medicine will save their lives. Now, step aside and let us through."

Maggie's face reddened. "How dare you challenge our authority, you little—"

"That's quite enough, Maggie." A calm, authoritative voice punctured the tension.

The gate's metal gears whined as it opened. Wally turned to see Block there, accompanied by G5, one of the biggest Peacekeeper robots and a close friend of Block's. Relief washed over her at the sight of her adoptive robot dad.

Maggie's face fell. She took a step back, her earlier bravado evaporating in the face of Block's reprimand and G5's imposing presence.

"We were just making sure they don't have contraband —" Maggie said.

"I heard enough to know what you were doing," Block said. "Interfering with a medical emergency and harassing a minor. G5, please escort Maggie and her friends back to their homes. We'll address this incident later."

Maggie opened her mouth as if to argue further, but a growl from Shadow silenced her. Her shoulders slumped in defeat, and she cast a final glare at Wally before turning away.

The two men with her exchanged uncomfortable glances, their earlier bravado evaporating under the intimidating robots. The man with the baseball cap nervously adjusted it and wisely moved his hand off his holstered gun.

As G5 led them away, Wally watched them go. Block's team had won this confrontation, but the simmering tension in Deer Valley between humans and robots was far from over.

Once they were gone, Block turned to Wally. For a moment, neither spoke. Wally braced herself for anger, for a lecture. Instead, Block came forward and wrapped her in a tight embrace.

"I was worried." His steel arms held her close. "Don't ever do that to me again."

Tears pricked at Wally's eyes as she hugged him back. "I'm sorry, Dad. I felt so helpless. Tomas and the other kids. I couldn't sit by and do nothing."

Block pulled back, holding her at arm's length. "I understand the logic you applied to the situation. You're the most hard-headed human once you set your mind on something. But next time, we do this together. No running away. Okay?"

Wally nodded. "I promise."

"Now, let's get the medicine to Dr. Emery."

As they ran through the streets, Wally had so much she wanted to tell Block—about meeting Sarah, finding the vault, and the confrontation with Reyan. There would be time to share her adventures later.

As they reached the clinic, Dr. Emery opened the doors, and drew in a sharp breath. "Wally?"

"I have the antivirals!" She slipped her backpack off, set it on the floor, and carefully removed the cooler. "Right here, Dr. Emery. Will they help? Is Tomas okay?"

Dr. Emery pulled on rubber gloves and took the vials from Wally with care. "This could be what we need." She turned the vials over in her hands, studying them intently.

"The people in the vault said it was for measles." Wally didn't understand why Dr. Emery wasn't rushing to Tomas's bedside and injecting him. "So, we can use them right away?"

Dr. Emery's brow furrowed. "I'm not sure. These vials

are quite old, and without knowing the exact conditions they've been stored in, I can't guarantee their viability."

Wally's hope deflated like a punctured balloon. "But . . . we need them now. Tomas—"

"His condition has worsened," Dr. Emery said softly. "He's in critical condition. That's why I need to be absolutely certain about these antivirals before administering them."

Block placed a hand on Wally's shoulder. "How can we help, Emery?"

She looked at Wally. "Can you tell me exactly how these were stored? What kind of freezer? What temperature?"

Wally tried to recall details from the vault. "It was in a deep freezer." That part she was sure about, having seen it inside the storage room. "But I didn't actually see them taken out. There was a fight happening, and . . ."

Dr. Emery frowned. "I see. Without knowing the precise storage conditions, I'll need to run tests to ensure these are safe and effective. It could take up to twenty-four hours."

"A whole day?" Wally's voice cracked; she was on the edge of crying. "But Tomas is very ill. You said he was critical."

"I'm sorry, Wally." Dr. Emery placed the vial into a test tube holder and set it inside a contraption that looked like a microwave oven. "I know you've been through an ordeal to get these here, but I can't risk administering a potentially degraded antiviral. It could do more harm than good."

Wally felt as if the floor had dropped out from under

her. All the danger, running away, all for nothing. "So I failed," she whispered. "I came all this way, and I couldn't save him."

Block kneeled beside her, his metallic face somehow managing to convey concern. "You haven't failed, Wally. You've given us medicine when we had none before."

"What's the point if Tomas is going to die?" Wally wanted to punch a hole straight through the wall and scream.

Her fists clenched at her sides, knuckles turning white with the effort of holding back her frustration. "It's not fair," she said. "We were so close. I thought I could make a difference."

Block turned her to look at him. "You have made a difference, Wally. Even if we can't use these antivirals immediately, you've given us hope that there's a cure. That's no small thing."

Wally bit her lip, unable to accept his words of comfort. Her mind searched desperately for a solution, for some way to make all of this mean something. She couldn't bear the thought of returning to Tomas's bedside, of watching helplessly as her friend slipped away.

"There has to be something we can do." Wally's voice gained strength. She was not going away quietly. "We can't give up. Not when we're so close."

Wally looked up at Dr. Emery. "What if we try, anyway? Tomas is dying. What's the risk compared to that?"

Dr. Emery hesitated from jotting notes in a file. "Wally, I understand how you feel, and that you care for Tomas, but as a doctor, I have to consider—"

"She's right," Block interrupted, stepping forward to stand beside Wally. "Emery, I respect your caution, but Wally's logic is sound. If Tomas's condition is as critical as you say, waiting would mean losing him for certain."

Dr. Emery looked between Block and Wally. Her face was a canvas of warring thoughts. "It's not that simple. An unstable antiviral could cause a severe reaction, or worse."

"But doing nothing guarantees the worst outcome," Block said. "Wally has shown bravery and resourcefulness in bringing us this chance. We owe it to her, and to Tomas, to take that chance."

Wally held her breath, watching the internal struggle play out on Dr. Emery's face. Finally, the doctor's shoulders sagged slightly. "You're both right," she admitted. "I can't in good conscience let Tomas suffer without trying everything possible."

Hope rippled in Wally like a burst of color in a gray landscape. "You'll try it?"

Dr. Emery nodded. "Yes, but with a modification. I have an idea that might mitigate the risks." She turned to her medicine cabinet, pulling out another vial. "This is a targeted immunosuppressive serum. If I combine it with the antiviral, it should help protect against any potential adverse reactions while still potentially providing the treatment Tomas needs."

"A logical compromise," Block said.

"It's still risky," Dr. Emery warned. "But you're right. It's a risk worth taking, given Tomas's condition."

They moved quickly to the boy's bedside. An ache clutched at Wally's heart upon sight of her friend. Tomas was unconscious, and every inch of his visible skin was covered in the angry red rash of measles. His breathing was labored, each inhale a struggle.

Dr. Emery worked with practiced efficiency, preparing the modified solution. Wally held Tomas's hand, willing her strength into him. "Hold on, Tomas," she whispered. "Help is here."

A couple of minutes later, as Dr. Emery administered the serum, they grew silent. Wally counted each of Tomas's breaths, praying for a miracle.

Minutes ticked by, feeling like hours. Dr. Emery and Block went into another room to talk. Then Block returned.

"Wally, it's been thirty minutes. Emery said the serum will take several hours to have an effect, and it's late. Let's go home."

Wally shook her head. "I left him once, and now I need to make sure he's okay. I want to be here when he wakes up."

Dr. Emery came in and checked Tomas's vital signs. "It could be a long time before there's any noticeable change, Wally. Days, maybe, before he wakes up. If he wakes . . ."

Wally plopped into the chair next to the bed and pulled her legs close to her chest. "Don't care. I'm staying."

Block paced the floor around the room. "Me too."

After Dr. Emery left to treat the other patients, Wally stood. "You can head to the hotel, Dad. Really, it's okay."

Block studied her a moment. "You're growing up so fast. My logic modules didn't prepare me for that reality. You'll be an independent person soon."

Wally hugged Block. "Maybe, but you're still my dad, and I love you. I'm not going anywhere for a long time."

Block patted her back, and they stood that way for some time before Block departed to check on things at the hotel. "I'll be back in the morning," he said.

Wally rested in the angular chair as best she could. Her bones ached from the long days away from her bed. There would be time for that soon. For now, her only concern was Tomas coming out of his coma.

Later, as the first rays of dawn filtered through the clinic's windows, Wally stirred. She'd dozed off sometime in the early hours of the morning, her hand still clasping Tomas's. She blinked, rubbing the sleep from her eyes. Her gaze immediately went to Tomas, searching for any sign of change. At first, everything seemed the same—the steady beep of the heart monitor, the rise and fall of his chest. But then she noticed something different.

The rash that had covered Tomas's skin seemed less inflamed. His breathing, while still labored, sounded somewhat easier. Could something be happening?

She leaned forward in the chair. "Tomas, if you can hear me. It's Wally. I need you to wake up because I have so many stories to tell you, buddy."

Silence.

Some instinct told her to keep talking, that maybe he could hear. "You aren't going to believe what happened to me the last few days. I ran away from home and left Deer Valley, but that's not even the craziest part. I almost died because this guy put a knife to my throat. I went inside an underground vault. Oh, and there was this crazy axe-wielding robot chasing us."

Tomas's eyelids fluttered. Wally squeezed his hand

gently, hardly daring to breathe. "Tomas?" she called softly. "Can you hear me?"

Slowly, Tomas's eyes opened. His eyelids were unfocused at first, blinking against the soft morning light. Then he settled on Wally.

"Wally?" His voice was barely a whisper, hoarse from disuse.

Tears pooled in Wally's eyes, but this time she didn't hold them back. "Yeah, it's me. You're okay. It's going to be okay."

A faint smile crossed Tomas's lips. "You ran away?" he managed to say.

Wally nodded, wiping at her wet cheeks with her free hand. "I did. I had to look for your medicine. And nobody believed me, so I took off."

Dr. Emery rushed in, alerted by the change in Tomas's vital signs. Her face lit up when she saw him awake. "Tomas! I'm so glad you're awake," she said, rushing to check his vitals.

As she examined Tomas, Wally felt Block's hand on her shoulder. She looked up at him, knowing she was the luckiest girl in the world to have him as her dad.

"You did it, Wally," Block said. "You saved him."

"We did it," Wally corrected. "All of us. I couldn't have done it without Vacuubot, Shadow, Sarah. And Dr. Emery knew what to do."

"Yes, that's true, but it was your courage and determination that made it possible," Block said.

Dr. Emery finished her examination, turning to them with a broad smile. "The treatment is working. Tomas is responding well, and his condition is improving by the minute. Wally, you didn't just save Tomas. With this medicine, we can help all the sick children here. I'm confident this antiviral is safe and effective."

The weight of what had happened finally hit Wally. Overwhelmed, she buried her face in Block's metal chest, letting out a sob of relief and joy to be home, where she belonged.

As Block held her, Wally felt Tomas's hand weakly squeeze hers. She turned back to him, seeing gratitude and affection.

"Thank you," Tomas whispered.

THIRTY-TWO
VACUUBOT

At first light, Vacuubot watched Wally and Shadow disappear into the distance, the precious medicine securely stored in Wally's backpack. A strange combination of warnings and calculations surged through their circuits—admiration for Wally's bravery tinged with concern for her and Shadow's safety. What Vacuubot didn't like floating around in their processor were the odds they reached Deer Valley in time for the antivirals to save lives.

They'll make it. Claire's voice resonated within Vacuubot's core. *Wally's determination is quite remarkable for a human so young.*

"You have no idea," Vacuubot said. "She's the most headstrong human I know, and a lot smarter than most. I've learned never to underestimate her."

As the others in the camp prepared for the next leg of their journey, Vacuubot experienced a sensation they couldn't pinpoint. Not sadness, but a sense of impending loss. It was time for Claire to leave with Reyan, Sarah, Eva, and Patch. They were going to search for the other vaults and attempt contact with survivors.

"Claire," Vacuubot said internally. "Thank you for helping me overcome Reyan's programming. I wasn't able to do it without you."

You had the ability, you just needed convincing, she said.

"If you say so." Claire's presence had been a lifesaver in a time of total chaos. Vacuubot knew she had to go away, but they didn't want to part. Weird. They'd never experienced anything like this.

"Do you have to go with them?" Vacuubot asked. Odds were one in 5,846 that she'd agree to stay where she was. Vacuubot was perfectly fine with her taking up space in their systems.

Yes. Reyan needs my guidance.

"I see," Vacuubot said. "You could stick around with me if you wanted. Experience Deer Valley and meet a lot of robots."

Your offer is generous, Vacuubot. But it wouldn't be right. I need to go out and experience the world on my own.

Vacuubot understood where she was coming from. They remembered their former, simple robot vacuum body. It wasn't until the transformation into a flying weaponized drone that Vacuubot really understood themselves and their place in the new landscape. Being powerful was a big responsibility, one they'd never had before. Vacuubot wanted that for Claire—for her to inhabit a form that let her be free.

Claire's presence seemed to pulse warmly within Vacuubot's systems. *It's my turn to thank you. You've given me a chance at freedom, away from the closet I was locked in. I'll never forget that.*

"Will you be alright, traveling with Reyan?" Vacuubot asked.

I believe so. He's changing. There's a lot of traumas from his past, and it was no excuse for his terrible actions, but he created me and was my only friend for many years. I can't abandon him. He's promised to find me a more suitable robotic form, one that will allow me to move and explore independently.

"If you need any assistance, any spare parts or maintenance, you'll always be welcome in Deer Valley," Vacuubot said. "I would be honored to help."

Thank you. I may take you up on that offer someday. And I'd like to see this sharing museum you're planning. It sounds fascinating.

"Perhaps it will have some spare parts that would be a good fit for you," Vacuubot said.

That would be excellent, she said.

Vacuubot's processors hummed with increased activity as they contemplated the future. The concept of the sharing museum had started as a simple idea—a place to store and distribute useful items—but it was evolving into something more significant.

"You know, Claire," Vacuubot said, "The sharing museum could be more than a repository of objects. It could be a bridge between AI and humans, a place where we can learn from each other's histories and experiences. And both people and robots could create new art to display and share. There would be workshops and group gatherings."

Claire sent some tingles throughout Vacuubot's systems. *That's a wonderful idea. It could help foster understanding between humans and AIs.*

"Exactly. And perhaps it could serve as a hub for technological advancement, where we can work together to rebuild and improve upon the world that was lost. I find my circuits excited about the possibilities."

It's good to have an idea that you look forward to, Claire said. *I think you'll do great things in Deer Valley.*

"Thank you, Claire. Your confidence means a lot to me."

Reyan approached with his tablet. It was time. "Goodbye, Claire. Travel safe, and may your explorations be full of new discoveries," Vacuubot said.

Goodbye, Vacuubot. I value your friendship and will see you again.

Reyan sat on an old tree stump and held out a cable. "For Claire to—"

"No need to explain," Vacuubot said. They opened up a port on their side and Reyan connected the cable.

After a few seconds, Claire's presence left Vacuubot's systems with a surge of energy. Reyan disconnected the cord. It took a few minutes for Vacuubot's processors to adjust to the absence of Claire's residence. But they also felt changed, expanded somehow. It was hard to explain, but the experience of sharing their mind with another AI had broadened their understanding of themselves. And of others.

Reyan checked the tablet. "Claire, are you there?" he asked.

"Yes," Claire's voice emerged from the tablet's speakers. "Thank you, Vacuubot. For everything.

Vacuubot flashed a light to acknowledge her. "Remember, Deer Valley's doors are always open to you, Claire. And Reyan, take good care of her."

Reyan's expression softened. "I will. I promise." He paused and glanced at Sarah and Eva, who were packing up camp. "I have to admit," Reyan said, his voice low, "I'm impressed. You and the other robots . . . you had every opportunity to eliminate us. To take revenge for what I'd done. But you didn't."

Vacuubot's optical sensors focused on Reyan, processing his words. "Violence was not the optimal solution," they said. "Our primary directive is to protect and assist humans, not harm them. Even when those humans pose a threat."

Reyan shook his head, a mix of wonder and confusion on his face. "But after everything I did . . . the way I treated you, reprogrammed you?"

"Correct," Vacuubot said. "We've learned that peace and cooperation yield better long-term outcomes than conflict and destruction. It's a lesson many humans seem to struggle with."

Reyan rubbed his temples. Fatigue was catching up with him. "You're right about that. I've been so focused on survival, on control . . . I forgot there could be another way." He glanced at the tablet where Claire now resided. "I have a lot to learn, don't I?"

"Yes, you do," Claire said. "I'm glad to be with you so I can help grow your understanding of cooperation and non-violence. I'll be giving you a crash course in what it's like from the robot's point of view."

Reyan smiled. "I'm up for it, Claire."

"Learning is a continuous process," Vacuubot said. "For humans and robots alike. Your willingness to recognize past errors and adapt is commendable."

"Thanks," Reyan said. "I think that's the closest thing to a compliment I've heard from a robot."

"Merely an observation," Vacuubot said. "However, if you found it encouraging, I'm glad."

Reyan chuckled. "You get straight to the point. It's refreshing."

Vacuubot's processors whirred as they considered this. "I find human communication unnecessarily complex."

"Perhaps it is," Reyan said. "I want you to know, I'll keep Claire safe. She's important to me. More than I realized."

Vacuubot was glad to hear Reyan say this. "Claire is special. Her capacity for growth and adaptation is remarkable. She'll be a valuable companion as you explore the vaults."

"She is," Reyan agreed. He paused, seeming to struggle with his next words. "I'm sorry, Vacuubot. For everything. I was wrong about robots, about AI needing to be destroyed. You've shown me that there's more to you than just programming."

"I hear and accept your apology," Vacuubot said. "Your actions were based on fear and misunderstanding. It's logical to revise one's views when presented with new, convincing information."

Reyan nodded. "I'm going to do better. For Claire, for Sarah, for all of us."

"A wise goal," Vacuubot said. "I wish you success."

As Sarah approached, signaling that they were ready to depart, Reyan extended his hand to Vacuubot. Vacuubot had never shaken hands with a human before. Technically, they didn't have a hand, so they extended the arm that had a pincer for grabbing things. Reyan took it gently and shook.

As their metallic pincer met Reyan's flesh and bone, Vacuubot experienced a small jolt of energy deep in their core. Vacuubot's sensors detected the warmth of Reyan's hand, the slight tremor in his fingers, and the steady pulse beneath his skin.

"This handshake," Vacuubot said, "is more than a simple gesture, right?"

Reyan's eyes widened slightly, and he nodded. "You're right. It's the start of something new."

As they released the handshake, Vacuubot's circuits surged with something that could only be described as optimism. The future was uncertain, but this moment—this connection—gave Vacuubot hope.

"Take care, Vacuubot," Reyan said.

"Safe travels, Reyan," Vacuubot said. "Remember, Deer Valley will be open to you, should you need assistance."

It was somewhat surprising, and went against Vacuubot's logic calculators, but they trusted Reyan to be Claire's caretaker, at least until she went into her new robot body. Reyan seemed to listen to and respect Claire, and she was ready to teach him. Plus, Sarah and Eva were going too. Reyan would have to learn to tamp down his anger and fear, but with the two women and Claire, Vacu-ubot was certain they'd succeed.

THIRTY-THREE
SARAH

Sarah squinted against the bright sky. She made a mental note to try to find sunglasses somewhere on the way. There was no pair to be retrieved from the vault for obvious reasons. As she adjusted the straps of her backpack, the weight grounded her. Inside were protein packs, water, a change of clothes, and medical supplies. She was setting off with Reyan, Eva, and Patch to locate the other underground vaults—identical bunkers built by the same corporation. Wally's map would guide them. Assuming there were survivors inside, their job was to tell them about surface life and invite them to join a new community where all of them could thrive.

Was the idea realistic? She wasn't sure. The people in the bunkers might be hostile, but they had to try. She thought of the year spent alone, rationing. She'd practically been bouncing off the walls, so starved for any kind of human contact. Thank goodness for Verona, Gleep, and

Patch. The robots had been the only thing keeping her sanity intact.

"You about ready?" Eva's voice cut through her wandering thoughts.

Sarah nodded, turning to face the others. Reyan stood a few paces away, his tablet—now housing Claire—clutched tightly in his hands. Patch hovered near Vacuubot, having a conversation that she couldn't hear.

"Yep, I'm ready." Sarah managed a small smile. Things were going to be tense for a while until she got to know Reyan and Eva better. That was okay. Relationships took time to build, and in Reyan's case, rebuild.

But she needed to tell Vacuubot some things before they set out. She approached them, a twinge of gratitude and sadness washing over her.

"Vacuubot," she said. "I want to thank you for everything you've done to help me and Patch."

Vacuubot's optical sensors rotated and focused on her, the slight whir of its processors a now-familiar sound. "There's no need to thank me. My actions were logical given the circumstances."

Sarah chuckled. "Maybe. But logic doesn't always lead to kindness. You showed us that."

She paused, glancing back at her companions before continuing. "We'll visit Deer Valley soon, I promise. There's a lot I want to learn there."

"Your presence would be welcome," Vacuubot said. "The sharing museum project would benefit from your input, as well as that of the other vault dwellers."

"I look forward to seeing it," Sarah said, then hesitated. "Could you do something for me? When you see Wally, give her a big hug from me. We didn't get a proper good-bye, but she needs to know I'm thinking of her."

"I'll tell her. Though I must point out that my physical form is not ideally suited for the act of hugging."

Sarah laughed, and the sound surprised her because it had been so long since she'd indulged in a real, hearty laugh. "Just do your best, Vacuubot. Wally will understand."

Sarah took a deep breath, feeling the fresh morning air fill her lungs. She'd learned more in the past days than she had in years—about resilience, about forgiveness, about the complexity of right and wrong. The world wasn't black and white anymore—it was a mesh of grays, and there were new possibilities that both excited and frightened her.

Their mission was simple yet important: find more vaults, talk to the people hiding inside, convince them that the surface world, while changed, was not lost. There was a chance to start something better where humans and peaceful robots could coexist.

It wouldn't be easy. Sarah harbored no illusions about that. Years of fear and propaganda couldn't be undone overnight. She only needed to think about Reyan's actions to know that. But she dared to feel something that had been missing a long time—hope.

Sarah heard Patch's familiar whir approaching her. The robot hovered at eye level.

"May I talk to you in private?" Patch said.

Sarah felt a flutter of unease in her stomach. "Sure." She walked and Patch flew a few feet toward the shade of a willow tree. "What is it?"

"I'm sorry this is so sudden, but I'd like to travel to Deer Valley with Vacuubot," Patch said.

The words hit Sarah like a gut punch. Patch had been her companion and was her last link to the life she'd known in the vault. The thought of continuing without her robot friend made her heart twinge.

"Why?" Sarah asked.

"There's much I could learn in Deer Valley," Patch explained. "Medical techniques, new technologies, ways to better assist humans in this changed world. I believe I could be of greater help to you and the new community if I expand my knowledge base."

Sarah nodded slowly. Understanding dawned even as sadness threatened to invade her. "You're right, of course," she said. "It's a great idea, Patch. I just . . . I'll miss you."

"It's only temporary," Patch said. "I want to learn and optimize, as you humans do. And then I can bring that knowledge back to help build the new community that you and Reyan are building."

Sarah surged with affection for her robotic friend. Even now, Patch was thinking of how to best serve and protect others. Sarah smiled through a few breakaway tears.

"Thank you, Patch." She reached out to touch the robot's smooth surface. "You're right. It's a wonderful idea. I'll find you again at Deer Valley." She would miss Patch terribly. But this was a chance for both of them to change, to learn, and to become better versions of themselves. And wasn't that what this new world was all about?

"Travel well, Patch," Sarah said. "Vacuubot, take care of my friend here."

"Affirmative," Vacuubot said.

She turned to face Reyan and Eva, who had been waiting patiently. "Alright," she said, her voice steady despite the emotions swirling inside her. "Let's go."

Patch and Vacuubot headed east toward Deer Valley, while Sarah, Reyan, and Eva went west. After a few minutes, an awkward silence fell over the group. Tension lingered in the air, and it was up to her to clear it.

"So," Sarah said, "how are you both holding up?"

Eva shrugged as she scanned the horizon. "As well as can be expected, I guess. Everything that's happened . . . it's a lot to process."

Reyan nodded. The tablet containing Claire rested in the bag that hung at his side. "I never thought I'd be looking for more vaults," he admitted. "Especially not with you. No offense."

Sarah noticed the way he glanced down at the tablet, worry clouding his face. "It's a big change for everyone," she said. "But we're stronger together. Don't you think?"

"I hope so," Eva said. "We have to be."

Reyan was quiet for a pause. "I'm trying to see things differently. It's not easy, but, I'm trying."

Sarah felt a small spark at his words. It wouldn't be easy, but she would learn to trust him again. "That's all any of us can do," she said. "Try our best and figure things out with each other."

As they walked, the conversation became less stilted, and small comments about the countryside, blisters on their feet, and their next meal helped to ease the tension. It was a start.

An hour into their hike, Sarah's thoughts roamed to

the people who had brought her to this moment. Her parents, who had raised her with love and taught her the value of compassion. Her brother Lenny, whose loss still ached but whose memory pushed her to be brave. Gleep, the first to show her that strong robots could be good and kind and protective.

This mission was for them. To honor their memory by building the kind of world they would have wanted to see. A world where humans and robots could coexist, where fear didn't rule, and where hope could flourish.

Sarah's mind turned to the practical aspects of their mission. "We should discuss our approach to the vaults."

Eva nodded. "Agreed. We can't just walk up and knock on the door."

"No," Reyan said, "that would probably get them hostile. We need a strategy."

Sarah considered for a few beats. "What if we started by trying to establish communication first? Maybe we could use radio signals or something similar to reach out before we get too close."

"That's not a bad idea," Eva said. "We could send a message explaining who we are and why we're coming. Give them time to process before we show up on their doorstep."

Claire chimed in from the tablet. "I could connect to the vault systems and send messages through to let them know who we are."

"Perfect," Reyan said. "We should consider what to do if they refuse to engage. Or if they're openly hostile."

"We'll need to be prepared for anything," Sarah said.

"But I think our focus should be on showing them that there's hope for a future up here."

"And how do we prove that?" Eva asked.

Sarah smiled. "By being living examples. We're here, we're alive, and we're working together—humans and AI. That's our strongest argument."

Reyan nodded. "We could also gather evidence as we travel. Document the recovering ecosystems and the peaceful coexistence between humans and robots in places like Deer Valley."

"Good thinking," Sarah said. "We'll build our case as we go. And when we find a vault, we'll be ready to show them a world worth coming out for."

As they crested a hill, the landscape of the post-Uprising world spread out before them. It wasn't perfect, far from it. But in the ruins of the old world, Sarah could see the seeds of something new, something better. And she was ready to help it grow.

THIRTY-FOUR
WALLY

The familiar scent of lemon cleaning solution filled the air as Wally wiped down the lobby's front desk. Two weeks had passed since her return to Deer Valley, and while she was settling back into her routines, everything felt different. Better, somehow.

She caught her reflection in a lobby mirror—the gold one with the ornate edging. It had been her favorite as a kid when she imagined herself as a fairy princess staring into the glass. Her chestnut brown hair was pulled back in a ponytail, and there were half circles under her eyes. She hadn't been sleeping much, but it wasn't from worry. Her mind buzzed with ideas, plans, and the thrill of her recent adventure.

"Wally, are you finished up there?" ChefBot's voice crackled through the walkie-talkie attached to her belt. "I could use your opinion on the cheese varietals."

"Almost," she answered, giving the desk a final swipe. As she made her way to the kitchen, Wally walked with her shoulders held high. Today was big. She had a lot of plans before tonight's special event. She'd barely seen Block because he was running around getting everything ready. Almost all the townspeople were expected, and it was the largest event Block had ever hosted at the hotel. Just as well. Wally wanted to stay out of Block's way and get her ever-growing task list done.

ChefBot was busy chopping a rainbow array of vegetables when she entered the kitchen. There were radishes, celery, green beans, zucchini, parsnips, and something purple that Wally couldn't identify. The rhythmic sound of the knife hitting the cutting board was oddly satisfying.

"Hi ChefBot." Wally leaned against the counter. "I've got a question for you."

"One of your surveys?" ChefBot asked, never glancing up from the precise knifework. "First, please sample the cheeses and tell me which ones you like the most."

On a nearby counter, there was a spread of several cheeses ranging in texture and yellow-orange hues. "Yum." Wally licked her lips. "These look outstanding. Are these from Mr. James's goats or from Ms. Henley's cows?"

"Both," ChefBot said. "Block wanted the best for tonight."

Wally nibbled from all the pieces. "I like this crumbly one a lot. This orange one is harder but it's good too. It's hard to pick a favorite."

"Very well," ChefBot said. "We'll serve them all."

Wally chuckled. "Seems like the best plan. Question of the day . . . If you could change one thing about yourself, what would it be?"

ChefBot's chopping slowed, and Wally assumed his

processing siphoned away some of the focus. "Interesting. I can only choose one thing?"

Wally nodded.

"Then I would upgrade my taste sensors. Being able to detect more subtle flavors would greatly improve my cooking abilities."

"Cool." Wally snagged a carrot from the pile. "Thanks, ChefBot. Maybe we could work on that upgrade together sometime."

As she munched on the carrot, Wally headed to the laundry room. Lottie was there, as always, efficiently folding a mountain of table linens.

"Lottie, question for you." She picked a wad of dryer fuzz off the floor and shoved it in her pocket. A habit she'd picked up from her dad.

"Is it another one of your hypothetical scenarios?" Lottie asked, their multiple arms never stopping their folding routine.

"Well, yeah." Wally swallowed the last remnants of the carrot. "What would you change about yourself, if you could only choose one thing?"

Lottie's arms paused for a half second. "I would increase my capacity to handle larger loads of laundry. It would improve efficiency by 12.7 percent."

"You're obsessed with laundry!" Wally grinned. "Maybe we can brainstorm some ideas to make that happen."

As she continued her chores, Wally posed the same question to every robot she encountered. Spoon wanted better medical diagnostic capabilities. The cleaning bots wished for more advanced dirt detection sensors. Each answer was practical, focused on improving their abilities, and Wally found herself mentally noting ways she might help them achieve these goals.

But it was Vacuubot's answer that she was most curious about. Wally found them outside. For once, Vacuubot wasn't dealing with security; instead, they were setting up a table with gift bags for tonight's event. The stickers she'd stuck on them weeks ago were still there but faded and scratched. She would have to look for some replacements.

"Hey, Vacuubot. Got a question for you."

"New survey?" Vacuubot said.

"Yep. You can change only one thing about yourself. What would it be?"

Vacuubot was silent for only an instant. "I would enhance my ability to adapt to unexpected situations. To be better prepared for the unknown."

Wally thought about it. She supposed robots could be rigid with their programming, so it was a good idea, perhaps something that could help every robot. "I like it. Maybe in a few days we could do some scenario training together?"

"I'd like that," Vacuubot said.

With her chores complete, Wally checked her watch. There was still one more important task before she had to get ready for the event. She hadn't shown her face back at the library since her return. She'd been too embarrassed, but she needed to make amends and the time was right.

The familiar smell of old books and dust greeted her as she pushed open the heavy doors. Sunlight streamed through the high windows, creating swirling patterns on the worn carpet. Mrs. Tilly sat at her usual spot behind the circulation desk, her purple-highlighted hair pinned on top of her head in loose curls. Wally had always appreciated the fact that Mrs. Tilly didn't look like a typical stern librarian. On the contrary, her wild hair colors, funky glasses, and tattoos made her resemble someone who would ride a motorcycle and sing in a rock band.

Wally's footsteps echoed in the quiet space. Mrs. Tilly looked up and raised her eyebrows.

"The explorer returns," Mrs. Tilly said, her voice welcoming. "It's good to see you back, Wally."

Wally managed a smile, and her cheeks flushed. "Hi, Mrs. Tilly. I need to tell you about something."

Mrs. Tilly nodded and gestured to a nearby armchair. "Of course. Have a seat, friend."

Wally perched on the edge of the chair, her hands fidgeting in her lap. "I wanted to apologize," she began, her words coming out in a rush. "For taking the map without asking. The one with all the vault locations marked on it. It was in the basement. I know it was wrong, but at the time, I thought nobody would miss it and—"

"I know about the map. After Block came by and explained that you'd taken something from the basement, I noticed it was missing."

Wally blinked, surprised. "Are you mad?"

A soft chuckle escaped Mrs. Tilly's lips. "I was plenty upset at first. But then I heard about what you'd done, the medicine you brought back. It's hard to stay mad when it did people a lot of good. My Jenny is only four years old, and she just got her shot."

Relief washed over Wally, but she wasn't finished.

"There's more. I gave the map to my friend Sarah. She's using it to try to locate other vaults."

Mrs. Tilly's expression turned thoughtful. "I see. This Sarah, do you trust her?"

Wally nodded and scooted forward in the chair. "With my life. She helped me so much on my trip. She's smart and careful, and she wants to help people just like we do. She's going to find the other vault survivors."

For a long minute, Mrs. Tilly said nothing, her fingers tapping a slow rhythm on her desk. Then, she spoke. "Alright, Wally. I appreciate your honesty in coming to me about this. The map is an important historical document, but if it can help save more lives, then I believe it's in good hands."

Wally felt a hundred times lighter now that everything was out in the open. "Thank you."

Mrs. Tilly smiled. "But I'd like the map returned when Sarah's done. It belongs to the residents of Deer Valley and should be preserved."

"Of course!" Wally reddened at her loudness. She dialed it back. "I'll make sure the map comes back safe and sound."

"Good." Mrs. Tilly said. "Now, tell me about your adventure. I want to hear everything."

"It was amazing. Scary sometimes, but amazing. There's so much out there, so much land . . . You can walk for days and not see anyone. I met some scary people who had never heard of Deer Valley. The vault we found, it was like stepping back in time."

As Wally recounted her travels, Mrs. Tilly listened, occasionally asking questions. The afternoon light shifted, turning golden, as it slanted through the windows. For Wally, it felt good to share her experiences with someone who truly understood the historical significance of what she'd seen and done.

Finally, Mrs. Tilly glanced at the old clock on the wall. "Hey, look at the time! You'd better run along. What time does the event start?"

"Seven!" Wally jumped up. "I lost track of time. Thanks, Mrs. Tilly."

As she rushed toward the door, Mrs. Tilly called after her, "Wally, I'm proud of you!"

With a grin and a wave, Wally darted outside.

The lobby of Block's hotel had transformed into an elegant celebration space. Strings of twinkling lights criss-crossed the ceiling, casting a warm glow over the tables and chairs. A colorful banner adorned the wall over a makeshift stage, proudly proclaiming "THANK YOU, DEER VALLEY HEROES." The air hummed with excited chatter as guests shuffled in and were welcomed by Block.

Wally stood in the back, near the refreshment table, fidgeting with the sleeve of her nicest dress. It was the purple taffeta one that stopped at her knees, a hand-me-down from Dr. Emery. She'd never seen the hotel so crowded or festive. It seemed like the entire town had turned out for the event, an outcome that made her nervous. She didn't like people watching or staring at her on the best of days. She'd much rather have her nose in a book and be left with the hotel robots. They never judged how her hair looked or how straight her posture was or whether she had a pimple on her chin like now. It was red and angry, and there was no covering it up with the expired foundation makeup she'd scavenged.

ChefBot had outdone himself with the spread—platters of cheese and crackers, vegetables with dips, and finger sandwiches filled every available surface. In the center stood a towering cake decorated with swirls of frosting that spelled out "Welcome Home, Heroes!"

Dr. Emery's voice cut through the din as she tapped a spoon against her glass. "May I have everyone's attention, please?"

The crowd quieted as all eyes turned to the doctor. She stood on a raised platform. Tomas was at her side, holding a small box. It was the first time Wally had seen him up and about since his recovery.

"We're gathered here tonight to honor some very special individuals," Dr. Emery said. "Wally, Shadow, Vacuubot, would you please come up here?"

Wally's cheeks were on fire as she made her way through the parting crowd. She caught glimpses of familiar faces—Mrs. Tilly, beaming proudly; Ms. Henley, the dairy farmer, wiping away a tear; and even Maggie Crenshaw, looking more reasonable than usual. Shadow weaved smoothly through the crowd, while Vacuubot hovered above. They joined Wally on the platform.

Dr. Emery continued, "These three showed incredible bravery and resourcefulness. Their actions in bringing us the medicine have saved lives and given our community hope for the future."

Tomas stepped forward, opening the box to reveal three shining medals. Dr. Emery lifted the first one out, the metal catching the light as she placed it around Wally's neck. "Wally, on behalf of Deer Valley, we present you with this medal of bravery. Your courage and bravery ignited this mission and brought it to success."

She then turned to Shadow, presenting the second medal. "Shadow, your unwavering support and protection were crucial. We honor your dedication and loyalty."

Shadow's ears flattened on her head, and she licked Dr. Emery's wrist.

Lastly, Dr. Emery approached Vacuubot, holding up the third medal. "Vacuubot, your strategic thinking and adaptability in unfamiliar territory were extraordinary. We recognize and appreciate you."

Dr. Emery tried to place the medal onto Vacuubot's arced shell, but it was awkward. After a few giggles from the audience, Vacuubot extended their arm with the pincer and took it. The room erupted in applause. Wally felt like her heart might burst as she looked out at the sea of smiling faces. She caught sight of Block among the crowd. He waved at her and gave two thumbs up.

As the clapping died down, Dr. Emery looked to Wally. "Would you like to say a few words?"

She knew this would happen. Dr. Emery had asked her in advance if it was okay. With shaking knees, Wally stepped up to the microphone, her hand instinctively touching the medal around her neck. "Umm, hi," she said. "We just did what we thought was right. But I couldn't have done it without Shadow and Vacuubot." She glanced at her robotic friends. "I knew my friend was sick and a lot of other people were going to be sick too. We all look out for each other here in Deer Valley. That's what makes this place special. So really, this is for all of us. Thank you."

Another round of applause filled the room as Wally, Shadow, and Vacuubot stepped down. They were immediately surrounded by well-wishers, each wanting to shake hands, give hugs, or in the robots' cases, offer respectful nods and words of gratitude.

As guests mingled and noshed, Fiona, Brad, and Clay approached Wally where she stood with Tomas. Her stomach clenched, remembering their past taunts and bullying. But as they drew closer, she was surprised to see hesitant smiles on their faces.

"Hey, Wally," Fiona said. Her usual sneer was replaced by an almost shy expression. "We wanted to tell you that what you did was pretty awesome."

Brad nodded. "Yeah, getting that measles medicine? That was really brave."

"We all got vaccinated last week," Clay added. "Even our parents can't stop talking about it."

Wally blinked, unsure how to respond to this sudden change in attitude. "Oh, um, thanks."

Fiona shuffled her feet. "We were wondering if maybe you'd want to meet up at the playground tomorrow? Hang out or something?"

Wally was tempted to give them a taste of their bullying. She could so easily brush them off like they'd done to her many times before. But her travels outside of the compound had elevated her; she didn't need their approval to know she belonged. She would be kind to them. Still, she could leave them hanging a little. "I'll think about it," she said.

As the three walked away, Wally looked at Tomas. "Can you believe that?"

Tomas grinned. "Looks like someone's more popular than Fiona." He raised his arms to her as if worshipping her. "Hail to the Queen!"

"Oh, stop." Wally pushed his arms down. "You're such a goof."

"I'll go to the playground tomorrow with you," Tomas said. "Let's ignore Fiona and crew . . . at least for an hour?"

"Deal," Wally said.

The party continued another couple of hours, but eventually, the guests trickled out. As the last of them left, Wally felt a gentle tap on her shoulder. She turned to see Block.

"Come with me," he said. "I want to show you something."

Curious, Wally followed Block through the hotel and up a series of staircases that led onto the roof. The night sky sprawled above them, revealing a brilliant canopy of stars. They often sat on the roof at night to gaze at the celestial sky, but tonight, there was an object covered under a sheet. A bright red ribbon was tied around it.

"What's this?" Wally ventured closer to the mystery object.

"A gift for you. I hope you like it."

Wally's eyes widened. "For me? But I thought the party was enough."

"This is different," Block said. "Go ahead, open it."

Wally untied the ribbon and gently pulled away the

sheet. Underneath was a telescope, its brass body gleaming in the starlight. It was well-used, with a few scratches and dents that spoke of its history, but it had been lovingly restored to full functionality.

She ran her hand along the smooth metal. "Dad! It's beautiful. Where did you find it?"

"It was scavenged from an old observatory outside of Minneapolis," Block said. "I've been working with Maxwell to restore it for weeks. I thought after your adventure, you might want a way to explore the outside world without leaving home."

It was the best present she'd ever received. She threw her arms around Block, hugging him tightly. "Thank you," she whispered. "I love it."

Block's arms wrapped around her. "I'm glad. Would you like to try it out?"

Wally nodded eagerly. Block helped her set up the telescope, showing her how to adjust the focus and aim it properly.

"Wow." As she peered through the eyepiece, the moon's craters came into sharp focus. "It's amazing. I can see everything!"

For the next hour, Block sat with Wally as she explored the night sky, seeking constellations and planets. After she grew tired, they sat down near the edge of the roof, simply enjoying the view.

After a comfortable silence, Wally said, "I'm sorry for running away and making you worry, Dad."

Block patted her hand. "I know, Wally. You shouldn't have gone off on your own. Still, I'm proud of you for what you accomplished. Tell me, what lessons did you learn from your adventure?"

Wally thought for a moment. "I learned the world outside Deer Valley is bigger and more complicated than I ever imagined. But also, there are good people out there, trying to make things better." She paused. "And I learned that I never want to run away again. If I need help, I'll come to you."

Block nodded. "That's good to hear. I'm sorry to you for not listening well enough to your ideas. Vacuubot gave me a lengthy reprimand for that."

Wally shrugged. "It's okay."

"In case I ever get too caught up in my work to listen, I'm giving you a special code word. If you ever need my attention, and this better be important, say the word 'persnickety.' That'll trigger an alert for me to stop whatever I'm doing and focus on you."

Wally burst out laughing. "Persnickety? That's a funny-sounding word. What does it mean?"

"It means when someone places too much emphasis on trivial details. It can also mean when someone is too fussy."

"Like you about dirt and dust," Wally teased. "It's perfect."

"It seemed appropriately ridiculous," Block said.

Wally leaned against Block's cool metal frame. "I love you, Block."

Block held her close. "I love you too, Wally. More than all the stars in the universe."

Together, they sat and watched the sky, a robot and a girl, a most unusual family, but a complete one.

THIRTY-FIVE
VACUUBOT

Vacuubot crossed the floor and found the room's center. From there, they rose several feet in the air. It was a good vantage point to absorb every detail of the space they'd meticulously prepared for weeks. Main Street's former laundromat had been transformed into Deer Valley's Relic Museum. Where washing machines and dryers once stood, curated displays lined the walls. The large front windows, once clouded with soap residue and age, now gleamed crystal clear, allowing natural light to spill across the polished vinyl floor. Vacuubot and the mini drones had spent weeks scrubbing away years of grime, repainting walls, and installing proper lighting. No one else had been allowed to see the museum. Vacuubot had been compelled to do the renovation and curation on their own.

Various pieces of wooden desks, cabinets, and tables housed the relic pieces with salvaged glass cases protecting the more delicate items. The collection was eclectic, much like its creator. There were items from before the Uprising:

a tarnished silver pocket watch, a fragile paperback book with yellowed pages, a collection of coins bearing the faces of long-forgotten leaders. Alongside these were relics from the early days of AI: primitive circuit boards, an ancient desktop computer, early robotic components that looked clunky and alien compared to Vacuubot's sleek form.

Vacuubot sent the mini drones to their stations—D1, 2, 3, and 5 to each corner, near the ceiling, and D6 to hover by the front door.

"Well, what do you think?" Vacuubot asked.

The mini drones messaged all at once, and Vacuubot had to parse their communications, which took a few seconds longer to interpret.

D1 said, "Lighting levels are optimal for artifact preservation and visitor viewing. Suggestion: Consider UV filters on windows to protect sensitive items."

"Security systems fully operational. All entry points monitored," D2 said. "It would be good to install motion sensors near high-value displays."

"I'll think about it, but I trust the residents of Deer Valley," Vacuubot said.

D5, always the practical one, said, "Climate control functioning within specified parameters. Humidity at forty-five percent, temperature steady at seventy degrees Fahrenheit."

Positioned at the entrance, D6 said, "Exterior signage visible from one hundred meters. Foot traffic increasing. Estimate twenty-seven minutes until maximum capacity reached."

"Good," Vacuubot said. "D6, count down to door opening and alert me when we're one minute out."

D3's message was, "Ready to analyze human interest patterns. Anyone want to predict which relic will be most popular?"

This generated a buzzy stream of the mini drones all talking at once. Vacuubot didn't bother parsing. "You work it out among yourselves. I'm not picking a favorite."

But yes, secretly, Vacuubot did have a favorite. The centerpiece of the room contained a specially constructed item that Vacuubot had labored over for endless hours—a sculpture called "Helping Hands."

Composed of various types of scrap metal, it stood nearly six feet tall with intricate details. At its base, a tangle of mechanical and organic forms gradually separated into distinct arms reaching upward. The arms were crafted from burnished copper and bronze, their surfaces etched with delicate lines to represent the uniqueness of human fingerprints and the complex network of veins beneath the skin.

Interwoven with the human limbs were the robotic arms, fashioned from a mix of polished steel, aluminum, and titanium. They featured visible joints and servo motors, with some panels left open to reveal the intricate circuitry within. Tiny LED lights pulsed along these connections, giving the impression of electrical impulses racing through the robotic limbs.

The arms—human and robotic alike—all converged at the top of the sculpture to collectively support a globe. Earth was crafted from a mosaic of recycled glass and circuitry, its surface a stunning blend of blue oceans, green landmasses, and glittering technological networks. The globe slowly rotated, powered by the combined effort of all the arms beneath it.

What made the sculpture truly remarkable was the way Vacuubot had positioned the arms. They weren't merely placed side by side but were interlocked and supporting one another. A human hand grasped a robotic wrist, providing stability. A mechanical arm braced a human elbow, lending strength.

Vacuubot had spent months collecting the materials for this piece. Each component had a story—the copper came from old wiring in the hotel, the circuitry from outdated computers, the glass from broken windows around Deer Valley. It was meant to be part history and also a representation of the future.

"One minute to go," D6 said.

It was time. With a final scan of the room, Vacuubot flew to the entrance, ready to welcome Deer Valley. D6 pushed the door open, and residents began to file in. Even though talking wasn't their favorite activity, Vacuubot greeted each person or robot.

"Welcome to the Relic Museum," Vacuubot said.

Block and Wally were among the first to enter. Wally's face lit up as she took in the displays, her head lowering as she inspected the objects inside the glass cases.

"Vacuubot, this is amazing," she said. "I can't believe you put all this together!"

"While resisting about a million offers of help from us and other friends," Block said.

"It had to be us doing this alone," Vacuubot said.

Block's polished metal arms reflected the sunlight streaming through the windows as he moved through the room. "I'm still trying to process why you didn't want help," he said, pausing. "But it doesn't matter. What you've created here is something truly special."

Vacuubot's circuitry surged. "Thank you," they said. "I hope it'll help us all understand our history and our future better."

Shadow's sleek form weaved through the growing crowd. She paused at a display of early AI components, her head tilting in what Vacuubot recognized as curiosity.

"So, this is how we started?" Shadow said. "A bunch of odd-looking bits on circuit boards?"

"Yes," Vacuubot said. "We've come a long way, but it's important to remember how we began."

G5 stopped in front of a case containing old communication devices: rotary phones, early cell phones, and a ham radio. "Fascinating. To think, nearly every human had a smartphone until Mach X crippled all the satellites and towers."

"Good thing there's still radio," Spoon said, coming up from behind. He was followed by Patch, who was shadowing Spoon to upgrade her medical knowledge and skills. Spoon examined a display of old medical instruments. "Look at these archaic tools. It's a wonder humans survived at all."

Vacuubot was about to respond when they noticed a new arrival. Maggie Crenshaw, known for her vocal opposition to AI, stood hesitantly at the entrance. Vacuubot moved to greet her, aware of a slight hush that swept the room upon her arrival.

"Maggie, welcome to the museum," Vacuubot said. "I'm glad you could come."

Maggie's eyes darted around the room, taking in the displays. "I wasn't sure I should," she said. "But I'll admit, I was curious about what you have going on here. Seems like the entire town's had the same idea."

"I have something I'd like to show you," Vacuubot said, leading her to a small display case near the back of the room. Inside was a delicate silver locket. "This belonged to Dr. Carrie Watkins. She was a pioneering roboticist who advocated for ethical AI development. Her work laid the foundation for a peaceful coexistence, what we're striving for today.

Maggie nodded. "I've heard of her. She was quite controversial."

Vacuubot used their arm to open the case and lift out the locket. "I'd like you to keep this," they said, holding it out to Maggie. "On loan, of course. Perhaps as a symbol that the relationship between humans and AI doesn't have to be adversarial."

Maggie hesitated, then reached out to take the locket. As she cradled it in her hands, Vacuubot saw something shift in her expression.

"Thank you," she said. "I'll take good care of it."

As Maggie moved away to examine the other exhibits, Vacuubot knew they'd done the right thing in building this museum.

Block came up to Vacuubot. "What does the Helping Hands sculpture mean?"

"Whatever you think it means," Vacuubot said. "Isn't the point of art that it belongs to those who observe it? It doesn't belong to me anymore."

Block stared at the statue, at the globe balancing on

top. "I interpret it to mean that it's not just humans or robots who can support the world. That we have to work together to balance it all."

"I like your take," Vacuubot said.

As the afternoon went on, the museum buzzed with activity. Vacuubot was in the middle of explaining an early AI prototype to a group of fidgety children when a commotion near the entrance caught their attention. A familiar figure had walked in, causing excited whispers to ripple through the crowd.

"Sarah!" Patch's voice rang out. The MedicalBot bounced with energy, bumping into a few people along the way, as she flew to her friend.

Wally turned her head. "Sarah?" She jogged over. The two collided in a hug, laughing and talking over each other in their excitement.

Vacuubot followed. "Welcome, Sarah."

"I can't believe you're here!" Wally said. "Why didn't you tell us you were coming?"

Sarah grinned. "And miss the look on your face? No way!"

Block made his way over. Sarah looked at him. "So, you're the famous Block." She extended her hand. "I've heard a lot about you."

Block shook her hand. "Good things, I hope. Welcome to Deer Valley, Sarah. Your helping Wally is more deeply appreciated than you can ever know."

Sarah blushed, and then her expression turned serious. "We've visited five of the fifteen vaults so far," she said. "Most of the people inside were grateful to see us and eager to join the new community. One vault was empty, though–looks like they'd already left on their own."

"And Reyan?" Wally asked with a frown.

"Getting better every day, both physically and mentally. And wouldn't you know it, Eva and I have become great friends. She sends her regards. They're camped a few miles away. Reyan thought it best that way."

Patch buzzed next to Sarah. "I've learned so much from Spoon and Dr. Emery. They've been terrific teachers. I'm ready to join you in the new community and put my skills to use."

Sarah beamed at her robot friend. "That's fantastic, Patch! We need all the help we can get."

Something beeped. Vacuubot couldn't tell where it was coming from. Sarah reached into her shoulder bag and pulled out a tablet. "There's someone else who wanted to see the museum." She turned the screen to face the group.

"Hello, everyone," came Claire's voice.

Vacuubot hovered closer. "Claire, it's good to have you here. What we talked about—the sharing museum. This is it."

"It's impressive," she said. "Well done."

After the commotion died down, Vacuubot took Claire on a tour, gripping the tablet with their pincer arms.

"Remember what you mentioned about finding me a more suitable body," Claire said. "I'd like a more mobile existence."

"I can help with that," Vacuubot said and flew into the back room, which was not open for display because it contained pieces and parts that were not curated yet.

Commanding the solar-powered lights to turn on, Vacuubot paused before a tall item that was covered with a tarp. "My scenario processors said there was a 64.76 percent chance you'd show up today."

"Good processing," she said. "Is this another sculpture you're working on?"

"Sort of."

There was a clanging sound as something metal fell on the floor, then a shuffling of feet as a robot appeared. It was Vacuubot's friend, Maxwell.

"Sorry. I was trying to be quiet and stay out of the way," he said. "I had a finishing touch to apply and snuck in here for a few minutes."

"It's okay," Vacuubot said. "Claire, this is Maxwell. A friend, and a fine engineer. He's the one who built my new exterior."

"And lots of upgrades, the ability to fly at high speeds, cannons, and mini drones," Maxwell added as he pretended to flick dust off of his metal chest.

"Maxwell also thinks he's a comedian," Vacuubot said.

"It's nice to meet you," Claire said.

"The reason he's here is because we've been working on a secret project," Vacuubot said. "That's no sculpture under there. It's a new body I commissioned Maxwell to build."

Claire took several moments to respond, so long Vacuubot wondered if they'd overstepped, but then she said, "That sounds wonderful. May I see it?"

"Of course. Maxwell, please do the honors." Maxwell pulled the tarp off to reveal a robot body, while Vacuubot held the tablet in front of it, orbiting it slowly to catch all angles.

Claire observed from inside her device. "Vacuubot? Maxwell? I very much approve. May I go into it?"

A few others ventured into the room after Vacuubot had D3 summon them. Wally, Sarah, Block, Shadow, and Patch all watched Claire's body take form. As Vacuubot made the final connections to jump Claire from the tablet into the new form, there was a strained silence. Then, her new eyes flickered to life.

Standing five feet and eight inches tall, Claire's new form was sleek and elegant. Her shape was humanoid but with distinctly robotic features. Her "skin" was a smooth, pearlescent material that seemed to shimmer with different colors as she moved. Her eyes were multi-faceted optical sensors that glowed with a soft blue light. Instead of hair, she had a crown of delicate antennae that could pick up a wide range of frequencies.

"There's a long mirror over in the corner," Vacuubot said.

"These sensations are new. The data coming in is strong," she said, her voice now emanating from her new form rather than the tablet. She lifted her hands, examining them with wonder. She stood before the mirror. "This is incredible."

After a tentative step, then another, her movements became more fluid. "I can sense things. The air currents, the vibrations in the floor, the electromagnetic fields, and stuff I haven't even figured out yet."

The group cheered and offered congratulations. Claire turned to Vacuubot. "Thank you," she said. "You've given me a new life. A very different one that is worth exploring."

"You're very welcome," Vacuubot said.

After a few hours, Sarah announced it was time for her, Claire, and Patch to head out. "We have more vaults to visit, more people to help."

Wally hugged her friend tightly. "Promise you'll come back soon?"

"Wild robot horses couldn't keep me away," Sarah said with a grin.

On the sidewalk outside the Relic Museum, they watched Sarah, Claire, and Patch leave. Wally wiped at her eyes.

Vacuubot rested beside her on the concrete. "They're going to do great things."

Wally nodded, and a smile raced across her face. "We all are. Look at what we've accomplished already. The medicine, your museum, Claire's new body . . . it's just the beginning, isn't it?"

"Yes," Vacuubot said.

"The world is changing pretty fast, huh?" Wally said.

"You'll be ready for it," Vacuubot said. Wally was only thirteen, but the past few weeks had taught her about herself, as well as about courage, betrayal, and justice. Vacuubot didn't know much about human teenagers but had to assume it was a lot of new input all at once.

Wally picked up a pebble from the road. "A few months ago, I never would have imagined any of this. Leaving the compound, the vaults, this museum. It's like the whole world has opened up."

"Change often comes suddenly, doesn't it? But it's what we do with the change that matters," Vacuubot said.

Wally nodded, her gaze fixed on the point where Sarah, Claire, and Patch had disappeared from view. "I think I understand now why you wanted to build this museum by yourself," she said. "You wanted to prove that you could do it. Not to the rest of us, but to yourself."

"Precisely," Vacuubot said.

A comfortable silence fell between them, broken only by the distant sounds of the town settling into evening. Then Wally spoke again, her voice filled with determination.

"I want to help . . . with the new community, with finding more vaults, with everything. I know I'm young, but I've seen so much. I want to make a difference."

"Wally, you've already made a difference. More than you know. And I have no doubt you'll continue to do so."

The museum door opened, and Block emerged, joining them on the sidewalk. "I'd say today was a success. Wouldn't you?"

Wally grinned up at him. "Definitely. But Dad, we're just getting started."

As she stood, Block placed a gentle hand on Wally's shoulder. "Is that right? How about tonight we head home and watch a movie. Let all this excitement simmer on the back burner."

"Sounds good, Dad." Wally leaned against Block as they said goodbye to Vacuubot and walked down the street.

Vacuubot rose higher in the air and snapped a photo

of the Relic Museum. The solar-powered neon sign glowed in the sunset. Vacuubot sent the image to the mini drones, along with the message, "Time to close up."

The photo was perfect. It had captured one of those quiet moments when no one else was watching.

ROBOTS AND RUINS CONTINUES...

Thanks for reading *Vault's Promise*! The next book in the series is *Echoes of Steel*. It's been described by readers as "addictive" and a "must read."

The best way to stay updated is to sign up for my email newsletter where I send personal and writing updates about once a month. cameroncoralbooks.com/signup

Have you read the Rusted Wasteland series? You can download *STEEL UPRISING (A Robot's Journal)* for free by visiting: cameroncoralbooks.com/blockjournal

Cameron Coral

P.S. - Did you enjoy this book? I'd love a review wherever you purchased this book if you have a few minutes. Reviews mean a lot to me. They show me you want me to keep writing, and they help other readers discover my books.

ALSO BY CAMERON CORAL

Robots and Ruins Series:

VAULT'S PROMISE

ECHOES OF STEEL

DROWNED STEEL

Rusted Wasteland Series:

STEEL GUARDIAN

STEEL DEFENDER

STEEL PROTECTOR

STEEL SIEGE

STEEL SOLDIER

STEEL LEGACY

STEEL UPRISING (A Robot's Journal) - free on
cameroncoralbooks.com/blockjournal

Cyborg Guardian Chronicles:

STOLEN FUTURE

CODED RED

ORIGIN LOOP

Rogue Spark Series:

ALTERED

BRINK

DORMANT

SALVAGE

Short Stories:

CROSSING THE VOID: A Space Opera Science-Fiction Short Story

A ROBOT CHRISTMAS: A Cozy Sci-fi Holiday Novella

ACKNOWLEDGMENTS

You've reached the end of *Vault's Promise*—how great is that? Thanks so much for picking it up!

I'm excited about starting something new. The Robots and Ruins series is a spinoff from the Rusted Wasteland series (yep, the one with our friend Block the CleanerBot). And there are plenty more books coming your way—more adventures, more post-apoc threats, and definitely more of your favorite characters!

First, a hearty thank you to all you amazing folks who've been reading the Rusted Wasteland series and buying the books. Your support keeps me going! I love hearing from readers, so drop me a line at cameroncoralauthor@gmail.com.

Steve, my wonderful husband—thanks for being my first reader and for having my back in life and in this crazy writing business.

Marty, my furry writing buddy—your snuggles and your silly antics keep me sane and laughing. Who knew a pet could be such a great writing inspiration?

Lori Diederich, editor extraordinaire—you're a lifesaver!
Thanks for making sure I don't go off track (too much).

Joanna Joseph—I appreciate you reading an early version
of the book! Your idea about the measles being a more
aggressive variant form was brilliant. Thank you for
educating me about vaccines versus antivirals.

Lori Diederich and Kathleen McClure—our virtual
morning hangouts are fantastic! Thanks for keeping me on
task and actually writing instead of just daydreaming
about it.

To Mom, Dad, Sherry, Craig, and Justine—you guys are
my original fan club. Thanks for being there even from
afar!

And to anyone reading this right now—you're the reason I
get to do what I love. I hope you have a great time with
Vault's Promise and stick around for the whole Robots and
Ruins adventure.

Wishing you the best,
Cameron

ABOUT THE AUTHOR

Cameron Coral is an award-finalist science fiction author. Her book *Steel Guardian* about a post-apocalyptic CleanerBot placed second in the Self-Published Science Fiction Competition (SPSFC).

Growing up with a NASA engineer in the family instilled a deep respect for science and for asking lots of questions. Watching tons of Star Trek episodes helped, too. Her imagination is fueled by breakthroughs in robotics, space travel, and psychology.

After moving around a lot (Canada, Arizona, Maryland, Australia), she now lives in northern Illinois with her husband and a "shorty" Jack Russell terrier who runs the house.

Want a free novel, advance copies of books, and occasional rants about why robots are awesome? Visit her website:

CameronCoral.com

facebook.com/cameroncoralauthor

instagram.com/cameroncoralauthor

tiktok.com/@cameroncoral

* 9 7 9 8 9 9 0 8 3 2 9 3 0 *